"Jill Eileen Smith's *Sarai* gives 'the rest of the story'—Abram and Sarai's journey toward faith. Don't hesitate to open this rich biblical drama for new insight and a new perspective on the patriarch and his family. A well-written story filled with human emotion."

—**Lyn Cote**, author of *Her Abundant Joy*

"What a marvelous retelling of an old and sacred story! Though I knew it well, I could not put *Sarai* down. Smith takes us into the minds of the characters as they struggle with their flaws, fears, and disappointments, armed only with an often fragile faith. *Sarai* is an inspiring offer of hope for all."

—**Linda Windsor**, author of the Brides of Alba series

"Jill Eileen Smith's research shines in this gem of a novel detailing the lives of Abram and Sarai. Fans of biblical fiction will be delighted by Smith's retelling of two of the most beloved personalities from the book of Genesis."

—**Kacy Barnett-Gramckow**, author of the Genesis Trilogy

"I've read Jill Eileen Smith's writing with great interest since before she was published, and I've enjoyed watching this talented woman be discovered as a powerful novelist. Jill has a special insight into her characters and a great love for biblical stories. I highly recommend her latest novel, *Sarai*. You will not be disappointed."

—**Hannah Alexander**, award-winning author of *Eye of the Storm*

"In *Sarai*, Jill Eileen Smith takes the reader back to ancient times and the nomadic life of Sarai and Abram. This is an absorbing visit to the past, filled with wonderful details and fascinating characters, including Abram's nephew Lot and his wife. Smith reveals timeless doubts and struggles, along with the triumphs of some and the ill-fated but fascinating paths of others. Remarkable research is folded into a story that builds to an unforgettable ending. Smith truly brought the era to life!"

—**Maureen Lang**, author of *Springtime of the Spirit* and *Whisper on the Wind*

Books by Jill Eileen Smith

THE WIVES OF KING DAVID
Michal

Abigail

Bathsheba

WIVES OF THE PATRIARCHS
Sarai

Sarai

A Novel

JILL EILEEN SMITH

Revell

a division of Baker Publishing Group
Grand Rapids, Michigan

Published by Revell
a division of Baker Publishing Group
P.O. Box 6287, Grand Rapids, MI 49516-6287
www.revellbooks.com

Printed in the United States of America

Library of Congress Cataloging-in-Publication Data
Smith, Jill Eileen, 1958–
     Sarai : a novel / Jill Eileen Smith.
         p.   cm. — (Wives of the patriarchs ; bk. 1)
     ISBN 978-0-8007-3429-9 (pbk.)
     1. Sarah (Biblical matriarch)—Fiction. 2. Bible. O.T.—History of Biblical events—Fiction. 3. Women in the Bible—Fiction. I. Title.
PS3619.M58838S27   2012
813'.6—dc22   2011038065

Published in association with the Books & Such Literary Agency, 52 Mission Circle, Suite 122, PMB 170, Santa Rosa, CA 95409-5370, www.booksandsuch.biz.

12   13   14   15   16   17   18   7   6   5   4   3   2   1

To my dad, who longed for a better country—a heavenly one—a city with foundations, whose architect and builder is God (Heb. 11:10, 16).

In Loving Memory
of
Leonard C. Smith, Jr.
1922–2011

Prologue

Sarai glanced across the courtyard, catching Abram's gaze. His half smile and the twinkle in his eye warmed her more than the wine she had tasted at the start of the ceremony. Music drifted around them as the bridal couple—their nephew Lot and his new wife, Melah—took their seats on the bench beneath the canopy and accepted rich foods from the hands of the servants.

"This whole wedding is a disgrace, you know." Sarai's sister-in-law Milcah stood at her elbow and leaned close to her ear. "Why her father agreed to the marriage after Lot had already humbled the girl . . . Though I suppose he didn't have much choice. Who else would want her after she'd already given in to Lot's charms?" Milcah batted at a fly, sending it away. "I can't imagine why Lot couldn't wait with such a one. It's not as though she's a beauty or a temptress. It seems like he could have done better." The last words came out in a whisper as Milcah moved in close again.

Sarai turned from watching the bridal couple to meet Milcah's pinched gaze. "If it is true that a babe is already on the way, it is better they marry." She had wearied of the heated debate and shame Lot had brought down on her household, particularly on Abram.

"Abi Terah seems pleased with the arrangement." Milcah touched Sarai's shoulder and pointed toward their father. "Though his conditions did seem a little harsh toward Lot, while Melah came away already with child and married to a man who can never put her aside or take another. I might have given in to Nahor before our betrothal for such a promise." She laughed at that, then shifted her ample bulk, bursting with child herself, to face Sarai once more.

Sarai stifled her hurt at the critical words, remembering her own wedding promises, hers and Abram's. She smoothed imaginary wrinkles from her skirts and avoided Milcah's perusing gaze.

"I see I have upset you." Milcah patted Sarai's arm. "Your time will come, Sarai. At least you can rest in knowing Abram loves you. If he didn't, he might have broken his vow to you long ago." She placed a protective hand over her middle and shook her head, her gaze pitying, though Sarai sensed, as she always did, a hint of arrogance in Milcah's tone. The beautiful Sarai was barren. She'd become a fool. A laughingstock.

She clenched her jaw and held herself erect, lifting a jeweled hand to her throat. "Thank you, Milcah." She forced a smile. "If you will excuse me, I must check on the food." She glided away from the bench along the courtyard wall, skirted the crowds, and hurried into the house, the vows at her own wedding feast suddenly sharp in her ear.

"I promise never to take another wife," Abram had said, his gaze full of love for only her.

"I promise to give you a child." Sarai had gazed into his handsome face, her heart doing a little dance at having finally convinced her father to let them marry.

"I hold you, my son Abram and my daughter Sarai, to your

promises this day. If you, Sarai, do not fulfill your vow to my son, his vow to you is null." Her father's unwavering gaze had held her fast.

How easy such a promise had seemed then.

But after thirty-two years of marriage, she had yet to conceive. And here Melah was already with child even before her wedding day. She blinked back stinging tears. Conversations and laughter filtered through the open windows while a harpist played quiet music in the background. After the meal, there would be singing and dancing, and guests would remain until well past nightfall, only to return again on the morrow for several more days of feasting.

She rested her head against the cool limestone wall aligning the comfortable sitting room, unobserved by the servants as they rushed down the halls from the cooking rooms with platters piled high with food. She had no reason to be jealous. She was mistress of a wealthy estate, wife to one of Ur's finest nobles, whose father had long held the king's ear. A princess of Ur, if ever there was one.

But she could not stop the pain Milcah's presence always evoked. Milcah already had one son who had weaned only three months before. She did not deserve another so soon.

"I thought I might find you here." At Abram's voice and his touch on her shoulder, she turned into his comforting embrace. "What's wrong, dear one?"

Sarai released a troubled sigh and leaned back to better see his face. "Milcah."

He nodded, but at his quizzical look, she knew he did not understand.

"She is flaunting her swollen belly, and I have no patience for her criticisms."

"Ah," he said, pulling her close again. "Milcah is jealous of your beauty, dear wife. She has nothing else to flaunt." He patted her back, but the action did not soothe.

"I would rather have a child than beauty." The words were a

mere breath against his chest, but when his hands stilled, she knew he'd heard.

"And I would rather have you just as you are." He held her at arm's length, his gaze searching. "Do not trouble yourself or deny joy to others, dear one. You have nothing to fear."

She looked into his handsome face and cupped his bearded cheek with her hand. He still carried the vigor of one much younger, and she rested in his strength as he held her. "But I do fear, dear husband. I fear I have failed to give you what you most deserve. Perhaps if I had been as Melah, you would already have a son."

"I deserve nothing, Sarai. What I possess is only a gift. Adonai will give what He will." He lifted her chin to look into her face. "Lot will have to live with his errors the rest of his days. Trust me in this, Sarai. A man who takes a woman before the proper time lives with long regrets, whether he realizes it or not."

"Do you think Lot regrets marrying Melah?" she whispered. Abram often had Lot's ear, and Abram had given the younger man a scathing lecture after the truth had come out.

"Lot is too brash and too charming, though he did repent of his act and agree to the marriage. But then, Father gave him no choice. He would have lost any inheritance if he had refused. Father has his honor."

"Lot should have had his own." Sarai looked into her husband's loving gaze, grateful all over again for such a man. A man whose character surpassed most men in the city, even those in her own family. A man who had earned her devotion and her respect.

Abram bent to give her a gentle kiss. "Come, sit with me at the feast. You need not endure Milcah's pity on such a day."

Tears rose again at his kindness, at how astute he could be to her emotions. He brushed the tears from her cheeks and slipped her hand in his. "Do not fear, Sarai. In His time, Adonai will give us a son. And if He does not, we will discuss what to do about it then."

She nodded, following his lead as he guided her back through the house to the courtyard. But as the music played around her and the well-wishers shouted blessings of fertility to the bride and groom as they entered the sparkling bridal tent, Sarai could not stop the worry or the fear.

How flippantly she had promised her husband a child in order to convince her father to give her to Abram.

She did not know how much that vow would cost her then.

And how impossible it all was now.

Part

1

Terah became the father of Abram, Nahor and Haran. And Haran became the father of Lot. While his father Terah was still alive, Haran died in Ur of the Chaldeans, in the land of his birth. Abram and Nahor both married. The name of Abram's wife was Sarai, and the name of Nahor's wife was Milcah; she was the daughter of Haran, the father of both Milcah and Iscah. Now Sarai was barren; she had no children.

Genesis 11:27–30

The LORD had said to Abram, "Leave your country, your people and your father's household and go to the land I will show you. . . ."

So Abram left, as the LORD had told him; and Lot went with him.

Genesis 12:1, 4

❋ 1 ❋

Sarai looked up at the great ziggurat of Nannar and took a step backward, overwhelmed as she always was at the enormity of the temple to Ur's patron god. The steps rising upward, forever upward, drew her gaze to the triangular peak, its god's-eye view gazing down at her, watching. She shivered, certain the feeling came from more than the soft breeze blowing down from the north.

Abram would not approve of her being here. Even protected by her male slaves and accompanied by her maid, Lila, her niece Melah, and her servants, Abram would still consider Ur unsafe for his beautiful wife. And if he knew her reason . . .

Why had she come?

"Did you bring the likeness?" Melah stopped on the cobbled street and turned to look at her. Her niece's face, still rosy with the freshness of youth yet well tanned by the sun, held a glint of excitement.

"It's here." Sarai patted the pouch at her side, tucked into the pocket of her robe. "But I still don't see what good this will do."

The image was carved of olive wood, a pregnant likeness of Sarai with crescent moons—symbols of the god—painted into the clothing designs. But could the gods really give Sarai the child she craved or the son Melah longed for—one who would live? While Abram's brother's sons lined his table like olive plants sprung up beneath an ancient flowering tree, Abram's own table stood quiet, empty.

Sarai would sacrifice her beauty to fill that void, to give Abram a son.

Melah frowned, crossed her arms over her chest. "It won't do any good at all if you don't believe, Sarai." Her gaze dropped to Sarai's flat stomach. "Obviously you need help."

"Obviously." She couldn't keep the sharpness or the sarcasm from her tone, especially in front of this upstart niece, or the pang of guilt and sadness from piercing her heart.

"Nevertheless, you should have done this years ago." Melah's patronizing tone made Sarai bristle. "You can't ask others to do the sacrificing and petitioning for you. The goddess wants your devotion. If you want a child, you must worship the mother goddess. For even Inana came by her fertile power through her mother Ningal. You've known this since childhood." Melah turned, then looked back again. "Of course, if you'd prefer Inana's fertility rites . . ." She smirked as though the thought amused her, whether because she disdained Abram's faith or because she could not imagine Sarai submitting to Inana's sexual practices. Probably both, considering Melah's blatant interest in the love goddess and her impassioned ways.

Sarai lifted her chin and tilted her gaze away from Melah. She nodded to her slaves and continued around the ziggurat to the streets behind until she came upon the courtyard fencing in Ningal's temple. Columns stood on either side of the gate with steps leading to two great, sculpted doors, where bulls carved into the wood gave silent otherworldly protection to all who dwelled therein. Incense, the breath of the gods, burned spicy-sweet in tall sconces on either side of the doors, where real guards in bronze helmets and brass greaves held tall spears at attention. From their vantage point, they saw every movement in the courtyard.

Sarai stared at the scene, taking in the gleaming gilded columns. The dappled light made the bulls appear to move, their horns bent forward as though to strike. The temple seemed to pulse with its own breath, making Sarai's catch in her throat. Her sandals felt suddenly weighted, stuck to the stones like dried mud to baked bricks.

She shouldn't be here.

"Are you ready?"

Sarai slipped a hand over the image in her pocket and slowly turned to look at her niece, the wooden image burning the flesh of her palm as though heated by the sun's sharp rays. Had Ningal's son Utu come to block their path? The gods were always bickering over one thing or another. Perhaps the sun god did not want them to pay homage to his mother. And what if Melah was right? Inana was the goddess of love. Was she the one who could answer Sarai's prayers for a child? But the rituals involved . . .

She shook her head, releasing her grip on the image and letting the pouch hang from the belt at her side. Never! She would not resort to such practices, even if she paid someone else to do them for her. Still, Ningal did not exact such a cost.

She looked at Melah. "I . . ." She what? Words would not form. What did she want but a child? But was this the best way?

"I didn't come all this way to have you change your mind on me, Sarai. Do you want to keep your vow to Abram or not?" Melah flicked a gaze in Lila's direction. "Or perhaps you should just give him your maid and be done with it." Her scowl drew her narrow eyes into slits, making her forty-plus years look far older than Sarai did at twenty years her senior.

"Abram wouldn't hear of such a thing." She lifted her chin, but the action was more to put Melah in her place than to assert her confidence. If Abram knew where she stood right now, what she was about to do . . . might he take another wife? She glanced at Lila, who had become more like a daughter than a maid to her. Abram would never agree to such a thing.

The sundial in the courtyard moved a notch, and Sarai glanced at the sky. Clouds skimmed the surface of blue, pushed along by the increasing breeze. She braced herself, her hand closing over the pouch with the image once more. She must act, one way or the other.

"Well?" Melah tapped an impatient foot, hands on her ample hips. "Do you have the coins? Are you going to do this, or did I waste my whole afternoon, not to mention the months it has taken to convince you I'm right?" She gave Sarai a pointed stare, then turned to walk toward the temple doors. Melah would offer a sacrifice whether Sarai did so or not, so the day really wasn't as wasted as she'd like Sarai to believe.

Sarai stifled a smile. Despite Melah's hasty marriage to Lot and the subsequent loss of their firstborn, Sarai had come to accept Melah, even carried some measure of affection for her, though she could be as ornery as a she-goat sometimes. Both Melah and Milcah believed in Ningal and Inana and worshiped frequently at one or both temples. Both women had borne children, though in Melah's case only one infant daughter still lived.

The breeze brought the scent of incense toward her, and the chant of worshipers clustered to her right broke into her thoughts, sealing her decision. She lifted the image from the pouch and stared at its pregnant likeness. Once she paid the hefty sacrifice—coins she had taken from the dowry her father had given her years before—the priestess would take the image, set it before the goddess, and offer prayers on her behalf until the new moon waned. Time enough and, hopefully, prayers enough to invoke the goddess's favor and grant her a son.

She drew in a slow breath, willing courage into her bones. She could do this. Her promise to Abram was at stake, and time was not in her favor. She had to do something, anything to procure a child. If that meant a sacrifice to the mother goddess, despite Abram's certain disapproval, she had to take the risk.

Abram scanned the distant copse of trees and brambles for some sign of Sarai's favorite ram, the one bent on straying despite Abram's attempts to teach it otherwise. Sarai would say the ram followed the same instinct born in men, and her piercing gaze would remind him of his youth and his own selfish ways. He scowled. Later he would chuckle over such thoughts, but now he was faced with the task of finding the animal.

Using his staff to guide his steps, he moved from beneath the shade of a spreading oak, speaking softly so as not to alarm the ewes still grazing nearby. On the hill opposite the meadow where his flock grazed, his nephew Lot played a melancholy tune on a reed flute, the sound carrying to Abram. He almost envied the younger man's ability, yet felt a measure of pride that his sheep knew his voice above all others, even the flat sounds of his tuneless singing. One young ewe in particular stayed close, like a daughter. He plucked at his beard and gave in to a rueful smile. Perhaps she was as tone-deaf as he.

The young ewe followed him now, and he waited a moment before picking his way forward again. When she reached his side, he picked her up and placed her over his shoulders. Clouds blocked the sun as he approached the ridge, and a sudden breeze cooled the skin on his face. An unexpected shiver worked through him as he neared the brambles, and he slowed, a feeling of uncertainty prickling the hairs on his arms. He squinted, raising a hand to his eyes, his grip tightening on his staff.

He stopped and listened, shifting the lamb's weight, then took several more cautious steps forward, at last spying the ram caught by its thick wool among the thorns, its pitiful cry touching Abram's heart. The sky darkened further, and a chill wind brushed his face. He glanced heavenward, a sense of foreboding filling him. There had been no sign of a storm that morning, but if one was upon them now, he had best make quick work of releasing the ram and hurry back to the rest of the flock, which would not know where to go to find shelter without his leading.

Spurred by this sudden urgency, he set the ewe on the ground near a patch of grass and pushed aside the brambles with his staff to get closer to the ram. "And how did you expect to get yourself out once you got into these thorns?" he asked the animal, gentling his voice above its bleating. Thorns gripped his robe, but he ignored the ripping sound of the fabric as he worked to disentangle the animal's wool. "There, there," he soothed. But the ram kicked and fought Abram's efforts, wedging himself in worse than before.

Sweat poured down Abram's back as he worked the hook of his staff under the animal's belly. The wind picked up, the air suddenly heavy and damp. His arms ached from the strain as he finally wrapped the hook of the staff around the animal's body well enough to wrench it free, briars and all.

When they were a few paces away, Abram knelt beside the ram and picked the last of the briars from his wool, then took the horn strapped to his side and poured oil over the scratches, rubbing it into the animal's skin. The ram stood still, apparently sufficiently chastised. Abram looked from the ram to the ewe. To mate the two would bring sturdy, unblemished offspring. No others in his flock could compare to these specimens of perfection, though he knew from experience that producing young would not change the ram's behavior.

Then again, would producing an heir change him?

His jaw tightened at the thought. It wasn't his fault Sarai had been barren all these years. They'd been the perfect couple from the start, though now, after years of her barrenness, his brother and nephew did not glance at Abram with the same hint of jealousy because of his beautiful wife. At least their wives had borne them sons, though Lot's had not lived long enough to tell of it.

He glanced at the two animals beside him, noting their suddenly rigid stance, the wary looks in their eyes. He looked at the sky, wondering at the change, at the unexpected stillness. Light now seeped from beneath the gray clouds, sending shafts of blazing white in all directions. The wind picked up again, the breeze stiff yet warm. Strange.

Definitely time to head back.

He dug his staff into the earth and pushed to his feet, ready to call the animals to follow, when a loud rumble like thunder made him pause. The clouds drew together as he watched, dark and heavy again. Fear tingled his spine.

He darted a look in all directions. Nothing moved. Even the wind had stilled, and Lot's flute no longer filled the silence. He glanced at the two animals, but they too had stilled, their heads bent to the grass but their mouths closed, unmoving.

"Abram!"

A chill worked through him. He glanced around again, but there was no one in sight. Was he hearing things?

"Abram!"

The voice, louder, more insistent, and powerful, reached into the pit of his soul, stirring deep fear inside of him. He sank to his knees and put his face to the dirt.

"Here I am," he choked out, his own voice weak in comparison.

"Get out of your country, from your family and from your father's house, to a land that I will show you. I will make you a great nation; I will bless you and make your name great; and you shall be a blessing. I will bless those who bless you, and I will curse him who curses you; and in you all the families of the earth shall be blessed."

Abram shuddered at the words, unable to respond. *Who are you?* But he couldn't utter the question. Deep down, he knew exactly who spoke to him. Only Adonai Elohim, the Lord, the Mighty God, Creator of heaven and earth, could make a man tremble in fear at His voice. Only a mighty Creator could cause the breeze to still and make the sky ominous and foreboding. Only a great Creator could speak such words and make a man know they were truth.

I will do as You ask, he said in his heart, certain his voice would not hold the words steady. At his response, the breeze returned. Abram slowly lifted his head. The animals resumed nibbling the grasses as though nothing had happened. Abram pushed himself to his knees, shaking, but one glance around him told him nothing had changed. The threat of the storm had passed, and in its place an inviting landscape and sunny, cloudless skies greeted him.

Had he heard correctly? It had all happened so fast. But in his spirit, he knew. He must take Sarai and leave Ur and follow the Lord to wherever He might lead. Where would He lead them?

But Abram didn't need to know that yet. He needed only to obey.

He looked back at the two animals, perfect in body but opposite in spirit. One obedient and loyal, the other rebellious and wayward. He would not be like the rebellious ram. He would obey his Creator.

Which meant he would sacrifice all he had to do so—his family inheritance, his home, his relatives, his friends . . . his best.

He stood, still unsteady, his gaze resting on the animals now looking at him with wide, trusting eyes. He must build an altar and make a burnt offering to the Lord. His heart constricted with his decision. One of them must die in the sacrifice.

Sarai shivered at the sudden shift in the breeze. Red dust coated the tanned leather of her sandals as she crossed further into the courtyard toward the imposing doors of the goddess's temple.

Melah moved ahead of her to approach the guards who stood blocking the way. Sarai waited, motionless, as Melah dropped her coins into a wooden tithing box inlaid with shells and lapis lazuli set in crescent designs.

Behind Melah, her five serving girls bowed low, facing the temple but not moving to enter. Melah would not have paid their way, and few slaves could afford such a luxury as to enter the chambers of the gods. To Sarai's left, the sonorous chant of the Ningal singers' tuneless melody and the heady incense coming from the tall cones on either side of the ornate door nearly turned her stomach.

The gods of our people are idols, Sarai. There is only one Maker.

She whirled about, Abram's voice loud in her ear. But no. His words were a memory. She had heard them often enough to know better than to be here. She caught sight of her slaves still standing guard at her back, their faces somber, dark as flint. Abram's One God, El Echad, would not dwell in such temples built with human hands. Hadn't she watched the construction of the many projects the king had undertaken since her early childhood? Hundreds of men had slaved to build Nannar-Sin's giant ziggurat, and more besides to add palaces and temples to shadow its sprawling court. Would the One God need such a temple?

The breeze swirled about her in a sudden gust, lifting the filmy gauze and jewels from her headdress. She must not do this.

The carved image pressed heavily against her hip, and the precious coins from her dowry seemed suddenly too important to waste on such uncertainty. She closed her eyes, seeing Abram's disapproval, wanting desperately to please him. Would he take another wife as Melah had suggested?

Oh, but why could she not bear a child?

The familiar ache settled in her middle, and she wavered, staring up at the imposing temple to Ningal, wondering if the goddess truly had the power Melah had worked so hard to convince her of.

If Sarai did not do this, if she did not ask, would she be throwing away her last chance? She'd been barren for so long. Did this goddess have the power to undo her past and make her whole before it was too late?

The chants grew louder as Melah disappeared behind the yawning doors into the mouth of the goddess. Dark clouds blotted the sun. Was Ningal's son Utu hiding his warmth, displeased with her uncertainty? Or had El Echad sent the clouds and the wind to drive her away?

"Oh, Abram, what should I do?" The words vanished in the thump of the chanters' drum, but the act of speaking them spurred her to move.

She must flee.

Her feet suddenly loosed from their immobility, Sarai spun about, picked up her skirts, and rushed through the streets of Ur, fear making her legs spring with the gait of youth long forgotten. She would run home to Abram and his God and forget this day had ever happened. She would renounce all devotion to Nannar-Sin and Ningal and their offspring of gods.

But as she slowed at the outskirts of Ur's redbrick walls, waiting for Lila to catch up to her, a new thought struck hard. What if her visit today had already offended Abram's God? Was El Echad greater than the mother goddess that He could grant a child? If she had offended him, what would Abram say? What could she do?

She walked with weighted steps the rest of the way home.

Abram laid his staff on the ground and walked nearer the edge of the cliff, picked up a heavy rock, and carted it back to the grassy knoll. His heart ached with each footfall, as each rock placed on top of the other brought him one step closer to killing the animal and lighting the sacrifice. Which animal should he offer? His favorite or Sarai's? The good ewe or the rebellious ram?

The thoughts tormented him as he put the last rock in place and found kindling to lay on top of the stones. Sacrifices were not new to him. His father, Terah, had sacrificed animals, among other things, to the gods of Ur. And his brother Haran had lost a bet and been forced by the king to sacrifice a son as a substitute for the king's life—a yearly sacrifice required by the gods to ensure the land's fertility. Surely Haran's death soon after came from his grief over such an act.

Abram shuddered at the thought. The idea that a man could be killed and brought back to life was pure myth, a story the people believed the gods required and could do. But not once had a sacrificed man returned to walk the earth again.

The sun or moon held no such power. And Adonai Elohim had

not required such sacrifice of men. An animal's blood, not a son's, must be shed.

The thought strengthened his resolve, and Abram knew he could not put off what he planned to do, what he needed to do. He walked away from the altar, back to the two animals. He could go to his flock still visible in the distance and choose another, one less perfect. He could almost hear Lot's voice making the suggestion. His practical nephew would find a way out of such a difficult choice. And it would surely make Abram feel less torn—and make telling Sarai less painful.

But the memory of that other voice still resonated in his soul. Adonai had not asked him to do this, but how could he start a journey without showing his willingness to obey his God, or take one step forward without repentance for his own rebellious ways?

He placed a hand over his chest and looked from the two perfect animals to the heavens. He would sacrifice the one most like himself. The one who represented his own penchant for straying. Decision made, he pulled a dagger from his side and slit the animal's throat, then cut it up, burned its flesh on the altar, and worshiped.

Sarai stood at the threshold between the food preparation area and the courtyard of her home, hands fidgeting with her sash, gaze darting between the servants and the distant path. Abram should have been home by now. Scents of onion and garlic mingled with the aroma of roasting fowl, filling the house. Clanking bowls and the chatter of servants, so familiar this time of day, helped dispel the memories of her afternoon. An afternoon she would not soon forget, whose regret still lingered with each beat of her heart.

She patted her thigh where the carved image had lain in its pouch at her side, reminding herself that she was free of it now. She had tossed the accursed thing into the fire the moment she'd returned home, vowing never to go near a foreign temple again. Why then did she still feel so restless and carry such a weight of guilt?

Annoyed with herself, she turned to observe the servants at work preparing the evening repast. A distant *clop-hobble*, the distinct sound of her father using his walking stick, grew closer. He appeared at the threshold of the cooking rooms.

"Late again, is he?" Terah moved a step back toward the hall and motioned for her to follow him into the courtyard. He slowly lowered his body to the stone bench and patted the seat beside him. "Sit, daughter. You must not worry so. He'll come."

"Of course he will." Sarai walked to the edge of the court and peered down the path Abram always took from the sheep pens, then joined her father. "One of the animals must have gotten lost again, or he and Lot got to talking." Her nephew could outtalk a woman and often engaged Abram in conversation about El Echad, the One God. But the more likely scenario was that a lamb had gotten caught in brambles or stolen from the flock by a lion or a fox. In his quest to find it, Abram might not show up until nightfall.

She toyed with a smile, seeing in her mind's eye her strong husband leading his sheep, rescuing the lost, disciplining the wayward. Her favorite lambs had always been the ones bent on straying. Perhaps they reminded her of Abram's younger days before his visit with their ancestor Eber when he learned of El Echad. And before she had tamed his restless spirit after he took her to wife.

"What are you smiling at, Sarai? Do you see him coming?"

She had almost forgotten her father's presence. She looked again at the path, and indeed, he was coming toward her, a lamb draped across his shoulders. No doubt his favorite ewe. He treated the animal like a pet, even letting it eat at their table. Another reminder of how much he needed sons.

The thought darkened her spirit, the image of the temple to the goddess mocking her. But she wouldn't think of it now.

She turned to face her father. "He is coming." She patted his knee, then stood, lifted her skirts, and hurried through the gate to meet Abram on the path.

She stopped a few paces from him, shaken by the intense look on his face. "What is it?" Her jeweled hand moved to her throat, brushing the soft fabric of her robe. "Something has happened. Tell me, please."

Abram stood looking down at her, his eyes bright. He set the lamb on the ground beside him, patted its head, then took Sarai's hands in his. "Adonai Elohim spoke to me today." A look of awe and humility filled his bearded face, and she longed to cup his cheek with her hand to somehow transfer the joy in his eyes to hers.

"How do you know? Did he speak aloud?" A tremor passed through her. She knew this God of Abram's was real, and He terrified her.

Abram nodded, tightening his grip on her hands, his dark eyes ablaze with excitement. "He called my name. He told me to leave my country, my family, and my father's household and go to a land He would show me, that He will make my name great and make me into a great nation, and that in me all of the families of the earth will be blessed. He promised to bless those who bless me and curse those who curse me." His look bored into hers, then softened. He released one hand and cupped her cheek. "To make me a great nation means He will have to give me a son, Sarai. We will have a child yet. Adonai promised."

Sarai's stomach dipped as he drew her into his arms. She blinked away the sting of tears, grateful beyond words that she had not heeded Melah's advice, had run from the gods of her people. Abram's God would provide him an heir. She would bear a child after all!

She felt Abram's hand rubbing circles along her back. "Will you come with me, Sarai?" He whispered the question as though he were suddenly uncertain.

She pulled back from his embrace and touched his face. "Of course, dear husband. I am bound to you in all ways. Where would I be without you?" She smiled at him, pleased to see the joy return to his gaze.

He bent his head and kissed her, a passionate, lingering kiss that awakened her senses. Perhaps this God would indeed grant her a son if Abram's sudden ardent affection were any indication.

She giggled at her own humorous thoughts as Abram lifted his mouth from hers. "Supper awaits you, my lord, unless you were planning to help Adonai's promise come to pass before you fill your belly."

His stomach rumbled in response, and they both laughed. He patted his middle even as he wrapped one arm around her waist. "You do tempt me, dear wife," he whispered, nuzzling her ear.

She laughed lightly again, then noticed their father slowly coming toward them. "I don't think our father will wait for us." She kissed his cheek. "He's put off eating, waiting for you, and the food is past ready. But of course, he didn't know you were so unexpectedly detained."

She took two steps forward, expecting Abram to join her. When his feet didn't move, she halted, not wishing to depart his embrace. Her mind was still reeling with all that had happened. Was it true? Would she indeed bear a son of the promise?

"The voice did not detain me long. The sacrifice did." Abram's words carried tenderness. And perhaps a hint of regret?

She faced him again, her back to their father. "What sacrifice? Did your God require a sacrifice greater than the one He has already requested? Isn't it enough to leave our family, our father, our inheritance, our friends? What more could El Echad want?"

Abram cupped her cheek again, studying her, then his gaze skipped to some place behind her. "Blood sacrifice was handed down from the days of Noah, to make atonement for our sins.

Our ancestors Eber and Nahor both taught this to me, though our father has not done so. Adonai Elohim did not ask it of me, but I knew in my spirit it was the right thing to do. I sacrificed one of the rams to Him."

Sarai looked away, her gaze catching a glimpse of Abram's pet, the spotless lamb he favored. There were only a few perfect sheep in the flock, and even fewer rams. The only spotless one she knew of . . . She looked into his face again, surprised when his gaze met hers so intensely.

"Which ram?" She needed to know. Yet she already did.

He took her hand in his and turned her away, walking them both toward Terah.

She forced him to stop. "Which one, my lord? You must tell me if I'm to follow you."

His gaze darkened ever so slightly. "Did you not just tell me you were bound to me in all ways? Following me should have nothing to do with which ram bore the sacrifice."

She recoiled at his tone, suddenly irritated that he should use her own vows against her. He didn't have to remind her. Didn't she always obey his commands? Didn't she even today obey when she didn't sacrifice to the goddess? She didn't need his reminder. She needed him to tell her he had chosen a ram she didn't care for in the least. Not one she fancied.

"I chose the one most like me," he said at last. "There were only two choices, and he represented my sins better than the other one."

"So you would spare your favorite and sacrifice mine." The words came out more bitter than she'd expected. Selfish male! What man had ever looked out for a woman above himself? She turned away from him, about to stalk off.

He caught her arm. "Sarai." His voice, both gentle and commanding, beckoned her to pause. She let him slowly turn her to face him. He grasped both her hands in his again. "I saved this one"—he glanced at his pet, then looked back at her—"for you. If we are to seek the Lord's favor, we must both offer Him our best. They will both shed their blood to cover our sins. I will take you to the altar first thing in the morning."

His words pierced her conscience, humbling her. She lowered her gaze, undone. "I'm sorry, my lord. I've misjudged you."

He tipped her chin toward him. "It is an honest misjudging. We must each part with everything we love. Except each other." He kissed her again, then took her hand and called to the ewe who would give her life for Sarai in the morning.

3

"If your God told you to go, then you must go." Terah leaned heavily on his staff and sat down on the bench beneath the parapet along the perimeter of their roof. He took time to settle his bulk, gave a short cough, then looked at Abram. "I will go with you."

Sarai's feet stopped a pace behind Abram's as he walked across the roof, her breath catching at his words. Abram's God had told Abram to leave his father's household. But of course, they couldn't leave Terah behind. Who would care for him in his old age?

"Are you sure you are up to travel, Father? I would not expect you to leave all you possess to join me. Surely Nahor will welcome you, especially now that he will inherit my land portion." Abram sat on the bench opposite their father and crossed his long legs at the ankles. Sarai sat next to him, tucking her hand into the crook of his arm.

"Do you think me so old that I cannot ride a camel across the desert, my son? It will be good for me to move about more. These bones get too stiff sitting all the time."

Abram opened his mouth as if to speak, then shut it again, clearly at a loss. Sarai glanced from one man to the other. Did Abram actually expect to talk their father out of something once his mind was made up? By the look in his eyes and the set to his jaw, their father had come to an immovable decision much quicker than she'd anticipated. How was that possible after so many years living in one place? She herself was still reeling from the enormity of what such a move would mean. And yet a little thrill passed through her. Was it true? Would she finally bear a son?

She would go to the ends of the earth with Abram if it meant she could finally keep her vow.

"You can't possibly expect to travel alone, just the two of you. You will need provisions, servants, and your flocks. What would you eat without their milk and cheeses? You will need their wool to warm you. And Lot will join us, of course."

Abram stiffened at their father's announcement, then let out a long, slow breath. "Lot may see things differently, Father."

A feeling of relief flooded her, and she scooted closer to Abram. As if he sensed her need of him, he put one arm around her and drew her to his chest. She liked Lot well enough, but she would almost be glad to leave Melah behind—a constant reminder of all she did not have.

But, of course, if the promises were true . . .

"You will need a steward to manage your affairs, someone to oversee things as you travel. Have you considered Eliezer of Damascus? He seems capable enough."

Sarai's mind drifted as the two men continued to talk, to work out the details they would need to travel to . . . where? Abram's God had not told him where. He had simply said to go. But when they did go, they obviously needed to take many camels to carry all of the supplies. They couldn't go without servants, of course, and they would need flocks of both sheep and goats. She must set the servants to sewing tents made of goat's hair, and food needed to be gathered and stored . . .

She started as Abram squeezed her arm, drawing her attention back to him.

"We will leave within a month. That should give us plenty of time to gather all we need," Abram said, pushing to his feet and drawing her up beside him.

"Only a month, my lord?" Sarai glanced at Terah, who was slowly making his way to the steps. "There is so much to be done." Had she been lost in thought so long that they were ready to retire to their beds? Or was the urgency of leaving pushing them onward with unseen hands?

Abram held her back from following their father. "We must do all we can to obey Adonai soon. A month is a reasonable time." He bent closer, his dark, speckled beard grazing her cheek. "Make sure to pack plenty of things for the coming little one. You will bear my son yet, beloved." He nibbled her ear, making tingling sensations rush through her.

"Do not fool with me, dear husband. Unless you plan to do something to make this supposed promise come to pass . . ." She let her words trail off and captured his gaze with a twinkling one of her own.

Abram looked up at the sound of their father grunting his way down the steps, mumbling to himself. A small scowl drew a thin line between Abram's brows, and Sarai turned to follow his gaze. When their father was out of earshot, Abram pulled her closer. "He will make the trip difficult, but I could not refuse him."

"Of course not. He is our father."

He nodded, relief flooding his face. "I knew you would understand." A smile turned the corners of his mouth, and he bent to kiss her. "Now let's go below and find a way to see Adonai's promise fulfilled, shall we?"

Her heart sang as she smiled her response and let him lead her down the steps.

Abram stood in the courtyard of his father's vast estate, shading his eyes against the sun's afternoon rays. He would normally rest in the relentless heat, but the need to gather provisions and obey Adonai's call urged him to push harder, to finish the work. He had already dispatched Lot to purchase more servants who would come with them to tend the sheep and help with the move, while his brother Nahor had begun preparations to take over Terah's estate once Abram and Terah had departed. Would they truly be ready to leave by week's end?

He ran a hand along the back of his neck, watching the road in the distance. Abram had chosen to sell his portion of his father's lands to his older brother at a reduced rate in order to keep the ancestral lands in the family. He could not afford to simply give them away, lest they run short of needed funds to purchase supplies that they might need along the journey. The enormity of what he had done, what he was about to do, only skirted the edges of his thoughts. He would not allow it to sink in too deeply. Not until they were on their way with no chance of turning back in disobedience.

He scanned the area in front of him from left to right, at last spotting his servant Eliezer coming toward him across the field, leading a heavily laden camel. Abram stepped from the stones of the court to walk the worn path toward the edge of the gated estate. He passed beneath the shadow of the ancient terebinth trees that kept watch over the land, trees older than the flood itself. The camel snorted as it came to a stop behind Eliezer, obediently bending at the knees and lowering itself to the ground.

"Greetings, my lord," Eliezer said, dipping his head in respect to Abram. "I have secured the last of the items you requested— grain, herbs, blankets, fine linen, leather, knives, camp ovens, and skins of wine, plus gold, silver, and trinkets for trading. The items you sold brought a fair price." He moved to the camel's side and untied one of the sacks, pulled a pouch from it, and placed it in Abram's hands.

Abram undid the drawstring and poured the hefty weight of gold coins into his palm. He did a quick count and transferred them back into the bag, nodding his acceptance. Eliezer had proven his ability and his worth. His father had been right. He would make a good steward.

"If it pleases you, Eliezer, I would have you come with us on our journey. I need wise servants and someone who will be capable of overseeing my household goods. If you are willing, I would make you my steward."

Eliezer drew a hand over his square, bearded jaw, then rested it on the camel's neck. A young man in his early forties, Eliezer carried a sturdy, confident build and a character Abram had quickly learned to trust.

"I would be honored to be your steward, my lord. I have nothing to keep me here."

"Good. You will be in charge of all necessary provisions and trade and keep a financial record of all I have. I will trust you to secure information of new territories before we enter." Abram tied the pouch of gold to his belt.

A shadow passed through Eliezer's dark, intelligent eyes, and his gaze moved from Abram to something beyond him.

"Does something trouble you, Eliezer?" Abram motioned for Eliezer to move from the sun to the shadow of the great spreading terebinth. "I would know your mind before we set out rather than have you change it along the way."

Eliezer bent his head and kicked a small stone with the toe of his sandal before lifting his eyes to meet Abram's gaze. "There is something about me you must know. I wish to keep you from suffering my fate." Eliezer's face darkened, but his look remained unwavering.

"Tell me," Abram said, not at all sure he wanted to know the man's story, but certain he must. "Sit with me and explain yourself so I may know all that is in your mind."

Eliezer nodded, waited for Abram to sit first, then sat a few paces away from him. "As you know, I am from Damascus. My wife and I grew up there and married several years ago." A pained expression crossed his face, and he looked into the distance, in the direction of Abram's house. "We were married three years, but Jerusha had yet to bear a child."

Abram rested his hands on his knees, all too aware of the pain of a barren wife. He tilted his head in a slight nod but held his peace.

Eliezer's Adam's apple bobbed as he clasped his hands in front of his body. "One day my business ventures called for me to travel to Nineveh, and Jerusha wanted to come with me. She loved the idea of travel, and I had yet to take her outside of Damascus. I had heard the rumors of foreign kings and beautiful women, but I had not believed them, thinking no man would be so cruel as to steal the wife of his neighbor." His gaze met Abram's and held. "I was wrong."

Abram's stomach sank like a stone dropped in a well. He said nothing, waiting, his mind whirling with ramifications and fear, knowing already what was to come. The rumors were true then.

Eliezer seemed to find fascination with his feet, like a man ashamed of what he is about to say. "We went to Nineveh. I told Jerusha to veil herself, to hide from the perusal of men. But the king's spies were everywhere, searching for beautiful women to add to his harem. They came in the night and stole Jerusha from my bed and took her to become wife to the king. They tried to kill me, but a friendly guard allowed me to escape with my life. My goods, my wife—everything I had taken with me but the clothes on my back—were lost."

Abram drew in a sharp breath, finding the air suddenly too

painful to breathe. Sarai was the most beautiful of women, fairest of anyone in the land of Ur. But in Ur, where his presence was well-known, she was protected. No one would harm the wife of one of Ur's leading elders. What would become of her in foreign lands, where they were not known?

"What should I do?" The question formed before Abram had a chance to process another thought. He had to protect Sarai, yet he had to obey Adonai's call.

Eliezer looked up, his expression carrying a hint of surprise, as if a master should never need advice but would be the one to give it instead. "I don't know, my lord. Unless . . ."

"Unless what?" Abram ought to know what to do, should have considered the matter the moment he'd heard the rumors and planned for the unknowns of the future. But it was too late now to look back on what should have been.

"You could pretend to be your wife's brother. A brother has more rights, can protect the women in his charge. Men might seek you for her hand in marriage, but you would have the right to refuse them. Or at the very least put them off until you could get out of their city. It would buy you time."

Abram plucked a blade of grass from the ground and chewed on the end. Such a plan would be the truth, what he would tell of it. Sarai was indeed his half sister, as they shared the same father. And if it would ensure her safety, and his . . .

He pushed to his feet, noticing the mild stiffness in his back, the slightest twinge he'd not felt before. After seventy-three summers since his birth, he shouldn't be surprised at these initial signs of aging, but he was. Shaking the thought aside, he turned to find Eliezer waiting for instruction.

"I will speak to Sarai and request her to tell everyone who asks that she is my sister. Let those coming with us know of our plan. For Sarai's protection."

✽✽✽

Sarai sifted through her sewing supplies, running her fingers along the smooth, multicolored threads. Piles of fine linen fabric, balls of colored wool, and a variety of sizes of bone needles filled the basket to the top. She closed the lid at the sound of footsteps behind her and turned to find Abram standing at the threshold of their bedroom.

"My lord, I didn't expect you so soon." She looked into his strong, handsome face. The faintest hint of silver threaded the strands of his dark hair at the temples, and his full beard held a mix of black and gray with strands of red mingling in, as though the hair could not decide what color it should be. His bushy brows were drawn, and little lines appeared on his normally smooth brow. For his age, Abram was a striking man, still strong and virile, still her heart's only love.

She smiled as she took two steps toward him. He met her in the middle of the room, his hand extended.

"We must talk."

She placed her hand in his and accepted his kiss. Memories of their nights together since the One God had made His promises to Abram stirred her thoughts now, making her ache with longing. Surely El Echad had quickened their desire. Surely He would soon fulfill His promise.

"Talk about what, my lord?"

Servants' voices came to them from the halls of the house, and the clatter of carts and braying of donkeys filtered through the open windows. While they were making quick work of packing to leave, Nahor and Milcah were moving in, creating a chaotic commotion.

Abram glanced behind him, then looked at her again. "Let's take a walk."

It was on the tip of her tongue to remind him they still had much to do and didn't have time for a frivolous visit that could wait until they shared their bed that night, but she silenced the thought. She could read his expressions like a scroll, and his look told her to do as he'd asked. "Yes, my lord."

He released her hand and turned, leading them through the house, past the servants working in the courtyard, across the sun-drenched grasses to the shade of a spreading terebinth tree—the place he often came to in the afternoons when he took his rest. She waited until he had settled himself into a comfortable position on the ground, then knelt near him.

"What troubles you, my lord? How may I help?" She clasped her hands in her lap and studied his dear face.

He looked at her, his gaze tender. "There are rumors."

He paused, and she had to bite her lip to keep from trying to hurry him along. "What rumors, my lord?"

He shook his head as though his thoughts had been elsewhere and finally came back around to focus on her again. "I'm sorry, my love. I am distracted by many things. I should not have dragged you away from your work, but Eliezer has just told me something . . . It concerns me, concerns you." He paused again and reached for her hand. "I want you to promise me something."

"Anything, my lord." Fear coiled inside of her at the look in his eyes.

"Eliezer lost his wife to the king of Nineveh. He took her with him on a visit there and nearly lost his life when the king's guards saw his wife's beauty and snatched her from him." His gaze grew intense, and Sarai's fear grew with it. "I know you are a beautiful woman, fairer than any woman in Ur and beyond, and I fear that as we travel, we could suffer the same fate."

She drew in a sharp breath. "What will we do? We must obey the Lord and leave this place. But how will we keep this from happening to us?" Her stomach plummeted at the thought of being snatched from him. He had always been her protector, her keeper. Even as a child, he had shown an older-brother protectiveness of her. Who would watch out for her if he were killed along the way? But surely not. Surely his God would be their rear guard.

But the look in Abram's eyes told her even he didn't believe the matter would concern Adonai. They must take action themselves.

"I've given this much thought, Sarai, and I see only one solution." He squeezed her fingers, and she drew support from his strength. "This is your kindness that you should do for me: in every place, wherever we go, say of me, 'He is my brother,' that it may go well with me, that my life might be spared."

His words were barbs, wounding her, but as she read the fear in his gaze, she knew she could deny him nothing. Yet what would such a thing mean? She glanced down at their intertwined hands. If she must go back to the time when he truly was only her brother, they would not be free to share the intimacies they did now. Memories of those long-ago days when she'd tried so hard to get him to notice her, when she'd pined after him, despairing that he would ever consider taking her to be his wife—would they be forced to return to such an arrangement whenever they joined another caravan or visited a town or a foreign land? How could she bear it?

His fingers touched her chin, gently coaxing her to look into his face once more. "I need your word, Sarai. I wouldn't ask such a thing . . ." He glanced away. "It will mean, of course, that at times you cannot share my bed . . ." His voice trailed off.

"How will I ever bear the promised child then, my lord? And what if he grows even now in my womb? I would be a woman scorned worse than I am now, to bear a child without a husband. How can you ask this of me?" Tears thickened her throat. But she knew by the disbelief in his eyes that he did not think her womb had quickened and did not worry that such a thing would confront them. Was he worried only for his own life then? What of hers?

What if she was taken as Eliezer's wife had been? A shudder passed through her.

"You won't be taken. If the promised child grows within you, I will protect you as any brother would. As I did before we married."

"You barely noticed me then." Bitterness tinged her tone.

"I saw everything about you, dearest Sarai. Since the time of your maturity, I've loved you." He pulled her toward him until her head rested on his shoulder and she was encased in his arms. "It will only be for those times when we enter a large city where a king resides, where the danger would be the greatest. As your brother, my life would not be in danger, and I would be in a better position to protect you."

His words sounded so convincing, but how would he truly stop a king's men should they come for her? And how long would she be forced to sleep alone during such an arrangement? She wasn't getting any younger. If she didn't conceive Adonai's promised one soon, she might lose her chance. She shivered against Abram's chest.

His hand trailed along her arm, then drew circles along her back. "Please do me this kindness, beloved. Do not make me beg you."

She almost laughed at the thought of her strong husband begging her for anything. She pulled back to look at him again, seeing the hint of defeat in his eyes. If she pouted or pushed him, she could get him to change his mind, to put away this ridiculous plan. But she couldn't bear to disappoint him, despite the sacrifice to their marriage.

"I will do this," she whispered, hating her beauty that put her at such risk, hating the need that spurred him to ask, hating the wickedness of foreign kings who would kill a man for his wife. "But I will not like it." She frowned, making sure he noted her displeasure.

He cupped her face with his hand and smiled. "Thank you, dear one. I will not like it any more than you will. But whether you think so or not, you have just given me back my life." He kissed her then, as though he didn't care who could see. Heat poured into her face at the sound of voices coming closer, but he did not pull back or shorten his kiss. When he released her, leaving both of them breathless, she smoothed her robe and glanced quickly behind her. Lot strode toward them, leading a group of men, obviously seeking Abram to speak with him.

"I should go, my lord." She touched her mouth with the back of her hand, her lips still trembling from his ardent kiss. Would she feel such a kiss on their journey, or would every day be fraught with danger too great, relegating her back to the role of sister instead of wife?

Abram stood and helped her to her feet, then left her to meet his nephew. Sarai hurried in the opposite direction, away from the scrutiny of the other men, away from her own traitorous thoughts. Lot would have no such need to ask Melah to lie about their relationship. Melah lacked the beauty that men would want and Lot would fear. Besides, Melah had one child and carried another—if, God willing, it lived. Another reason why Lot would not worry that men would take her.

On the other hand, Sarai not only had no child, but apparently, for at least part of their journey into the future, she would have no husband as well.

4

Sarai rose from the hard ground, her back aching and her limbs stiff and sore. The dark interior of the goat's-hair tent let in little light, but the sounds of the stirring camp and the scent of flat bread baking told her it was time to rise and would soon be time to move on again. It had been only two weeks since they left their comfortable home in Ur, yet it felt as though they had been traveling forever.

She stretched her arms overhead, surprised at the creak in her bones. She could not continue this ridiculous arrangement. At the very least, she must speak to Abram and insist upon a mat of feathers, not this prickly straw she'd been forced to lie upon. How to transport such a thing would be up to the servants to figure out. She simply could not sleep on the ground one more night!

Voices grew louder outside the tent. Had she slept so long that the whole camp was already working without her? Feeling her way along the tent's wall, she found the tunic and robe she had worn yesterday and the day before, and too many days to count before that. The faded red and gold made her look like a peasant and had grown impossibly dust coated. Once they reached Harran, she would wash every dusty thing in her pack and not be so quick to change to fresh clothing. And she must insist Abram not push them so hard. Father was already showing signs of fatigue, and the servants had no time to rest or bathe in the Euphrates. What she wouldn't give to feel clean again!

She lifted the tent flap and stepped into the bright morning sunlight, squinting.

"The meal is ready to break your fast, mistress. The master is asking for you." Her maid, Lila, offered her a flask of water, then fell into step a pace behind her.

"Why did you not wake me sooner then?" Irritation tinged her voice, and Sarai checked herself as she walked toward the circle of men. She would never get her way if she did not sweeten her requests with a pleasing tone.

"I'm sorry, mistress. The master said to let you sleep." Lila stepped to the side while Sarai walked with practiced grace toward the central fire, straightening her back.

She tested a smile, sensing it more listless than eager to please, and finally settled for a mixed half smile that would convey to Abram her pleasure at seeing him and her displeasure at her circumstances.

She spotted female servants pouring batter onto the surface of a camp oven to bake the quick flat bread, a poor substitute for the soft, yeasty, sweet dough she was so well-known for in Ur. She was weary of flat bread and stews and goat cheese. Sheep cheese had a better flavor, but their supply had been minimal from the start, making her parcel it out most carefully. How much longer would it take to get to the land Adonai wanted them to reach?

Her smile widened just slightly at Abram's approach. "My lord." She gave a short bow, accepting the stone seat he offered her near the fire.

Abram took her hand and kissed her cheek. "You look well today," he said, giving her that charming smile she could never resist. He had a way of disarming her, distracting her from things that troubled her until she looked back on the matter and realized he had won the little game they played with hardly a contest. She must not let it happen this time. She could not keep up this pace.

"If I look well, it is an illusion, my lord." She kept her tone light and lowered her head, her expression reserved. "I cannot sleep another night on such hard ground. Send the servants to find feathers to fill between sheets of fine linen or shear one of the sheep and fill the linen cover with its wool. And make them pad it thick. I don't want to feel a single clod of dirt or stone beneath me."

He squeezed her hand, bringing it to his lips. "Such a thing would be a burden, dear one. Wait until we reach Harran. Then you can have your bed of fine feathers and we will rest for a short time." He released her hand as though the matter was settled.

"I cannot wait that long. I could barely walk this morning." It was an exaggeration of the aches she'd felt, but he didn't need to know it. She accepted a plate of flat bread and cheese from Lila's hand and nibbled the cheese, scrunching her nose at the sharp taste as she watched him. A hint of annoyance crossed his brow, causing her the slightest prickle of anxiety. She hadn't meant to anger him, but still . . .

He looked as though he were about to speak, but then appeared to discard his frustration, surprising her. He stroked the edges of his beard. "I will see what can be done to make your bed more comfortable."

She searched his face for some sign of weakening. He didn't usually give in so easily. "My bed would be just fine if my husband shared it." She was baiting him and she knew it, but she didn't care.

When his expression changed again to frustration, she wondered at her own good sense. But she wanted more than a bed of soft feathers. She wanted her husband to give her a child, and he couldn't do that when they were living apart. Let him be angry then, if it got him to change their traveling arrangements.

She lifted her face in challenge, meeting his scowl, but a moment later he gentled his look and cupped her cheek with one hand. "I miss having you at my side as well, Sarai. You know this."

She swallowed a bitter retort. He was making this harder than it should be. "If you miss me, then why do you avoid my bed?" She leaned in closer, her voice a mere whisper, embarrassed that she should even have to ask such a thing.

"You know why, Sarai."

"There are no kings about, no foreign spies. What other reason is there?" His actions of late had confused her so. Killing their pet lambs to appease his God and taking off on this journey to who knew where because of a voice he said he heard? It made no sense, and she struggled to understand.

"The journey is taxing, Sarai. I have little desire by day's end but to sleep."

His admission stung in its stark reminder that her husband was no longer the passionate man of his youth. While he still possessed the vigor of men much younger than he, his stamina faded sooner than it used to. And where desire had once shown strong, it now carried the fading sense of age. How could he possibly believe Adonai would give them a son when his body was nearly too old to father one? Though at seventy-three, surely it was still possible.

"Then we need to stop. If you are worn out, what of Father? Have you not noticed his fatigue? He is frail, my lord, yet you have pushed us to the limit every day without even a moment to wash in the river, until I can no longer bear the odor of my own flesh!"

Abram's hand on her arm told her she had spoken too loudly and said too much. She should have waited until they were alone in his tent to vent her feelings. Here the servants paused to listen, and no doubt gossip would spread among them until Melah heard a disjointed version of the truth. She didn't need Melah's meddling and had no desire to explain herself to her niece.

"I am sorry this has been so hard on you, dear one." Abram's voice drew her attention to his dark eyes, his uncertainty evident. He seemed at a loss for words. His chest lifted in a sigh, and he reached to put one arm around her, pulling her close. She leaned into him, feeling his strength, and suddenly wished she had kept her discontent to herself, wanting to comfort him.

"I will go with you, my lord, but please don't stay so distant even if you are too weary for love. I can't bear it."

He squeezed her shoulder and kissed the top of her head. "I will do my best."

Eliezer approached the fire. "Excuse me, my lord, but we are ready to move when you are." Abram released her and stood, leaving her side without another word. The loss pained her. Somewhere along the way, Abram had changed the rules of their relationship. Where once he had been playful, now he was nearly always serious, unresponsive to her banter. How was she supposed to treat him? She'd gotten her way by plying her charms, and he had won his way by confusing her efforts. The game was a trifle immature, but he had indulged her. Now he gave in without a fight, as though peace was worth any price.

What was wrong with him?

She snatched what was left of the flat bread from the plate and handed the empty dish to Lila to pack in the leather satchel. She had her own work to oversee. Call of God or not, she must get Abram to rethink what he was doing. Perhaps Harran would provide some answers and grant relief from her husband's confusing choices.

Red clay walls and gates ringed the city of Harran but did not block the taller cone-shaped and round-roofed buildings housed within. Abram stood at the head of their company, speaking to the sentries that were posted as guards. What was taking so long?

A braying donkey sounded behind her. Sarai turned at the sense of movement and maneuvered her animal to the side to allow Melah to sidle up beside her.

"I cannot wait to get inside, to find a room, and to make a trip to the river. The grime and dust are so thick I can no longer see the color of my skin." Melah made a futile attempt to brush some of the dust from her arm.

Sarai gave her niece a sidelong glance. "In this I will agree with you. I am glad we are stopping here to rest for a while." She had done her best to keep her complaints from Melah, which would only fuel the woman's critical spirit, but her own body ached from too many nights on hard ground and too many days riding on the back of an animal.

Melah drew closer, their donkeys almost touching. "Lot and I have been talking." She paused, and Sarai turned to meet her gaze "I think we should stay here." Melah motioned toward the city, where Sarai glimpsed Abram still in deep conversation with one of the men at the gate. "And I don't mean only Lot and myself." She pulled closer still, too close, and Sarai dug her heels into the donkey's side to move it forward a few steps.

"I think you should convince Abram to stay too, Sarai. Your father's health isn't good. The journey has aged him, and I think Abram would do well to settle here. At least for a time. You have Abram's ear. He will listen if you insist on it."

Sarai glimpsed her father's cart up ahead, where a handful of servants propped cushions and covered him with another blanket, trying to keep him comfortable.

"You are just as discontented as the rest of us. Admit it." Melah's tone held uncharacteristic empathy, as though for once she really did care about someone other than herself.

Sarai craned her neck to see behind her, where Melah's donkey had stopped a pace back, waiting with the rest of them to move into the city. She weighed the wisdom of trusting her niece with her true thoughts. A soft sigh lifted her chest. She was discontented, but her reasons were far more than the discomforts of the journey. She looked forward again, and Melah edged in beside her.

"God has called Abram to follow Him to Canaan, not Harran. Discontented or not, I have promised to do the same." The direction they were to go had come to Abram after they set out, and she had no reason to doubt him. The caravan finally moved, slowly crossing past the guards toward the gates. "But," she said, glancing once more at her niece, "I will speak to Abram. Perhaps a short stay will not be a problem."

The red clay bricks grew close enough to touch now, and she saw Abram coming toward her. He caught the donkey's bridle and pulled it to a stop. He leaned in but did not touch her.

"I have found us rooms to rent from a caravan merchant who is rarely at home. Father can rest there, and you can take care of him as a good daughter would." His pointed look sent a stab of fear through her. "As my sister has already done so well."

She swallowed, her senses grown suddenly dull, but not so faded that she did not miss his meaning. The look in his eye told her clearly what she had expected anywhere but here. Harran was a city like Ur, not a powerful kingdom whose kings held no regard for their subjects. Surely a man's wife was safe in his keeping here, despite her beauty.

Abram fell into step at her side, his hand slowly guiding the donkey. "A city whose god was conceived through the ruin of his mother breeds a people of suspect morality, dear one. I cannot risk it."

"Everyone knows Nannar was born of Enlil's love for Ninlil. We have heard these stories since our youth. We had no fear of such things in Ur. Harran is Ur's sister city. Why should it be any different?"

"Everyone in Ur believes that tale is one of love, yes. Not so in Harran. Here, the god Enlil forced Ninlil, who in turn birthed Sin. When a man forces a woman, there is no love bond there."

Abram stopped the donkey again and gave Sarai a look. They had reached the gate, and he would speak no more of this with her now. Perhaps in the seclusion of the house he had secured, he would further explain himself. But it would not be said in the intimacy of the dark at his side. He would not risk sharing her bed here. Any hope she had possessed of making a home, of resting at length in this place and re-creating what they'd had in Ur, was gone.

Abram stepped around her to the guard's side. "The woman is my sister and nursemaid to our father."

The guard lifted a brow even as his eyes roamed her features, what little he could discern from her disheveled, dusty, veiled appearance. She lowered her head, her submission to Abram an outward obedience, knowing it was what he expected to keep her safe. She should be grateful. He was only doing what was best for both of them. But her grip tightened around the leather reins in a vain attempt to curb her rising anger, to squelch the poisoned seeds of bitterness settling in her heart.

5

Abram jabbed his walking stick onto the hard-packed earth of the overcrowded and confining streets of Harran's marketplace. He passed a baker's stall, his stomach rumbling with the mixed scents of yeast and cinnamon and honey, knowing that if he had any sense, he should take some to Sarai as a peace offering. He paused a moment to glance into the stall, but was in no mood to wait behind three cackling women with small children hanging onto their skirts.

He hurried on. Children scampered out of his way, his stick making an added *thwack* to every step but doing little to release his mounting aggravation. How was he supposed to care for his father and obey his God at the same time if his father was too frail to continue on? Why hadn't the man stayed behind with Nahor? Hadn't Adonai told Abram to leave his father's household?

Guilt filled him. He came to an abrupt stop and lifted his gaze to the cloudy sky. *Am I doing the wrong thing?* He'd told the elders they planned to stay and live among the people for as long as it took until his father was well enough to travel. Their open acceptance should have warmed him, but mingled among the hospitality was a hint of greed, and Abram knew that these people would not accept his beliefs in Adonai Elohim. He almost told the truth about his marriage to Sarai, but decided they could live secretly as man and wife without the whole city having to know. She would remain his father's daughter in their eyes. It was safer this way.

He blinked against the sun as it spilled from behind a cloud. His heart calmed, listening for some response, some relief from the guilt he now bore, but it found none. When he looked again at his surroundings, he recognized the house where they were staying, the place that had already become too familiar. Sarai stood in the courtyard talking over the brick wall with a neighbor, her friendly demeanor and beautiful smile dispelling his foul mood. At his approach, she turned, her smile fading behind a careful mask. She dipped her head, then walked swiftly toward him and kissed his cheek.

"Brother," she said, her voice void of emotion, her mood obviously unchanged. "I trust your day was productive."

He looked down at her, his heart constricting. Despite the head covering, her thin veil revealed a full mouth and dark blue eyes full of longing. He stifled a groan and turned her toward the house, his hand at the small of her back, gently urging her forward. "How is Father?" He glanced at the neighbor and nodded his greeting. The woman's sharp eye worried him. The last thing he needed was a meddlesome gossip living beside them. Perhaps he could find a house closer to the city wall, a larger home, further from nosy neighbors.

"He seems better since we have settled, though I fear he is still too weak to travel, my lord." She turned to face him the moment he closed the door. "What did the elders say?"

He placed a finger over her mouth to still her questions, then took her hand and tugged her toward his private quarters, shutting the door behind them. He closed the shutters over the windows, and the heat quickly rose in the stifling room.

"I trust you do not say much to our inquisitive neighbor?"

Sarai removed her veil, shaking the combs from her hair. "Of course not. I asked her for a recipe for lamb curry. I smelled it cooking in her courtyard the other day and she let me taste it. I wanted to make it for you." She stepped closer and placed a hand on his chest, her soft fingers making his blood pump hot and fierce.

He released his grip on the walking stick and took her into his arms. She leaned into him, and he bent his head until his lips claimed hers. Her lips were honey and cinnamon, her love filling the longing ache in his heart.

"I've missed you," he whispered against her hair, pulling her down beside him on his bed. "But the time for secrecy has not passed." His kiss silenced her response.

She rested against his chest, her even breathing a greater comfort than he could have thought possible. How had he denied her so long? And yet even amid the question, the fear of losing her returned.

"You did not tell the elders the truth about us, did you?" She rolled onto her side and rose up on one elbow, piercing him with those dark, seductive eyes.

He shook his head, feeling as though he had somehow failed her.

"What happens if Adonai sends His promised seed and produces this long-awaited child in me? What will they think of us then, my lord? We cannot live a lie forever."

"We should not live a lie at all." But what else was he to do? "I don't plan for us to stay here that long."

"So we are leaving then?" She sat up, her long, dark hair falling far beneath her shoulders, its thick tresses framing her beautiful face. Her expression clouded. "We cannot force Father to continue."

"He should have stayed in Ur." Silence followed Abram's comment. "I could send for Nahor to come and get him, to take him home to Ur."

"I cannot leave him with Milcah. She never cared for him as I do. He would die too soon, and I would never know it." She glanced beyond him, her eyes filming, and his heart ached with her pain.

He drew her into his arms again, his sigh palpable. "Of course not." He rubbed her back, enjoying the feel of her head against his heart. "When the promised seed grows within you, I will tell the elders the truth. Until then, we will keep our love quiet between us."

She placed a hand over her middle, her own sigh deep yet quiet, as though willing the promise to come this moment yet certain it wouldn't. Surely it was possible . . . surely soon.

But when she rose to dress and looked down at him still resting among the cushions, he wondered whether El Echad would bless them now amid the lie they were living.

Sarai waited in the courtyard outside of Lot's home for Melah to fasten the clasp of her robe while her servant tied the leather sandals to her feet. Lila stood in the street just beyond the gate with Sarai's two ever-watchful male slaves. Lot's voice came from inside the house, his tone angry, but his words were indistinguishable. She looked toward the wooden door at the sound of footsteps and moved to the side as he burst into the courtyard with barely a glance at his wife. He nodded toward Sarai, stopping abruptly.

"I did not see you there, Aunt." He smoothed his hands along the sides of his robe as though suddenly uncertain what to do or how to act. "Is there something you need?"

She shook her head, her gaze skipping to Melah's, catching the soft glint of tears on her lashes. Had they fought? But of course they had. She looked back at Lot, clearing her throat. "I came to accompany Melah to market. The Akitu Festival is next week, and I thought to purchase some spices and games for the children so we might have a quiet celebration in its stead." Abram would never allow them to participate in the worship of foreign gods, but planning an alternative seemed like a good way to keep her father distracted and the household servants and their children at peace.

"The festival. Of course. I had almost forgotten." Though by the slight scowl along his brow, Sarai wondered if he spoke the truth. "I will leave you two to your plans then." He offered her a curt nod, not even a hint of his once-charming smile poking at the edges of his close-cropped beard. He strode through the courtyard into the street, turned a corner, and disappeared from sight.

Did Lot plan to allow his household to participate in the gaiety, to watch the act of sacred marriage or pretend the moon god had died and somehow come to life again? She knew too well the horrors of the sacrifice that accompanied the festival, of life lost because of such beliefs. Their brother Haran had lost his son to such a sacrifice in the years before Sarai was old enough to understand its significance. She shuddered at the thought.

"Are you ready?" Melah appeared at her side, her face barely a handbreadth from Sarai's.

Sarai took a step back. "I'm ready." She pointed toward the gate, allowing Melah to move ahead of her. They maneuvered the crowded streets, and Sarai could not help but note the festive atmosphere already present, as though the people were anxious to start the celebration. Men whistled as they passed, and as they stepped beneath the merchants' tents, smiles greeted them.

"Do you want to tell me what's wrong?" Sarai fingered a miniature table with its accompanying stool, bed, and doll, then snuck a glance at Melah. "Why was Lot so upset?"

Melah stood close, her hand grazing a selection of tiny animals—sheep, goats, birds, bears, and lions. "Kammani would love these." She picked up a lamb and turned it over. The wooden craftsmanship was superb, down to the fine lines depicting the wool.

"If you don't want to talk about it, that's fine." Sarai chose several tops and balls and small ships for the boys, along with some dolls and furniture for the girls. She enjoyed spoiling the children of her servants. It didn't quite fill the void of her empty arms, but the temporary joy it brought to the children and parents alike helped.

"We argued about the festival. He doesn't want me to go." She lifted her chin, a defiant gleam in her eyes. "But we've been here a year, and we missed it last time. I told him I was going whether he liked it or not." She met Sarai's gaze, her own challenging. "And I don't want to hear any lectures against the evils of watching the parade or listening to the stories of the gods. If it isn't real, there's no harm. And if it is, then it's good to keep the gods happy."

Sarai's stomach tightened and a shiver worked through her, as it always did whenever she and Melah got into a discussion about the gods. "I won't argue with you, Melah. Obviously Lot already tried that." She stepped toward the merchant with her purchases, exchanged a few words to barter the price, paid the man, then followed Melah to the next tent. She was in no mood to argue with Melah today, and by her tone, there would be no reasoning with her anyway.

"What are we looking for here?" Sarai glanced around the black goat's-hair walls, where multicolored tapestries hung with pictures of erotic art. Tables were spread with amulets and idols of gods she had seen in Ur all her life. She turned to leave, but Melah caught her arm.

"I need an amulet to keep the demons from stealing my baby." She laid a hand over the place where a child would lay.

"Kammani is to have a brother or sister?" Sarai could not stop the swift pang of jealousy, but she smoothed her expression and stuffed the pain away. She smiled. "How wonderful for you."

Melah lost her defiant look, her gaze suddenly troubled. She moved to one of the tables holding various stone pendants strung with leather strings to wear about the neck. "If the gods are kind to me. You know how many I have lost." Melah had miscarried several children before Kammani's birth.

"That one is the demon Pazuzu and is perfect for counteracting the evil of Lamashtu against you or your unborn child." The female merchant looked at Melah, taking in her appearance as if trying to judge what to think of her.

Melah picked up the amulet and held it to her chest. "I will take it."

The merchant gave Melah a semi-toothless smile, waiting while Melah fished the coins from her pouch. She accepted them and placed them in the pocket of her heavy leather girdle, then turned her attention to Sarai. "Can I interest you in such an amulet? I have all kinds—those for women with child, women who are sick with child, and even women who are barren and cannot bear a child." At her last words, she pointed to a leather strand with twenty-one small stones draped down the sides. "I've heard testimonies that this one really works." She gave Sarai a pointed stare. Could the woman read her thoughts?

Sarai stepped closer, looking down at the gleaming black stones, wondering what possible power such a thing could have to procure a child.

"It's not a bad idea, Sarai," Melah said at her side, their shoulders touching. "What can it hurt?"

The necklace was appealing. Would Abram recognize it as an amulet? It almost looked like the jewels she often wore, especially during festive occasions. But Melah's attitude stopped her.

"We better go." She looked at the merchant. "Thank you." Before Melah or the woman could respond, Sarai hurried from the tent, breathing deeper when she saw Lila and her guards standing close by.

"Why did you rush out like that?" Melah touched her arm, and Sarai took a step back, suddenly wanting to go home. But she had not purchased the spices yet or found the honeyed treats she hoped to secure.

"I have more important things to shop for than stone trinkets that will do nothing except be a weight around my neck." She glanced at Lila to follow her and hurried on to find the stall of spices.

"You're wasting a lot of good opportunities," Melah called after her. "You don't have to worship it. Just give it a try."

Sarai ducked into the tent, knowing Melah would follow and probably try to push the point, but Sarai had no intention of letting her. She did not need to tempt the fragile trust she had in Abram's God to keep His promise to them. If she listened too long to her niece, she would plunge headlong into despair and darkness.

She dare not risk it.

6

Palm trees lined the brick streets in the main section of Harran, leading a parade of people toward the city's temples. Carts carrying the image of Nannar-Sin, pulled by fattened oxen, were decorated with elaborate designs, while priests in grotesque face masks and wild costumes walked behind. Painted women in colorful garments danced, skirts swirling around the costumed priests, while guards flanked them before and behind, all leading the crowd toward the imposing ziggurat temple of Sin.

Melah stood on tiptoe, straining to see above the heads of other men and women, her heart beating with the pace of the drum. Terah, Lot's grandfather, stood at her side, clutching her arm in a grip far stronger than he'd exhibited in previous weeks.

"We should have found a roof to stand on to look down upon the parade." Terah's voice rasped like dried parchment. He cleared his throat. "We won't be able to see the king with the priestess from here."

"Abram would be glad we can see so little." Melah glanced at Terah, but his look told her he did not care whether his son was troubled by his choice to be here. Even Lot had acquiesced, allowing her to come once Terah insisted he would accompany her.

"Abram is too concerned with pleasing only his unseen God, my daughter." He patted her arm, motioning for her to follow him behind the crowds to the street beyond. "He does not realize the significance of the New Year's Feast. How will the gods shine upon the city or bless the ground with fertility if we do not please them? The grieving and contrition are important, to be sure, but the feasting and rejoicing matter too. What is one without the other?"

They maneuvered around donkeys tied to parked carts, and Melah lifted her robes to avoid a pile of dung in the dirt path. Terah's walking stick struck the uneven ground, and his breathing grew labored. He paused to catch his breath.

"Perhaps we should go back, Sabba. We do not need a better view." If Terah fell ill while in her care, Sarai would never forgive her. Not that she cared what Sarai thought. Sarai agreed with Lot, and Lot could learn a thing or two from his grandfather. What harm was there in watching a celebration?

"I'm fine." Terah stopped to take a few deep breaths, then continued on. They turned at the next street to the sound of trumpets and marching feet.

"The king is heading to the temple, Sabba. We must hurry!" Melah helped him climb the rest of the steps, then begged and pushed and prodded until a young woman finally took pity on Terah and allowed them a place to squeeze in beside her near the parapet. The ziggurat stood directly across from them, the steps clearly visible. Melah stood mesmerized, her heart beating faster as she watched the handsome king climb the steps to the temple doors, where the beautiful priestess stood waiting for him.

Music continued as the king declared his love for the priestess, then she spoke of her love for him in return. The words were poetic, their meaning erotic, as the flute and harp accompanied the spoken song. The crowds hushed, taking in the passion of their declaration, until at last the king pulled the priestess into his arms

61 *

and kissed her. The crowd cheered as the king lifted the priestess and carried her into the temple, and the great double doors swung shut behind them.

Melah sighed, drawn to the romance of such symbolic love, her heart yearning for more. Lot had treated her that way once. Back before they had wed, when he glimpsed her at Ur's New Year's Festival dancing in the streets with the other virgin daughters of the city. He had thought her a priestess at first, but when he realized she was free to marry, he had charmed her to the bank of the river, where the moon god's glow bathed the waters in ethereal light. He tempted and wooed her there, night after night, coaxing her from her father's house until at last she had succumbed to his desire. If only marriage had not changed him.

She looked back at the closed doors of the ziggurat, imagining the passion that was now missing from her own marriage, then shrugged the depressing thoughts aside. The parade continued with singing and dancing in the streets. A banquet would follow, and they should head to the palace grounds if they wanted a good seat.

She turned to face Terah. "Are you ready to head to the banquet, Sabba?"

Terah leaned against the parapet, but his face had gone gray, and a look of fear filled his expression. He slumped forward, his chest catching on the bricks, which stopped him from tumbling over the roof to the street below.

"Sabba!" She dove toward him, grabbing his shoulders and pulling him back, but the action made him lose his grip, and he crumpled to the ground. She looked around, frantic. "Someone help me!"

But the crowd on the roof had already headed down the stairs to join the celebration in the streets, and the sound of the drumbeat and the loud singing and chanting of the crowd smothered her insistent cries. Terah lay ashen and still. She leaned over him, listening for his breath, watching for the rise and fall of his chest, but he remained in his crumpled position, unmoving. She slipped her arms beneath him, grunting and groaning as she dragged him to the back of the roof near the stairs. She could not carry him home. She must get help.

Her pulse keeping time with her racing thoughts, Melah hurried down the steps and ran through the streets, silently thanking Nannar for the empty back alleys as she hurried home to find Lot and Abram.

Sarai sat limp and cold, unable to get warm despite the summer heat. Abram paced the length of the sitting room, his brows drawn low, his scowl hiding the worry she knew he felt. The door to their father's bedchamber opened, and a wiry, shriveled man emerged, the only physician not feasting and celebrating with the rest of the city.

"How is he?" Abram stood a head taller than the physician and looked twice as fierce. Sarai placed a hand on his arm in comfort.

"Very frail," the man said, craning his neck to meet Abram's gaze. "In truth, my lord, he hasn't much time. By all the gods, it is surprising he still lives at all. How old did you say he is?"

"A hundred twice and five years."

"Ah, that explains many things. By the look of him, I would have thought him a younger man."

"We are blessed to carry age well." Abram appeared to at last notice Sarai's hand on his arm and reached to tuck it closer, bringing her alongside him. "There is no hope for him then?"

The man shook his head. "His breathing—very shallow. And his life pulse beats so slow I can count to three before I feel the next." He adjusted the pouch holding his instruments and straightened his bent back, though it seemed to make little difference. "I will come again tomorrow, but you will be calling the mourners before I get here if my guess is right." He moved past them before Abram said a word in response.

Sarai looked at her husband, the shock she felt keenly evident in his dark eyes. "He seemed well this morning," she whispered, again wondering what had happened during the parade to bring such a thing upon him. Only Melah could tell them, and she, for once, wasn't talking.

Abram nodded. "We should go to him." He spoke to the room more than to her, and when he moved forward, he did not let go of her arm but coaxed her to follow.

They entered the room, where dark stuffiness greeted them. "Is that man trying to make things better or worse?" She quickly crossed to the window and threw open the dark shutters to let in the afternoon light. Her father would be in the depths of Sheol soon enough; he didn't need the darkness to take him there.

When she turned back from her task, she found Abram kneeling at their father's side, his large hand encasing Terah's equally large but thinner, veined one. "Father, can you hear me?"

She crept close, kneeling beside Abram, searching their father's weathered face for some sign of movement. Not even his eyes fluttered, and when she looked at the thin sheet covering his chest, she saw no movement. Was he already gone? A lump settled in her throat, and she swallowed hard against the threat of tears. *Not yet. Oh, please, not yet.*

As if he could read her thoughts, Terah's lips moved. Sarai leaned close until her ear nearly touched his mouth. His chest barely lifted, his breath too shallow against her cheek.

"Promise." His voice faded, and Sarai struggled to understand his meaning.

"Father, you must save your strength—"

"Keep."

She lifted her head to look at him. His eyes were open now, his gaze firm, taking her in. But in a heartbeat they closed again, the moment of intensity gone.

Abram's hand moved to touch Terah's throat, searching for the life pulse. He waited, bending low to listen for a breath. At last he leaned back and shook his head.

Sarai stared at Terah's face, waiting, watching to see if Abram's assessment proved true. What had he meant? That she must keep her promise to Abram, the promise she had made to Terah when he agreed to the marriage? Or to trust El Echad's promise to bring about what she could not? She stood, meeting Abram's gaze, certain he had not heard their father's final words.

"He never gave you the blessing." She wished Terah's thoughts had been directed to his son rather than to her failures.

"Adonai has already blessed me, dear one. Father could have added nothing to such promises as His." He rested a hand on her back.

She gave him a brief look, unconvinced. Turning once more to her father, she touched his face with her palm but did not linger. Life had gone out of him, and the feel of his skin made her shiver.

Never again would she listen to him give Abram sage advice or look on him with pride, bolstered by his endearing smile. Never again would she look into his eyes, hear his laughter, or touch his dear face.

She could not swallow past the lump in her throat.

How much she would miss him!

She felt Abram's arms drawing her close, turning her into his comforting embrace. She slumped into him, weeping.

7

Mourners' cries mingled with the joyous shouts of singing and dance from the remaining days of the New Year's celebration, and the steady beat of the drums caused a headache to form along Abram's brow. The rituals and worship of foreign gods had grown wearying, and Abram feared his household was being drawn away to follow after the ways of Ur and Harran rather than remaining true to Adonai.

The procession to the public cemetery on the outskirts of Harran stopped before a deep burial chamber cut into the ground. Stone circular stairs led downward into darkness, making him shudder. When the time came, he would find a cave for himself and Sarai rather than a pit, but his choices here were limited.

Four strong Arameans lifted the stone sarcophagus to the edge of a chamber and descended with Terah's body to place it in a crevice in the depths of the earth. The sounds of weeping swirled around him, and Abram's own tears flowed freely. Scents of dirt and the press of unwashed bodies stirred the gentle breeze coming down from the north and rustling the terebinth trees standing guard over the place.

"He lived a good life," Sarai whispered, her voice calmer than it had been a few days before, the day of their father's death. "He was a good man."

Abram nodded, but words would not come past the emotion in his throat. Gregarious in life, his father was well loved by everyone who met him. A careful businessman, shrewd yet giving, compassionate and understanding, yet not overly introspective. Unlike his thirdborn, whose introspective thoughts questioned where his father was now. What fate befell a man who worshiped many gods, adding El Echad to his plethora of choices rather than turning his devotion to Him alone? Did God judge a man for having a divided heart?

A ram's horn sounded, its lingering notes melancholy and haunting. Articles of pottery, clothing, furniture, and coins would have normally accompanied Terah into his tomb to keep him company in his rest, but Abram would have none of it. A man came into this life with nothing and could take nothing with him. Of that he was certain, whether Terah had believed it or not. When the last note died away, Abram released Sarai's hand and faced the crowd.

"We commit the body of Terah ben Nahor to his Creator this day, to return it to the dust from which it came. May he rest in Sheol in peace."

If only he knew that for certain.

What he did know was that the time had come to leave this place, to get his people away from the influences of other gods, to go as God had said to the place He would show him. Abram had waited in Harran long enough. It was time he obeyed and set things right.

Sarai stood at the side of the kneeling camel, not at all certain the animal could be trusted. Abram had acquired more of the long-necked beasts during their stay in Harran to help carry the added provisions and servants that were going with them to Canaan. And he expected her to ride on one of them, assuring her the journey would be pleasant, the ride one of relaxed ease. Looking at the beast's large eyes and deceptive smile, she didn't believe a word of it, and she was certain there was no way she could mount it, in any case.

"Eliezer will help you up, Sarai. Just put your right hand on the camel's back and the other on his shoulder. He will boost you up." Abram's amused tone did nothing to remove the sudden fear of heights that came over her.

She gave him a scowl. "Perhaps I should walk for a while."

He chuckled and she made a face at him. "Suit yourself. If you are too afraid—"

"I'm not afraid." She looked at him evenly, then back at the camel. Perhaps she spoke too soon.

"This one is gentle. I think you'll find the ride enjoyable, mistress." Eliezer smiled, offering her his hand. The younger man exuded a sense of charm and confidence, qualities that endeared him to both her and Abram and made him a good manager of the people in Abram's care. Surely she could trust him not to let her fall.

She nodded, running her hands along her robe and tunic. She had tucked them between her legs and girded them as men did during battle, except not quite so exposing, just enough to allow her to ride with ease over the long distances ahead. She looked to Abram, then Eliezer. "All right. I'm ready."

The animal shifted, jostling her ever so slightly as she lifted her leg over its back. She squealed like a young girl, then laughed at her own anxiety. But when Eliezer motioned for the beast to stand, she clung to the saddle until every muscle clenched. "I'm going to fall!"

The animal rose and shifted, tossing her gently from side to side. She dug her knees into the camel's sides, feeling Abram's hand on her leg. "You'll be fine. Would I let anything hurt you?"

She looked down at him, saw the serious glint beneath the humor in his eyes. "Of course not." But a small part of her doubted. The lie they'd been living had hurt them both.

"I will be up ahead with the men." He inclined his head toward the group of several hundred trained men he had worked with over the past two years, men he had acquired with the intent of keeping a small army to protect their ever-growing retinue. To protect her, he'd said. "I will come back to join you later."

She nodded, knowing later would mean many hours from now. He walked off, Eliezer at his side. Like a father and son.

The thought brought a pang of longing so deep it caused a physical ache in her middle. She tried to breathe, but the action only produced small whiffs of air. *Promise. Keep.* Her father's last words had continued to haunt her, their meaning clear.

The camel lurched, jerking her thoughts, making her heart beat wildly again. But within moments the animal took up a steady cadence, following the caravan lined up outside the city gates headed south and west. Her breathing slowed as she adjusted to the camel's stride, but her thoughts still churned as Eliezer rode up and down the lines, checking to make sure everything was in order.

He was a good man. Young enough to be her son if she'd been blessed enough to have one. Abram put great store by him. The man had proven himself during their time in Harran, and she had seen no guile in him to fear he had selfish interests at heart. Perhaps Abram should give the man the seal of adoption, choosing him as their heir to at least give them a more secure future.

She looked up at the sound of male voices coming closer and clung to her camel's hump as Lot and two of his men darted past, kicking dust behind them and shouting Abram's name. She lifted the veil to her mouth, coughing. Now what?

She glanced to the side as Melah's camel drew alongside hers. Her face looked pale as though she might be sick, her young daughter close in front of her.

"Would you take her for a time, Sarai?" Melah wiped a hand along her sweating brow. Her misery touched a chord within Sarai, and she suddenly wished her jealousy of the woman would not so often invade her desire to encourage and comfort.

"Of course I'll take her. But I have no idea how to make this beast kneel." She pulled on the reins, reading desperation in Melah's face. The camel slowed and came to a stop as Melah's did the same. The women behind her slowed as well, and she wondered how long it would take for the men up ahead to notice.

"Someone will come to help us once they see we are not moving." She sought to reassure Melah, but a moment later the woman turned her head to the side and lost whatever food she had eaten that morning.

"I think I need to walk for a while." But Melah looked too weak to hold herself upright.

"Perhaps you should ride a donkey instead. They might not bounce as much." The line of men continued to move ahead without them, until at last she spotted Eliezer coming toward them.

"Is something wrong, mistress?" His dark eyes held concern with no trace of impatience.

She smiled at him. "I am fine, Eliezer. But Melah is not." She motioned to her niece. "I need to take Kammani from her for a time, but I don't know how to get down or reach her." She suddenly felt helpless and determined she would learn to manage the animal despite her fear of heights. "Perhaps Melah could ride a donkey instead. The camel sways too much and is making her sick."

Eliezer nodded. "Of course." He commanded his own mount to kneel and hopped down, then walked over to the women's camels and bid them do the same. Hoofbeats drew closer, and Sarai glimpsed Lot astride his donkey headed toward them. She took Kammani from Eliezer's outstretched arms as Lot pulled his animal to a halt.

"What is the meaning of this? We are not ready to stop yet." He glared at his wife, who stumbled as Eliezer helped her to the ground, a hand clutched to her middle.

"Your wife is ill," Sarai said, not bothering to keep the disgust from her tone. She settled two-year-old Kammani against her chest and tucked the folds of her robe around her, breathing in little-girl scent and feeling her heart warm to the child. *Oh, Adonai, why do you withhold such blessing from me?*

Lot grunted as he dismounted his donkey and walked to Melah's side. He cast a glare toward Sarai, but she pretended not to see. He stopped near his wife but did not touch her. "Is it the babe?"

Melah nodded. "It will be better for me if I walk for a while."

A look of uncertainty passed over his features, but it quickly passed. "Take my donkey. I'll take the camel." Though by his expression, Sarai could tell the thought did not please him.

"If it pleases you, my lord, I'd rather walk for a while." Melah looked at her husband, her ashen face filled with something Sarai could not quite define. Longing? Irritation? Or a strange mix of both?

"Do what you want then." Lot walked back to his donkey, not bothering to leave Melah with an option to ride later. He gave both women a cursory glance, mounted the beast, and took off back toward the men at the front of the company.

Eliezer cleared his throat, as though the whole episode had troubled him. "I will see if there is another way for you to ride, mistress. Will you be able to keep up walking?"

Melah put a hand to her mouth, and Sarai wondered if it was an attempt to hold back tears, but from where she sat, she could not tell.

"I'm fine. I can keep up, I think."

"We'll go slow." Sarai nodded to Eliezer, who commanded the camel to rise. This time Sarai held on to the reins and didn't squeal.

She touched her knees to the camel's flanks after watching Eliezer do the same and take off with one last look in their direction. The steward was a better man than her nephew by far. Abram would do well to name him his heir, to give them security should something happen to them along the way. It was the only sensible thing to do.

Evening firelight dispelled the dark veil that had quickly replaced the soft colors of sunset. Sarai's body ached with every movement, her legs and back still feeling as though she were molded to the camel, the rocking sensation still clinging to her. Lila's deft fingers worked the knotted muscles in her shoulders while another maid dipped a cloth in water to wipe some of the grime from Sarai's feet.

She closed her eyes, enjoying the pampering, drinking in the scents of the fire and the flat bread baking on it. The only thing she missed was Kammani settled asleep in her arms.

A sigh worked through her as male voices came closer, and she looked up to see Abram deep in conversation with Eliezer. They paused at the sight of her. Abram sat on the raised stone beside her while Eliezer excused himself.

"How did you fare on your first camel ride?" His smile held a mixture of concern and amusement while he took in her maids' fawning over her as if she were a queen.

Lila's fingers stilled, and she bent close to Sarai's ear. "I will bring you some wine and bread." She slipped away before Sarai could answer, the servant at her feet following suit.

"You have scared them away," Sarai said, offering him a mock pout. "But I will forgive you for it just the same." She smiled then, leaning into him as his arm came around her. "The ride was not one I will soon forget. Perhaps I will walk part of the way tomorrow."

"The distance is long. But if you wish to walk part of the way, I will not stop you." His gaze traveled beyond them to the opposite side of the fire, where Lot and Melah and Kammani broke bread. "You would have more time to talk with our niece or listen to the gossip of the servants. But whatever you like."

She turned to him, playfully smacking his arm. "You make sport of me, husband." She lowered her voice. "In truth, I think Melah is lonely. Lot does not treat her as well as you treat me."

A scowl formed along his brow. "He is not harsh with her, is he? I will not tolerate a violent man among us."

She shook her head. "No, no. But he does not seem to care when she is sick. I wonder if he resents the child."

"I think he resents the wife more than the child, dear one." Abram leaned close and kissed her nose. "I will talk with him." His boyish smile caused her heart to skip a beat. His dark eyes flickered in the firelight, their meaning clear. She would not sleep alone tonight.

Lila returned with two clay mugs of spiced wine, a loaf of flat bread, and a bowl of lentil stew. Abram took the mugs from her hand and gave one to Sarai, while Lila placed the bread and bowl on a rock before them and retreated.

They ate in silence for a moment, the buzz of voices mingling with the lone melody of a reed flute. Sarai sipped her wine and glanced in the direction of the sound to find Eliezer sitting on a rock almost out of the circle of light from the fire, playing the flute.

"Eliezer is a man of many talents, is he not, my lord?" Sarai watched Abram closely as she ripped a piece of bread from the loaf, dipped it into the stew, and handed it to him. "A man whose father must be proud of him, if he had such a father."

Abram took the offering from her hand and tossed it into his mouth, his gaze thoughtful. "Eliezer has no family. His parents died soon after he married, and I already told you what happened to his wife."

"It is hard to forget such a thing," she said, forcing her tone to remain even despite the bitterness the thought evoked. If not for Eliezer's hardship, they would never have known the evil of foreign kings. Perhaps ignorance of the matter would have been better, but she could never say so. "It is too bad Eliezer has no family. Perhaps we should seek a wife for him." She held the flat bread to her lips and nibbled slowly, her expression neutral as his gaze met hers.

"Eliezer is old enough to take a wife for himself, Sarai. He does not need a father's permission." Abram's mouth held a grim line, but his eyes belied a hint of amusement. "Are you suggesting someone in particular, or do you just enjoy the women's game of matchmaking?"

She turned her head, pretending offense. "How can you say such a thing? I do not engage in such foolishness." Though if she'd had a handful of sons by now, she would have gladly helped choose their brides-to-be. But she hid that thought, smiling into his eyes. "I simply thought how much Eliezer looks up to you, how much like a father you must seem to him, and thought you might help him get over his loss by finding another wife for him."

Abram glanced toward Eliezer, and she noticed his shoulders visibly relax at the gentle tune coming from his simple instrument. "If I were his father, I would do just that, dear one. But a master and a father are not the same. I can suggest, if that would please you, but nothing else."

"Perhaps you should change his status and yours." The whispered words seemed to echo between them.

He turned in his seat, one hand loosely gripping the mug, the other resting on her knee. "What are you suggesting, Sarai?"

"Isn't it obvious, my lord? If something should happen to us along the way, Lot would inherit all you own. But would he care for the servants or the flocks as you do? Would he care where we were buried or say the blessing over us? I would not wish to see him made wealthy on your account." It was no secret between them what she thought of Lot's weaknesses or Melah's complaints.

Abram ripped another piece of bread from the loaf and looked away, his mind obviously working as he popped it into his mouth and chewed. She sipped the spiced wine again, warmth spreading through her, relaxing the tight muscles and easing the aches from riding all day. There was nothing more to be done now but wait as he pondered what she had said.

He finished his meal, downed the last of the wine, and wiped his mouth with the back of his hand. Standing, he offered her his hand. "Come, wife."

She smiled at the twinkle in his eye, knowing their conversation about Eliezer was at an end. Their conversation of a different sort was just beginning.

8

The skies changed little and the days ran into each other, a blur of monotony from dawn until dusk. After a month of riding the camel, breaking at noon, then riding some more until the sun left little light by which to set up the tents, Sarai had almost become used to the routine. But the day finally came when they passed through to the land of Canaan, past the town of Shechem, and moved on to the large oak tree of Moreh, where Abram stopped the caravan and gave the command to pitch his tents.

Servants moved in a familiar pattern, unloading donkeys and camels and pulling tents and cooking utensils from wooden carts. Women guided children in small tasks and set about preparations for the evening meal. Sarai moved to join them when she caught sight of Abram and Eliezer talking a stone's throw from where the servants were setting up Abram's tent.

The sight was nothing unusual. Abram often consulted with his chief steward, but when Eliezer dropped to his knees and kissed the hem of Abram's robes, Sarai's curiosity propelled her to move closer. Abram extended a hand to Eliezer and helped him to stand again.

"Once the tent is set up and everything is unpacked, I will draw up the contract and place my seal over it. Until Adonai sees fit to give me a son of my own body, you will be my heir." His arm drew an arc pointing toward the people and herds that spread out before them as far as they could see. "Adonai has promised to give me descendants, and I do not doubt His promise." Sarai moved closer, and when Abram saw her, he beckoned her with his arm. "I do not doubt that Adonai will do all He has said. But I also do not know when that will be. It is wise in the eyes of the law to have an heir." Abram looked at Eliezer, and Sarai breathed a sigh of relief at the man's nod of agreement.

"I will be honored to be your heir, my lord. And I will be pleased to be second to any son you might have as well. I will do all in my power to protect what is yours, and if you should die, I will make sure you find a safe resting place. May Adonai bless you, and may His face be turned toward you, to bring His promises to pass."

"Thank you, Eliezer." Abram pulled the man to him and kissed each cheek, patting him on the back as he did so. "Come to my tent this evening. I will have witnesses there and give you the adoption seal."

Eliezer bowed low, then stood. "It will be as you have said."

Abram dismissed him then, and Sarai watched the man's lithe gait as he moved among the busy servants, checking their progress as he went.

"Did I do the right thing?" Abram slipped his arm around her but kept his gaze straight ahead, his voice so low she knew only she had heard. "It's not that I don't believe the promises. Adonai said He would bless us." He turned to face her then. "I know He will, Sarai. We cannot doubt."

"Of course He will." She patted his arm, hoping her smile reassured him. "But it is not wrong, as you said, to do the wise thing. We don't want Lot and Melah taking control of what is ours. It's not that I don't care for our nephew, it's just . . ."

"I know. I feel as you do." Abram stroked his beard. His look grew thoughtful. "When Adonai gives us the promised child, there will be no need to worry about such things. But you are right. Eliezer is a better choice than our nephew. I was probably wrong to allow them to come with us in the first place."

Sarai offered him a smile and slipped her arm in his. "You made the right decision, my lord." She leaned closer and kissed his bearded face. "I will see to supper." She moved away from him to oversee the work of her maids.

※✛※

Later that night Sarai watched Abram unclasp the lapis lazuli cone-shaped seal from his wrist and press it into the clay adoption tablet. Most adoptions were handled with verbal agreements, but she knew Abram would take no chances that Lot would try to usurp Eliezer's place.

Eliezer took the sealed document from Abram, slipped it inside a leather pouch, and tied its leather straps about his neck. "When Adonai keeps His promise to give you a son," he said, his gaze fixed on Abram, "we shall together break this clay. I will gladly remain your trusted servant."

Tears filled her eyes at Eliezer's words. Words that were as valid as the sealed clay he now owned. They had made a wise choice, perhaps wiser than they knew.

The familiar female discomfort and cramping came upon her suddenly, and she hurried from Abram's tent to her own. There would be no sleeping at Abram's side this night, just as there would be no promised son anytime soon. Another month lost. One more proof of her barrenness. Were Abram's hopes pinned on false promises? Had he truly heard Adonai say such things? Where was the sign of the child's promised coming?

She lay down on her reed mat and accepted from Lila's hand the herbed tea that would ease her discomfort. She tried desperately to console herself knowing that at least Abram now had an heir, albeit an adopted one. When her week of uncleanness passed, she would ask him if the adoption released her from her vow. Perhaps he would be kinder than her father had been and give her this grace. If he would not, she didn't know what she would do.

Abram rose early the next morning, a sense of disquiet settling over him. He was glad to have given Eliezer the seal of adoption. The younger man had become like a son to him during their stay in Harran, and Abram was relieved to know he had someone to care for him and Sarai during the forthcoming years. But what of the child, the descendants promised to him? Did Adonai still intend to keep those promises? And what of the land where they had now pitched their tents? Canaanites, some as tall as small trees, roamed the cities they'd passed through. Some had been inviting and friendly enough, but others wore looks of malevolence, and the gossip Eliezer had heard in the camp had Abram's trained men on alert. How long would he be able to keep Sarai safe?

The camp had yet to stir, wisps of sunlight brightening the sky. His sandals touched the dew-drenched earth as he strode from his tent up the rise to the hill where the oak of Moreh stood proudly, its branches like great arms stretching high above him. He came to a stop at the tree, his gaze taking in the plain beyond. A lone figure strode toward him as big as the giants of the land, his bearing straight and sure, his clothes golden and white, nearly blinding. When he drew near, his gaze pierced Abram's soul.

The rush of fear cut deep, and Abram's knees suddenly felt aged, too weak to hold him upright. His thoughts unfurled, his questions, his every doubt exposed. He sank to the earth, put his face to the ground.

My Lord and my God! The unspoken words filled the air between them, musical and glorious, unlike any Abram had ever spoken or thought before. His blood pumped hard and his breath came fast. *How is it that my Lord honors me with His presence?* Surely he would die for having seen God.

"To your offspring I will give this land." The voice, both powerful and soothing, filled him with peace.

Strength returned to him, and he felt the man's hand grasp his, pulling him to stand. The man's eyes drew him, and he saw in a moment's gaze such perfect love that he wondered if he had stopped breathing altogether. Warmth enveloped him, and joy so deep he could not help the smile or the laughter that followed. The man smiled in return, and Abram felt as though he never wanted to leave this person or this place.

But a moment later, the man disappeared from his view, his words lingering on the quiet morning air. *To your offspring I will give this land.*

Not to Eliezer. To Abram's offspring. Children that would issue from his own body. Sarai's own son.

Thoughts of Sarai reminded him of her quick retreat the night before, and he knew in the look that had passed between them that her time had come upon her again. Another week would pass before he could go to her to comfort her, to remind her of the promise.

In the meantime, he must build an altar to Adonai, to offer a sacrifice of praise to His name.

Sarai measured cumin, fennel, and coriander seeds and dumped them into a wide, three-pronged pot set over the embers of the dying fire. With a long-handled utensil, she moved them back and forth lest they burn, while a short distance away another pot of water sat over a fire, waiting to boil. She drew out some raw mustard from a pouch at her waist, then pulled a few cucumbers out of the basket near her feet. The smoke from Abram's sacrifice still lingered on the breeze, but the meat would be in her hands soon enough to add to the broth.

She hummed a soft tune as she stirred the seeds, saw that they were done, and lifted the pot from the ashes to cool. She stretched to loosen the crick in her back, then grabbed a sharp flint knife to cut long, thin slices of cucumber.

"Do you need help with that, Sarai?"

She hadn't heard Melah approach, and she started, causing the knife to slip. She nicked her finger and quickly put it in her mouth. "You can prepare the bread if you like." She checked her finger, saw that the nick was small and not bleeding, then resumed slicing. Melah went to the bags of grain and scooped wheat kernels into a stone bowl. She picked up a pestle and worked the grain.

"I wonder how long we'll stay this time. Lot is ready to settle here if Abram agrees." Melah looked toward the distant hills. "It is beautiful here."

Sarai lifted her gaze to the lush hills, the sun glinting off the grasses, making them shine like burnished gold. "It's breathtaking." They had lived near the terebinth of Moreh for nearly a year when Abram declared they must move on again. Now, here in the hills between Bethel and Ai, she felt at peace.

"I have no idea how long we will stay here." Longing filled her to put down roots and have the promised child. She glanced at Melah, then moved closer to the boiling water and tossed in the raw mustard, stirring once.

The sound of stone against grain filled the silence between them. Servants' voices drew closer as more women came to help with meal preparations, and children awoke from naps, then ran off to play in the nearby grasses where their mothers could keep watch over them.

Melah finished the grinding and stood as she lifted the grains through a sieve to let the chaff blow away. She stepped closer to Sarai, nearly touching her arm. "Now that we are here, and assuming we stay for a while, it might do you good to offer prayers and a sacrifice." She paused, glanced before and behind, then leaned closer still. "If you want proof the goddess can help you, just look at Kammani and Ku-aya—two healthy daughters." Her chin lifted. "The images are in my tent. If you change your mind—"

"I'm not going to change my mind." Sarai took a step back, scowling, even as her heart gave a twinge, betraying the truth. If only it were that easy. But an image could not bring about a child. Though Abram's God had not brought one either in the three years since the promise. How long were they supposed to wait?

"I'm just saying, if you do . . . well, I won't hold it against you for ignoring me all these years." Melah gave her a pointed look, yet despite the suggestion, her gaze held kindness. "You know I only want your best. You do know that, don't you, Sarai?"

Sarai turned back to the roasted seeds and stirred them, then moved to the pot with the boiling water and lifted the lid, watching the steam rise upward. Male voices drew near, and Sarai breathed a relieved sigh as she turned to see Abram and Eliezer bringing a portion of the sacrificed lamb.

"Ready for the meat?" Abram smiled down at her as he and Eliezer lowered the thick slab of lamb's breast and thighs. "Do you want help cutting it up?"

She straightened while Eliezer positioned the lamb's meat on a flat stone and took a sharp knife to chop it from the bone.

"Thank you, my lord, but the servants can tend to this." She smiled into Abram's appreciative eyes.

"You put such preparation into the meals. Thank you." He gripped her shoulders and pulled her close, kissing her forehead.

"It is nothing any wife wouldn't do."

He glanced beyond her to where Melah sat, then gave her a sly wink. "Not every wife," he whispered in her ear.

She chuckled softly, knowing Lot had undoubtedly voiced his complaints long and loud about his wife when she was not within earshot. Had he also complained about the constant need to uproot and move on? Would Lot and Melah stay behind if Abram said it was time to go again? The thought almost pleased her, but Melah's hinted offer made her pause. Should she take advantage of Melah's gods while they were still together, while there was still time? Would it hurt to do so if Abram never knew?

She looked into his dark eyes, saw the love and trust he put in her evident in his fervent gaze. How could she do such a thing knowing how he would feel? But a part of her wondered. If the end result brought a child, what should the means to getting it matter?

"Supper will be ready in a few hours. Can I get you anything now, my lord? A mug of beer, perhaps?" The homemade drink from malted grain was among his favorites. She touched his arm, amazed at the youthful vigor she felt beneath his skin. He seemed stronger than he had in years, since the day he said he'd met his God face-to-face. If only Sarai could have met Him too.

"I have work to attend, but I will enjoy some with you after the meal." He smiled and kissed her cheek, then strode off toward the main part of the camp. Eliezer soon followed, and Sarai returned to her tasks.

"Any time you change your mind, Sarai," Melah said as she added water to the flour and shoved her palm forward, kneading the dough, "my tent is always open."

Clouds hid the sun from view as Sarai trudged to the area outside the camp, carrying the basket of soiled linens on her hip. Lila and two other maids followed, hefting jugs of water from the nearby well and an empty cooking pot to heat the water. Two months had passed in this place, this sanctuary between Bethel and Ai, but Sarai drew little comfort from it today.

The servants set about building a fire to heat the water above the flames, while Sarai knelt in the grass and pulled one of Abram's soiled tunics from the basket. Melah's constant comments had worn her down until she almost believed them. At the very least, she'd doubted the promise, doubted Abram's God.

Would a simple prayer to the goddess hurt?

Tears pricked her eyes, and she blinked hard, squeezing them back, forcing her mood into submission. The camp need not know of her anxiety or the despair that dogged her every step. A new recipe for the evening meal would surely cheer her. She would pull out her finest spices, the ones she had been hoarding since they left Harran, and see if the servants could find some wild leeks and fresh olives.

She could dig out the yarns she had finished carding and gather some plants to mix new dyes. A colorful new robe for Abram would please him.

She turned at the sound of rustling grasses and the voices of women. Melah approached with Kammani and two servants, while a third carrying her infant daughter, Ku-aya, trailed slightly behind. She lowered her burdens to the grass and knelt at Sarai's side. Melah slipped her hand into the pouch tucked along her belt and removed a small object. She leaned closer and laid it beneath the folds of dirty tunics in Sarai's basket, gave a small nod, and stood, taking her basket closer to the cooking pot.

Kammani chattered as Melah gave her a wooden toy to play with, distracting her from toddling too close to the fire. Today of all days, seeing the child and hearing the baby coo brought Sarai's wistful longing into sharper focus. She looked away, glanced down at the object in her basket, and pushed the folds of cloth away to get a better look. A small idol, like the one she had burned in the ashes in Ur, lay serenely among the folds. She studied its rigid posture, its arms supporting full breasts. She glanced up to find Melah looking at her, giving her another nod.

Sarai looked at the object again, her spirit recoiling yet drawn to it at the same time. Melah's actions spoke louder than any words she could have uttered. It was time Sarai did something to help procure this promised child. Melah's living daughters were proof enough that the goddess had heard her prayers. So why not Sarai's as well?

What could one prayer hurt?

Later that evening, as Sarai bent over the grinding wheel, her thoughts churned with each turn of the stone. Female servants hovered near. Her maid Lila, whose status had risen since her marriage to Eliezer the month before, chatted along with several others while they worked alongside her.

Sarai felt Melah's eyes on her from where she sat across the circular hearth. She glanced up, wiping sweat from her brow with the back of her sleeve, and saw Abram striding toward her, staff in hand.

She rose, brushing the soft dust of the grain from her hands, and walked to meet him, accepting his kiss of greeting. "You are early, my lord. Supper will not be ready for hours yet. Is something wrong?"

Abram looked toward the women, who had paused in their work to listen to their master. He acknowledged them with a smile and turned back to her.

"The grasses are drying up with every day of the summer heat. It is time to move further south toward the outskirts of the Negev. We already started moving the flocks, so I came to tell you." His look was apologetic as he glanced once more at the women, who one by one had resumed their tasks. "You will need to finish this up and start packing." He touched her arm. "The men will help load the animals."

"What of the supper I've prepared? Will we not eat?"

At her tone, petulant even to her own ears, he gave her a quizzical look. "You can complete the tasks when we stop for the night, can you not?"

"To stop and start again will not be easy, my lord. Could we not wait to move until morning?" The sun's peak had already passed the halfway point in the sky, and she did not relish the idea of moving so late in the day. It was time to be thinking of relaxing with good food and barley beer, fellowship and laughter.

He looked at her, his jaw tightening. "All right," he said, but his tone and the dark look in his eyes clearly told her it wasn't. "We will send the animals on ahead, but the rest of the camp will leave at dawn. When you are done grinding grain, see to it you start packing." He turned then, his manner brusque, and walked with strong, measured steps away from her.

She watched him leave, feeling suddenly bereft, knowing her lack of quick acceptance and obedience did not sit well with him. So he wanted to hold a grudge against her? Let him! Men could be so unrealistic when it came to planning things or moving such a large company. She did not care for his dark moods, though they came far less often than they did in the early years of their marriage, when they first discovered her barrenness. She would grow obstinate and he would brood, but as they matured, both had set aside their selfishness and had learned to accept what was—most of the time. Today was not one of those times, and she was not happy to see him walk off in anger.

She moved back to the grinding stone, feeling the weight of the image Melah had given to her press against her thigh. She picked up the stone, her thoughts churning and angry once again, and pounded out her frustrations on the grain as she worked. When the bread was set to bake and the stew was bubbling over the fire, she would visit the small shrine in Melah's tent. She would pray for the child she so desperately desired, and she would pray that Abram would stop brooding and not find out what she had done.

Abram, Eliezer, and Lot returned with several other men from the camp, sooner than Sarai expected, and took seats around the open hearth. The bread had barely finished baking and the stew still needed time for the barley to soften. But the servants could see to the rest. She moved to the goat's-hair tent that had become their home, not sure she wanted to listen to the men talk of plans for the move toward the Negev. She was weary of change, and she didn't want to leave this place where she had found some small sense of peace.

Sighing, she moved to her sleeping area and pulled the bronze mirror from a leather sack, examined her disheveled appearance, and tucked loose strands of hair behind her head scarf. She should wash and put on fresh clothes before entering Melah's shrine, but there was no time for such luxuries.

She smoothed her hands over her tunic, brushing loose grains and dust from its folds, and slipped out of the tent. Dusk was falling, something she would use to her advantage. She glanced to her right, toward the large, open hearth where Abram and his men still sat drinking clay cups of beer, legs stretched out in front of them. Female servants hovered nearby, the clattering of bowls telling her they were ladling the stew and taking bread to the men. Sarai skirted the cooking fires and headed across the rows to Lot's tents opposite Abram's. The distance was similar to the city blocks back in Ur, and as Sarai picked her way along the rocky path, she envisioned the cobbled pavement and mud-brick homes she once knew. The city with Ningal's temple. The one she had previously spurned.

Glancing over her shoulder lest she be followed, Sarai ducked her head, pulled the scarf over her face, and quickened her gait. Her jeweled sandals were always coated in a thin layer of dust now, and she rarely brought them out of the wicker basket she had packed them in. These unadorned ones sufficed, though in truth she missed dressing herself in fine clothes and turning the heads of the nobles who came to visit. Her beauty was the only thing she had in her favor, perhaps the only thing keeping Abram from taking another wife. A wife who would give him this promised heir.

She stepped around a dropping of animal dung, probably from one of the milk goats Melah kept for curds and cheese. Glancing up, she spotted the small black animal tied to a rope attached to a peg in the ground. Melah's tent stood just beyond, the wide awning stretching above the open enclosure. She paused. Should she enter unannounced? She had done so many times before, but never for such a purpose.

She turned, darting quick looks in all directions, then ducked through the door. If anyone was watching her, they would wonder why she appeared so skittish.

"Melah? Is anyone here?" She smoothed both hands on her skirts again, her fingers brushing the hard object in the pouch as she did so.

Silence met her ears. She moved to the area marked off as a sitting room, squinting to see in the dim light coming through the door. She had not thought to bring a lamp and would pay for her foolishness as she made her way back to the hearth. Her sandals would probably end up coated in the animal dung if she could not recall where it was in the dark. Chagrined by her wayward thoughts, she shook herself, reminded why she had come.

Just hurry and be done with this. Where did Melah keep the shrine? Sarai chided herself for not having asked, and she had not been here often enough to notice. Perhaps it was hidden behind a cushion.

Irritated, she moved through the tent, going from the sitting area to the private area where Kammani and Ku-aya would sleep and Melah would keep her personal items. She shoved a cushion aside with her foot, hoping Melah did not notice the mess she had made. At last she spied a smooth, carved stone table with the image of a goddess sitting on a golden throne carved with symbols. She was dressed in a layered, flowing, golden robe, hands clasped at her waist, a golden headdress encircling her plaited black hair, her look serene.

Sarai studied the statue, transfixed. Could Ningal hear her prayers? The image was somehow comforting.

Sarai's heartbeat slowed as she knelt before the image, extracted the wooden carving of her likeness from the pouch, and placed it before the idol. *Can you hear me?*

No sound emerged, and no returning thoughts made her think there would be a response. But what did she expect from an image of gold? Perhaps her prayers would reach the moon and the goddess would hear from her home in the stars.

Grant me a son. Please. I beg of you to hear me, to do what I cannot. Let me fulfill my vow to my husband and bear a son to carry on his name.

A gust of wind blew the tent's flap. Sarai jumped up, her fear rising. "Is anyone there? Melah?"

Only the hot breath of wind responded. She glanced from the shrine to the door. Darkness had fully descended now, and Abram would wonder where she was. Bending low, she left her image at the feet of the miniature golden goddess. She should make some kind of sacrifice, promise the goddess something, but what? She would not sacrifice the child—the very gift she requested. There was nothing else.

Uneasiness filled her at her own uncertainty, and the growing darkness made her shiver. She replaced the cushion in front of the shrine, hurried to the tent's entrance, and slipped into the night. She attempted to fill her lungs but could draw only a shallow breath. Fear accompanied the shadows, whispering, haunting. She stilled, listening. Across the compound, light flickered from the hearth fires, drawing her, beckoning her.

She glanced back at Melah's tent. The wind's breath on her neck made her shiver again, the darkness deepening as the moon quickly rose. She glanced up. Had the goddess heard her? Would she speak with her here? For a heartbeat she wanted to believe it, to know that her prayers were answered. But as she picked up her pace and hurried toward the camp's fire, she wondered at the wisdom of her choice.

❈ 10 ❈

"I looked for you. Where were you?" Abram accepted the clay bowl of stew from Sarai's hands and angled his head to the side, motioning for her to sit beside him on the smooth rock that served as a bench.

Sarai sat, nerves tense, hands clutching a small loaf of bread and a flask of barley beer. "I went to Melah's tent, looking for her." She avoided his gaze, though she felt it resting on her, sizing her up, certain he could read her thoughts.

"Melah has been here with the women since I returned with Lot and Eliezer. Why would you go to her tent when she is obviously here?" He set the bowl of stew between them, taking the loaf from her hands. His fingers brushed hers, and she recoiled, surprised at the shock the intrusion of his touch brought. "Your hands are cold." His gaze fully fixed on her now did nothing to still the rapid beating of her heart.

"I'm not feeling so good." It wasn't a lie, for in truth, the closer she'd come to Abram's side, the more her insides churned, and she could not shake a sudden overpowering sense of dread. He would never understand or approve. She should run back to Melah's tent even now and retrieve the image, cast it into the fire. She should

Sarai

expose Melah's idol worship to Abram and put an end to her niece's errant ways.

Concern etched his brow, and he touched her cheek, stroking her skin. "Your face is flushed. Perhaps you should lie down. I will send Lila to bring you some wine and herbs. Have you not slept well?"

She closed her eyes against the feel of his hand, guilt a heavy weight over her heart. She shook her head, unable to speak. She should confess all to him now . . .

"If you need rest, we can wait another day to move south. The shepherds can handle the flocks along the way." He reached for her hand then and pressed it to his lips. "Talk to me, Sarai. What troubles you?"

She could not look at him, and yet she knew if she did not, he would suspect more than she dared tell him. Swallowing hard, she met his gaze, undone by the tender look in his eyes.

"I'm sorry for this afternoon. If that's what this is about—"

"No, no. You did nothing wrong. It is time to move, as we knew it would be. I just have to get used to this nomadic life. It wearies me sometimes. I thought Adonai told you this land would be ours, but if that is the case, I don't see why we have to move about so much." She hadn't planned to complain, but the words sprang to her lips, a quick escape from the guilt of what she couldn't say.

He leaned away from her, his chest lifting in a deep sigh. Silence passed between them for the space of several heartbeats, disturbed only by the sound of other conversations about them. At last he broke off a piece of the bread loaf and dipped it into the stew, then handed it to her.

"It is the life of a shepherd to go where the grass can feed the flocks and herds. This new land Adonai has sent us to is not like the irrigated lands of Ur or Harran." He broke a piece of bread for himself and scooped up a large chunk of lamb and lentils. He chewed and swallowed and smiled at her. "Very tasty. No one can surpass your ability to bake and cook, my princess." He handed her another piece. "I must adjust to this nomadic life as well. It is not at all what we've known during these first fifty years of our marriage, but then, it is a great adventure, is it not?"

His twinkling eyes put her at ease, and she accepted a drink from his clay cup, wrapping her hands around his as he gently lifted it to her lips. When he pulled the cup away, he leaned in and kissed the few drops of beer left on her lips.

"Mmmm . . . even after fifty years, you still taste good." He touched a finger to her mouth and leaned close. "The next fifty will be even better, Sarai. Our God has great things in store for us." His gaze traveled to her middle as his hand covered hers, over the place where a child had never lain. "You will bear the promised one, Sarai. I am sure of it."

Heat crept up her neck from his intimate comments and the feel of his hand over hers. He still knew how to stir her emotions, to make her feel like a new bride when he wanted to, though those times were fewer and farther between. Had her prayers to the goddess somehow sparked his ardor? Or was his God trying to show her through Abram's constant reminder that she had nothing to fear?

But it was a woman's place to give her husband an heir. The law of the land of her birth declared it so, and her father had held her to her vow even on his deathbed. She could not sit back and hope Abram had heard correctly from the God he feared. It was Abram's kindness that kept him from putting her aside. She could have been divorced or reduced to a lesser wife's status, or at the very least forced to share him years ago, if not for his strength of character and his faith in his God.

"I hope you are right, my lord." She squeezed his hand, willing his words to take root within her. Perhaps even this night . . . but her faith was not great enough to hope for it so soon.

"I am right. Never doubt it." He settled back to finish his meal, turning his attention back to the conversations going on around him. "There is Melah," he said, turning to her moments later. "Do you want me to summon her here?"

"No . . . no need." Her calm shattered again at his comment, and she realized that he had not forgotten his initial question. "I found what I needed. Don't trouble yourself."

He nodded, his brow lifted in puzzlement, but he turned to his stew a moment later, sharing the last of the bread with her. The food, mixed with the lie, tasted like dust in her mouth.

❋❋❋

Hot, dry winds whipped the sands of the Negev into a storm fiercer than Sarai had ever seen. The camp had moved from Bethel in search of greener pastures two weeks earlier, but summer's heat had scorched even the outskirts of the desert grasses, forcing Abram to push on further south in the direction of Egypt.

Sarai stood at the tent's closed flap, listening to the sand slap its fine grains against the sturdy goat's-hair enclosure, her stomach knotting with barely concealed dread. Abram had wrapped himself in his cloak and hooded turban, brandished his staff, and gone out into the storm.

Where was he? Two days had passed if her guess was correct, though with the darkness and relentless whistle of wind, it was impossible to tell the passage of day or night. And still he had not returned.

"He will come, mistress. You must not fret so." Lila spoke from behind her, and when Sarai turned, she could barely see the outline of her maid's face in the dimness. They could not risk a lamp during what little daylight a day afforded, lest the wind shaking the goat's-hair enclosure somehow seeped beneath and whipped the tent into flames.

"Then where is he?" Sarai drew in a shallow breath. It was

hard to even breathe in the confines of the tent. He should have been back by now, unless something awful had happened. Was this sandstorm a punishment sent from Abram's God because she had prayed to the moon goddess?

"He and Eliezer and the others had a long way to go to reach the flocks. The camels can survive in the storm. I'm sure the master's God will go with them." Lila touched her arm, something she rarely did, the action somehow more comforting than Sarai had expected. Since Lila had married Eliezer, the relationship of servant to master had changed. Though Lila still served Sarai, she was not a slave, and Sarai considered her like a daughter.

"Yes, I know. Abram's God will not let the storm harm him." Hadn't Adonai promised to make Abram a blessing to nations? But that did not mean Abram would suffer no loss in the meantime. Especially if his God held him responsible for what she had done.

Guilt filled her. Was such a thing possible? Abram knew nothing about her choices, her failures. He could not know how rising each day took more strength than she had. If only she could stay beneath the bedsheets and never rise again until she could fling aside her barrenness like the unwanted covers.

A prick of tears surprised her, and she hurried back into the tent's sitting area lest Lila somehow see her pain. Feeling along the wall for the spindle and distaff, she unwound the yarn and sank onto the dusty cushions. She was so tired of dirt and dust and lack of water and travel . . . Where *was* he?

Her hands moved to the rhythm of the spindle she knew so well as Lila began dinner preparations. If the men did return, they would be as hungry as camels. She lifted her head to the sound of the wind, wishing she could pray for their safety but knowing nothing she could say would be heard.

❋❋❋

Abram kept his head bent against the sand-coated wind, pushing and prodding the last of the sheep toward one of the caves of the Negev. It had taken thirty men the past two days to round up the herds and hurry them toward shelter. He had no idea how many sheep they had lost to the desert. A count would be taken when the sandstorm abated.

The cave's entrance suddenly drew near, a break in the wind guiding his way. He lifted the last tottering lamb into his arms and used his staff to prod the others. At last inside, he made his way back and pulled the turban from his eyes. Adjusting to the dim light, he spotted some of his men further on, heard the bleating of worried sheep.

He set the small lamb onto the hard earth and watched it totter off toward its mother, then made his way toward the huddled men. Eliezer stepped forward, and the two men embraced.

"You are safe." Eliezer's voice held relief, as though he feared Abram incapable of surviving such a feat.

"I am old, but not quite so old." Abram unwrapped the turban the rest of the way and rubbed a hand over his gritty beard. "I think that's the last of them."

Eliezer rubbed the back of his neck. "Hard to tell for sure until we can count them."

Abram nodded, untied the skin of water from his side, and allowed a few drops to wet his throat. He'd rationed it as best he could, troubled by the sight of the skin's sagging sides. No telling what the storm would have done to the wells or the wadis. "After we assess the damage, I want you to lead the men and herds further south. This storm, added to the already sparse grass and drying riverbeds, is only going to make things worse. The animals will not survive long in a famine."

Eliezer tucked his hands behind him and followed as Abram walked further into the cave and slowly sank to the earth. "Egypt is not likely as hit by the famine as Canaan," he said, squatting opposite Abram.

Abram laid his staff on the ground beside him and called one of the ewe lambs over to him. The animal obeyed, and Abram pulled it to him like a pet, sifting his fingers through the lamb's sand-coated wool. "Have the men brush the sand from the sheep as best they can." He looked up, meeting Eliezer's gaze. "Egypt is not my first choice. Adonai called me to Canaan."

"Adonai would not wish us to die in Canaan, though."

"Adonai will not let that happen." But doubt pricked him just the same. Adonai had allowed the drought and sandstorm, which only worsened the threat of famine. What else could he do if he hoped to save his flocks and the people entrusted to his care? He could not, would not return to Mesopotamia, nor retrace his steps north toward Eliezer's Damascus. That left only Egypt or the Great Sea.

"I will see to the flocks." Eliezer rose and walked away. Abram absently brushed the ewe in his lap, weighing his options. If Nineveh had posed a threat to Eliezer, taking his first wife, Jerusha, from his bed, how much more would the king of Egypt do to a man with a wife as beautiful as Sarai?

Dare he risk his wife and his own life for food?

❊11❊

Sarai's jaw clenched and her hands gripped the reins of the donkey, her emotions rising and falling with each look forward at Abram's stiff back. He walked ahead of her, staff in hand, the determined speed of his gait raising her irritation all over again. That he had returned to her safely after the storm was a relief beyond measure, but the next words out of his mouth had dampened the relief, angering her instead. She did not want to go to Egypt!

"We have no other choice, Sarai, unless you would like to starve and watch everyone we love die of hunger and thirst. The famine is not going away anytime soon. Egypt has both food and water in abundance. Besides, it's not like we're going to stay there indefinitely."

His words had ended the discussion, though she would not call it that. He had not listened to her complaints and had obviously decided before he ever stepped into her tent to greet her with just exactly what he planned for their future.

I thought Adonai wanted us to live in Canaan. But she hadn't voiced the thought because her persistent guilt had stopped any further attempt to change his mind. Had her actions brought on the famine? Should she tell Abram what she had done, confess her wrongs, offer a sacrifice? Perhaps the famine would swiftly end if she did, but the damage the sandstorm had caused was already too evident. The herds needed grass and water, and both were in short supply.

She loosened her grip, her anger abating slightly at the thought, reminding herself yet again that she had agreed to follow her husband wherever he led. She forced a smile as he turned, easing his gait to let her donkey catch up with him and walk beside him.

"We will reach the border crossing into Egypt by morning." He looked beyond her toward the distant rise they were approaching.

She waited for him to say more, not sure how to respond. Should she tell him this was a good thing, let him think she was now pleased to have arrived at the destination she feared? She checked her spirit. Why did she fear Egypt? No logical explanation surfaced other than the fear she faced at every new city. She closed her eyes, silently begging him not to ask it of her again.

"The guards at the checkpoints will inspect our belongings. I'm told the pharaoh exacts a tax on visitors to his country, and garrisons are posted along the main highways. Pharaoh's hand is mighty, and like all kings, he makes use of his power to ensure everyone knows he has it." Abram gripped the donkey's neck, coaxing it to stop. The rest of the men and women following did the same, waiting for Abram to move on again.

Sarai looked into his dark eyes, reading the truth in his imploring gaze.

"I know what a beautiful woman you are." He hesitated, looking down toward his feet as though embarrassed to repeat the request he had voiced too often before.

"Please, Abram . . ." Her voice dropped in pitch. "Don't ask it of me again." The whispered words fell like darkness between them.

He rested his hands over hers, the ones fisted over the donkey's reins. "When the Egyptians see you, they will say, 'This is his wife.' Then they will kill me but will let you live. You know it's true, Sarai.

Should we escape the famine only to find my life ended because of a king's desire?"

She gripped the reins tighter, stiffening at his words, reading in his expression the full import of what he would not say. If she had a son, he would not ask this of her. But until she produced an heir, his death would mean the end of much more than his life. The promises of Adonai would go unfulfilled, and she would end up the property of a foreign king. His request was meant to protect her, though she had a hard time feeling protected at all.

"Say you are my sister, Sarai, so that I will be treated well for your sake and my life will be spared because of you."

His words set her teeth on edge. The constant clenching caused a headache to begin along her jaw and travel to her temples.

"It would be nice if you cared for my life as well." The words hissed between her gritted teeth, and she turned her head away, avoiding his pleading look.

His touch on her shoulder was gentle, a caress. "Of course I care for your life, dear one. I have loved you since childhood, and not just because of your beauty." He coaxed her to turn and look at him again. "If you were not so unimaginably beautiful . . . Do you not wonder how hard it has been to shield you from the gazes of unscrupulous men over the years? Even in Ur and Harran when you were either my wife or my sister, I have warded off the advances of other men who approached me on your behalf. Believe me, beloved, there have been too many to count."

Her eyes widened at his revelation. "You never told me that." Was he saying so simply to get her to go along with the lie?

"I didn't want you to know. I didn't want you to hunger for another man, since I have never given you the son you so desire." He prodded the donkey forward again, glancing behind them. The buzz of conversation in the distance told her they were alone in the crowd, that his comments had not been overheard.

But his words warmed her in a way nothing ever had. No man would ever admit to such a thing. If a woman did not conceive a child, it was her fault, not the man's. And it was her place according to custom to supply a substitute if she could not bear a child on her own. That Abram had never asked Sarai to give him a maid—to prove his innocence and bear his child—spoke of his deep love for her, something he rarely said openly.

She touched his arm, meeting his gaze, her heart softening toward him. "It is I who have failed you, my lord. I have wanted a son for your sake. I could never love another man, nor want one—ever."

His boyish smile brought a dimple to his left cheek, just above his beard. "You do me great honor, Sarai." He fingered her veil, his palm caressing her face. "Then you will go along with the ruse one more time? As your brother, I will do all in my power to protect you. You know this."

She nodded. "Of course."

But as they made camp for the night overlooking the lush land of the pharaohs, the historic heritage of Noah's son Ham, the fear she had battled on the journey remained.

Abram approached the border crossing, an uneasy fear warning him to turn back. But he had been through every option open to him too many times to count. If he turned back, they would die. There was no place to go.

Two guards stepped forward, their chests bare but for collars inlaid with gems across their necks and shoulders, their short tunics revealing bare legs. A quiver of arrows was slung behind their backs, and they each held a bow in their left hand. A colorful sash was tied at their waist, and tall helmets rose high above their dark heads. Abram attempted a smile as he approached, but the stern looks he received in response made his smile quickly fade.

"State your business," one young guard said, his bearing like a prince, his gaze cool, assessing.

"I have come with my household to seek shelter from the famine in Canaan. We wish to stay only until the lands to the north are fertile once again." Abram waved an arm behind him to encompass the group at his back. "My people are your king's willing servants."

The guard's gaze moved beyond Abram. "How many are in your company?"

"Right now we are one hundred and fifty men, plus women and children."

"What are these herds, and what is this bleating of sheep I hear?" The guard's grim mouth tipped in a scowl.

"We have only a few sheep and cattle, to keep our families supplied with food and shelter." Abram sensed distaste from the man but said nothing, waiting.

The guard motioned the first in the group forward, and Abram held his breath as the servants and their families were allowed into Egypt. During the night, Abram had arranged his people into a specific order, putting Lot and his men with the flocks near the front, Sarai and her maids and the children in the middle, and Eliezer with the rest of the men near the end. He hoped in so doing, the women clustered around Sarai would pass through as a group, unnoticed and protected.

He stood silent, watching as more guards emerged from the mud-brick houses near the outpost and headed his way. They consulted the man Abram had spoken to, then made their way down the line of men and sheep, headed toward the women with obvious purpose. The Egyptian outpost surely saw a daily influx of people seeking escape from the famine. Were they planning to accost the women in his company right before his eyes?

Abram glanced in Sarai's direction, the fear he'd fought during the night returning in full force as the Egyptian guards came to the middle of the group and paused before each woman. He hurried forward.

"Is there a problem?" He stopped several paces from Sarai, hoping to draw the guard's attention to himself.

"No problem at all. The pharaoh likes beautiful women." He fingered the edge of his bow, his dark-lidded eyes looking down on Abram as though he were of no consequence. "Do you have any beautiful women in your company?"

Abram glanced purposely away from Sarai, his heart beating thick with dread. The guard walked away, apparently not willing to await an answer, but the two guards weaving in and among the women, assessing them, made Abram feel powerless.

The guards moved on at last, and the women and children passed through unharmed into Egypt. Abram released a slow breath, his heart rate returning to normal.

They camped on the outskirts of Succoth, grouping their tents together in a circle as they did everywhere they went. Abram considered keeping Sarai with him, leaving her tent to her maids, but quickly changed his thinking, recalling the almost malevolent looks of the guards. If the governors or viziers or any of the princes of Egypt thought him to be Sarai's husband, things would not bode well for either of them.

He should never have brought them this far. Though the pharaoh's arm had weakened in recent years, he had united Egypt again, his influence reaching even north into Canaanite lands. Abram should have known better than to trust such a foreign power with his family, his livelihood. This pharaoh could be no better than the kings of the east from which he'd come. And probably worse.

As night descended and the voices of his people fell to whispers around him, Abram stepped from his tent, glancing once more toward Sarai's quarters, wishing he could go to her for comfort.

For in truth, he needed her warmth, her smile, her assurance to tell him he'd done the right thing.

Three weeks of constant waking at every noise, every shift of the wind, left Sarai groggy and anxious. She had work to do and should rise this very moment, but her limbs felt ancient, her motivation gone. How long must they stay in this land of gods she did not know, living in fear of what they could not see? Abram's faith, always so strong, seemed to have slipped behind him in a place he could not reach. And she was powerless to help him if he did not come to her. Her faith in his One God was too weak to stand without him.

Voices drifted to her, pulling her from her melancholy depths. Hurried footsteps padded over the thick-carpeted fabrics spread over the earthen floor.

"Sarai, you must come at once!" Lila burst into the sleeping room of the tent, short of breath. "Egyptian princes have come to the camp. They are speaking with Abram even now."

Lila's whispered words sent a dart of fear straight through her. "Whatever could they want?" But instinctively she knew. The fate that had befallen Eliezer's first wife—the fear she had lived with since they had left Ur—would surely be hers. Her heart beat too fast as she scrambled from the cushioned bed and let Lila help her dress.

Lila pulled Sarai's best deep-blue gown from the basket of robes and tunics. "You will need to pack for at least two weeks, to journey to Thebes and back again." She snatched the stone casket lined with soft linen holding Sarai's jewels. "They insisted you pack your finest clothing," she said as she lifted lapis lazuli earrings and a matching lapis lazuli, gold, and pearl necklace from the case. "The pharaoh wants to meet you."

· Lila draped the jewels about her neck, their weight feeling like a prisoner's rope. "I can't do this." Sarai's voice sounded weak to her ears, and numbness settled over her. She sank to a low stool, her strength fading.

"I know. But what else can you do?" Lila's mouth formed a grim line as she hurried to apply kohl to Sarai's eyes.

"There must be something." They could tell the truth. But her stomach twisted at that thought. Abram would not agree.

"Perhaps as your brother, Abram can tell the pharaoh you are promised to someone else. Or he could say you are widowed." Lila coiled her hair with jeweled combs beneath a veil of soft, dark fabric.

"Don't say such a thing!" Could saying the words make them come true? A tremor worked through her, and she gripped the sides of the stool for support.

"I'm sorry, Sarai. Didn't you and Abram plan for what to do if such a thing came to pass?"

A shadow fell across her tent opening, interrupting their conversation. She turned to see Abram standing there, blocking the light. She rose slowly, not trusting her legs to hold her, and went to him.

"Sarai." Her name on his lips came out strangled. "The pharaoh . . . he is asking to meet us . . . to meet my sister."

Her feet held her fast as she took in his gaze, the one that would not quite meet hers. His hands clenched and unclenched, and he shifted from foot to foot.

"You said it would not come to this. You said you would tell them I am not available." Her words came out low and harsh, her anger the only thing keeping her from swaying and fainting straightaway.

Silence met her ear until at last he looked her in the eye. "I tried, Sarai. But apparently Pharaoh Mentuhotep II has an eye for beautiful women. His princes and guards and viziers and governors are all commissioned to keep a lookout for them. They report any they find directly to the king, and they reported you." He moved into the tent and took her hands in his. She did not pull away, not knowing whether she would feel his touch again after this meeting. "I should never have brought you here."

His look of dejection touched a chord within her, melting her anger, and his fear became her own. She pulled one hand from his to stroke his beard. "The famine." And her foolish sacrifice that caused it. "There was nothing else we could have done." The words tasted like ash.

He darted a quick look behind him, then turned and wrapped her in his arms, crushing her beneath his kiss. He broke free too soon and released her, the loss acute. He nodded once, turned, and strode from the tent. Heart racing, she followed him.

She squinted against the angle of the morning sun, spotting bare-chested Egyptian princes decked out in short crowns of gold, jeweled collars, and sashes, their rich, colorful skirts covering them from waist to knee. Five princes surrounded by twenty guards stood at attention, awaiting her. Their strange beauty impressed and repulsed her. Did they come to show off their military might or their judicial power? What were twenty guards against the one hundred and fifty trained men in Abram's company?

And yet she knew Abram's men would not fight on her behalf. The Egyptian guards were a small show of force against Egypt's greater might. She and Abram were at the mercy of the king. If she did not cooperate, Abram could die and all would be lost.

She stepped forward, her heart crying out within her, begging Abram's God for help, for rescue from whatever lay ahead. If her folly with the moon goddess was responsible, let her offer a sacrifice and be forgiven. What good could come to Abram, the man called by Adonai to start a new nation, if he fell prisoner—or worse—to a foreign king?

She shivered beneath the veil covering all but her kohl-darkened eyes, but as she approached the guards, she forced courage into her will and did not cower as they took in her appearance. Neither would she cower before this Pharaoh Mentuhotep II. If he were determined to meet her, she would show him an air of pride and dignity. He would not win or woo her easily as Abram's sister, princess of Ur. Even if he took her into his harem, as she knew Abram feared, she would not let him touch her.

If Abram could not protect her, and if his God would not rescue her, she would do what she must to help herself.

❋ 12 ❋

Two Egyptian slaves took Sarai's arms and tugged her away from Abram. She twisted and shrugged out of their grip. "Don't touch me!" But they only looked at her strangely and muttered words she could not understand.

She turned toward Abram, extending a hand. But the slaves grasped her upper arms again and tightened their grip, dragging her away. She thought to twist and writhe beneath their grasp, but the sight of the five princes brandishing golden swords beside an elegant, colorful litter made her resist the urge. She clenched her hands but could not still the shaking.

A prince nodded and pointed to the litter, offering a hand to help her inside. She gave him a disdainful look. His laugh incensed her, and she climbed inside without his assistance.

Four Egyptian slaves lifted the litter's golden bars to their shoulders, taking her with them. As the litter shifted, she stifled a cry, fearing she might fall, but the slaves quickly fell into a rhythm, marching at a brisk trot. She twisted, peering through the filmy curtain to see if Abram would follow, but she lost sight of him. She could only assume, alone in a sea of horses and men.

Would she see him again? Her heart quivered, and she fought

the urge to be sick. The litter stopped a short while later, and the sounds of lapping water met Sarai's ears. The curtains parted, and the same prince stood nearby, a smug smile on his lips. Anger shot through her. She ignored his outstretched hand and climbed out on her own.

The port city bustled with life, but a quick glance showed no sign of Abram. Sarai's stomach did an uncomfortable flip as the two slaves came alongside her again.

She turned on them. "Where is my brother? Keep your hands off me!" She glared at them, but they only shrugged, not understanding.

They reached for her again, but she waved her arms, batting them away. Uncivilized Egyptians! How dare they treat her like a slave to be auctioned! She whirled about, showing them her back. Laughter erupted from behind, and she cursed the Egyptian prince's arrogance. She waited a breath until he stepped up beside her. He bowed at the waist and motioned toward the barge, but she did not miss the amusement in his gaze. He thought her a foolish one! She would show him who was the bigger fool.

She walked the wooden planks to the dock where a barge waited, whose flags and insignias could only be that of the Egyptian king. She stepped aboard, clinging to the rail to keep her balance. Her stomach churned harder as she stumbled toward the seat beneath a colorful linen canopy.

"Sarai." She jumped up at Abram's welcome voice, spotting him with Eliezer near the pilot at the bow.

"Abram!"

He hurried to her. She gripped the marble columns holding the canopy, trying not to slip on the platform of gold. She felt his arms come around her, then pull quickly away. She ached to hold him, to cling to him.

"We cannot do this, Sarai," he whispered against her ear. "You must be brave."

"How can you ask this of me? You need to help me escape," she hissed through clenched teeth.

"The only escape is to leave Egypt," he said, "and you can see how impossible that is now."

Her gaze caught Egyptian slaves milling about, readying long poles for the water. The barge pushed away from the bank, and she gripped the marble column. The annoying prince stepped onto the golden platform, motioning for her to sit. She glared in response, but at Abram's touch on her shoulder, she obeyed.

"What will become of me?" She looked at Abram, whose scowl followed the Egyptian prince's back as he returned to the bow. "Is there nothing to be done then?" Her voice shook like one of the reeds along the river's edge.

"I don't know." He looked at her then, his expression a mixture of anguish and anger and fear. Bile rose in her throat at the realization of just how helpless he was. And just how hopeless.

Abram stood at the river's edge later that day as the barge stopped for the night, staring out over the dark, moonlit water. A splash nearby made him step back a pace. He did not wish to be food for crocodiles.

"Abram?"

"Sarai." She rushed toward him, and he pulled her down beside him on the bank, hidden among the reeds. Her lips tasted sweet as honey and salty as tears. "Sarai, my most beloved." He breathed the words against her ear, clinging to her.

She sobbed against him, though no sound accompanied her shaking. "Oh, my husband!" He winced at the title she used. He did not deserve to be called such a name. What kind of husband allowed his wife to be in such danger?

He crushed her to his chest, memorizing her feel, her scent. How could he protect her from these people, from Pharaoh?

"You must get me away from here. We could run even now to the barge and set out across the water to the other side."

"The barge is guarded night and day, Sarai. And it takes at least six men to operate the poles on a craft that size." He raked a hand through his hair, listening to the whisper of wind in the reeds.

"Then we will swim to the other side. It will be no different than when we played as children in the Euphrates." She gripped his arm so tight her nails pinched his flesh.

"The crocodiles would catch us before we stepped fully into the water." He loosened her grip. "We would need men to help us and a boat small enough to manage ourselves." He looked into her stricken gaze and brushed the tears from her cheeks. "Oh, Sarai, I wish there was a way. But we cannot even speak the language of most, and there are none who will betray their pharaoh to help us."

The admission made his gut clench hard, and for a moment he feared he would break down and weep with her. He pulled her to him instead, fighting the emotion.

"Why is this happening to us?" Her words were a whisper.

"I learned long ago not to ask such questions, beloved." He stroked her back, closing his eyes against the sting of the half truth. He had asked the question of himself too many times, certain he was to blame for bringing them here.

He leaned back and searched her face, visible only in the slim slice of moonlight. She met his gaze, and something flickered in her eyes that he couldn't define. She opened her mouth as if to speak, then closed it again.

"I don't want to live in Pharaoh's palace. I don't want to lose you."

"Nor I you."

She drew in a breath. "Then you must do something. We have a week, my husband, until we reach Thebes. You must find a way to help us escape, before it is too late."

❊⁘❊

The enormity and splendor of the Egyptian capital of Thebes filled Sarai with a deep sense of dread. The week had passed too quickly, with no more chance to meet her husband alone by the river's bank and no plan to get them away from their Egyptian hosts. Egyptian guards came alongside them as they stepped from the barge and quickly escorted them down a brick lane, halting beneath a shaded colonnade.

Slaves appeared from behind marble columns to brush dust from Sarai's robes. One offered her a golden goblet of wine. She waved a hand to refuse but caught Abram's look. He accepted the drink, sipping some dark liquid. She followed his lead, tasting pomegranate wine.

Sweat gathered along her brow, and the scent of cumin and garlic that hung in the air churned her stomach. She moved closer to Abram. "What are they waiting for?"

"We have to wait our turn." Abram took her hand and tucked it over his arm.

Moments later, the thick double doors opened. Guards motioned them forward, and trumpets blared as they stepped over the threshold. Rows of men and women lined the hall—a wall of interest. Abram's steps slowed.

"Keep moving." A guard prodded them, pointing a sword at Abram's feet.

Sarai stumbled. Abram's grip tightened, and she clung to his arm. The room stretched on for an eternity, but all too soon they stopped before the steps of inlaid stone and Pharaoh's gilded throne. Abram knelt, pulling Sarai down with him, her face to the tiles, her emotions curling into a tight fist in her middle.

"You may rise." The voice came from the left, not from the man seated on the throne.

Sarai rose, a shudder working through her. Pharaoh Mentuho-tep II sat straight, his striped headpiece resting from his head to his shoulder, draping to his chest over a vulture-shaped, jeweled collar. His chin held a fake beard, narrow and woven, and a golden cobra and lapis lazuli vulture stood out on his forehead as though ready to spit fire. A golden shepherd's crook and a flail of fine leather cords and brass circles extended from each of the pharaoh's hands, symbols of protection and judgment.

The pharaoh spoke to a man at his side in a tongue she did not recognize. His voice was deep, and his proud, possessive look turned her blood cold.

The man responded, and Sarai's fear rose higher. How were they supposed to communicate to one whose tongue sounded like babble?

The man spoke again, this time the words familiar though diffi-cult to discern. "Yes, my king. She is the man's sister." He pointed at Abram, and Sarai knew the man had spoken for their benefit. Sarai barely dared to breathe.

Pharaoh Mentuhotep set his gaze on Abram, studying him, then flicked his kohl-rimmed eyes toward Sarai. He took in her appearance slowly, as one tasting many flavors at a meal, leaving Sarai feeling vulnerable and exposed.

"Remove her veil." The command, impossible to misinterpret, startled her, but her protests died on her lips as two female servants hurried to do the bidding of the king's servant, dislodging one of Lila's carefully placed combs in their haste. Several strands of Sarai's thick hair tumbled to her shoulders. She snatched at her hair and tried to tuck it into another comb, but the effort failed, loosening it instead. Heat filled her cheeks, and she could not look at anything but the floor.

The pharaoh spoke again, his tone sounding almost amused.

The man responded in the Egyptian tongue, then Sarai clearly caught his final words. "She has beautiful hair."

They were talking about her as though she were a slave to be sold. The thought chilled her. Was that not exactly what she had become? Despite Abram's impassioned words, she was only a sister now. A woman free to marry another, to be sold to the king at whatever price could be had. Would Abram do nothing to stop such a thing?

More words were exchanged in the Egyptian tongue until at last they stilled.

"I accept."

Sarai's head snapped up at the pharaoh's words. He had spoken their language. Had he played them for fools from the start? But of course, coming here proved that was exactly what they were.

"Accept, my lord?" Abram bowed. "I do not understand."

"I accept your sister as my wife." He extended the shepherd's staff and motioned Abram to touch it.

Abram glanced at her, his dark eyes flickering with raw pain. But in an instant, he masked the expression and turned, saying nothing. He moved forward, hand lifted, and touched the tip of the crook.

"It is done then." A guard clapped his hands, making Sarai's taut nerves nearly shatter. "Take this woman to the queen's quarters."

Before she could catch her breath, guards escorted Sarai from the audience chambers and down several gleaming corridors, each one filled with carvings of animals—vultures, cobras, cats. And faces of gods she could not name. More servants speaking foreign words passed them, some smiling, others impassive.

They forced her to stop at a gated courtyard. "Welcome to the Hall of Queens." The female servant spoke in a dialect of the Canaanite tongue, and Sarai caught the meaning, if not every word.

Panic rushed in on her, made her heart beat too fast as the young woman motioned her toward a set of rooms off to the left. "This is where Pharaoh's new acquisitions begin the purification process. You will stay here until your body has been perfumed and oiled and until the right clothes can be fitted for you." She looked Sarai over, her attitude sparking a hint of disdain.

"The clothes I have are perfectly fine." Sarai lifted her chin. How dare a servant act so above her. She was a princess of Ur, wife of Abram!

"The king likes his wives to be diverse, but he also has times he prefers they dress as Egyptians. You will be no exception, my lady." The last was added almost as an afterthought, reminding Sarai that while she might be a princess, even a queen now, she was no longer who she used to be.

He had lost her. Just as Eliezer had lost Jerusha, only worse. Eliezer had fought to save Jerusha from the king of Nineveh, whereas Abram had stood watching his beloved taken without saying a word.

Guilt lashed him. He should open his mouth even now and tell the king the truth, demand his wife's return. He glanced at the king's face, saw the threatening gleam in his eyes, and the words died on his tongue.

"You will be well paid for your sister."

Abram's thoughts snapped. Pharaoh Mentuhotep's honeyed tone seemed as false as his beard.

The pharaoh laid the crook and the flail across his knees and clapped his hands. "Take this man—what is your name?"

Abram swallowed the grit on his tongue and cleared his throat. "Abram ben Terah, my lord."

He nodded. "Take Abram ben Terah to my inner courtyard and bring the servants. He shall have his pick of menservants and maidservants. Then take him to the sheep pens and the donkey and camel stalls. Give him the best of my flocks and herds." He stroked his fake chin, eyeing Abram. "Your sister—what is her name?"

Abram's chest tightened, his heart beating faster. "Sarai, my lord."

Pharaoh Mentuhotep smiled, his teeth showing white above the thin beard. "My princess. How fitting." He snapped his fingers at his servants. "See to it the man is well paid."

Abram bowed low, somehow managing to thank the pharaoh. Servants guided him toward the palace courtyard, but his feet were weighted, his limbs bent and forced to move as though trudging through Canaan's tar pits. He drew in a shallow breath, but the effort made his knees weak. Eliezer somehow appeared at his side and caught his arm.

"How could this have happened?" Abram asked. He would surely awaken from this nightmare. It couldn't possibly be real.

A cacophony of voices filled the courtyard, men and women forming two lines like sheep heading to slaughter. Abram blinked, barely able to focus. What was he doing here?

Eliezer leaned close to Abram's ear. "We will get her back."

Abram shook his head, suddenly feeling aged, dead, yet somehow still breathing. "You above all men should know how impossible that is."

A guard summoned Abram forward to choose twenty menservants and twenty maidservants to join his company. Abram looked at the Egyptian overseer, disgust turning to bile in his gut. He whirled about, glanced at Eliezer. "You decide." He stormed off, his thoughts churning, consumed with his loss. He couldn't live without Sarai. Why had God allowed this?

He should never have come here. And now he had ruined everything.

God help him!

❄13❄

Hagar sat at the end of her mother's sparkling pool and dangled her feet in the water. A flutist played a cheerful tune in the sitting room nearby, and the voices of her sisters chattering and bickering intruded on her attempt at solitude. The music was meant to soothe, but nothing could release the tensions that flowed in her mother's rooms, especially when her father added a new wife to his bulging harem.

She moved the water with her toe and lifted it high, watching the water droplets dance on the surface as they dripped from her brown leg. Her mother's cat sauntered near and shoved its head against her arm. She laughed, petting the animal until it evoked a loud purr.

"Hagar, there you are."

Irritation stirred within Hagar at her mother's tone. She braced herself.

"Why are you sitting around lazing by the pool? Your father has taken a new wife. Now go!"

Hagar looked into her mother's scowling face. The woman seemed to notice her only when she wanted something. "I thought I'd give the new wife a chance to settle first." She was tired of playing the servant to appease her mother's whims. Though as a servant, at least she felt loved. Nitianu, her maidservant since her birth, was more a mother to her than the woman who glared down at her now, and Osahar, chief eunuch of her father's harem, was the father she would never have as Pharaoh's daughter.

"You are a lazy excuse for a daughter, and I have half a mind to sell you to the slave dealers." Her mother bent toward her and grabbed her arm. "Get up!" She yanked Hagar's forearm, her long nails digging into her flesh.

Hagar stifled a cry, scrambling to her feet. "All right then! Stop fussing at me. You can't sell me. I'm Pharaoh's daughter! Once in a while it would be nice if you realized that."

The sting of her mother's hand bit into her cheek. She staggered backward, hating the sudden emotion. She would not cry.

"Don't you dare speak to me like that again, Hagar. You may be Pharaoh's daughter, but you have nothing to offer him." Her kohl-rimmed eyes narrowed to slits, and her normally beautiful mouth curled in disgust. "If you had your sisters' charm and beauty or even talent, you would make a sure alliance with foreign lands. As it is, the only good you are to me is the information you bring me and the lies you tell the new wife. Once Pharaoh has had his fill of her, she will soon be forgotten. I need not remind you how important that is to our cause."

Hagar nodded, the heat of her mother's slap matching the fire in her glare. But the physical pain could not compare to the emotional wounds she was inflicting with every word. Her mother's cause? She did not care if her mother ever regained her favor as a wife instead of a concubine or won her father's heart. Her mother could go to Osiris, god of the underworld, for all she cared!

"Why are you still standing there? Go!" Her mother's voice rose to a shriek. The flutist hit a faulty note, and her sisters' arguments ceased.

"Yes, Mother." The word tasted sour as she whirled about and fled the courtyard. She would go to the new wife and learn what she could. But she would not lie to this one. She would do all she could to help the woman find favor in her father's eyes.

Sarai entered a room painted in brilliant colors, the smooth tiles of the floor gleaming white in contrast. Columns stood along one wall opening to a courtyard garden, where lotus blossoms floated on the blue water of a pool.

"This will be your room for the first month." A servant walked to the chest and lifted the lid. "Once you are ready for your audience with the king, you will move to another room across the courtyard." She waved a hand toward the columns housing the pool. "If he is pleased with you, you will be his wife. If not"—she shrugged—"you'll be his concubine. His choice will determine where you will live."

The girl lifted a white linen shift and sheer robe from the chest and spread them out on the bed. "These are your nightclothes. The other garments are in the chest. We will review them tomorrow. For now you are free to enjoy your rooms and rest. Food will be served to you here until you are ready to join the other women."

Sarai's head spun as she took in her surroundings. She eyed the young Egyptian servant. A developing youth, she wore little more than a skimpy white linen skirt that fell to her knees, tied with two straps over her shoulders. Sarai's breath hitched. The wide straps merely skimmed the edges of her small brown breasts. Did these people care nothing for modesty? She raised a hand to her throat and blinked hard, certain she had not seen the servant clearly, but when she looked again, the girl's appearance had not changed.

Heat warmed Sarai's cheeks, and she lifted her gaze upward, studying the girl's face. A black braided wig came to just below her chin, similar to that of every other servant Sarai had seen, enhancing a common Egyptian face. Dark kohl rimmed the girl's eyes like everyone else's, holding no distinction. What purpose was there in dressing everyone to look the same? And why did they think it normal to expose so much skin?

"If there is nothing else, my lady, I will leave you now."

"No . . . I mean . . . please, don't go." Suddenly the thought of being left alone terrified her. If she would plan a way of escape from this place, she must begin by making acquaintances of the servants. Servants often knew more than their masters.

The girl lifted a sculpted black brow as though pondering the thought. At last she nodded. "I will summon some fish with bread and honey, and then you can rest." She went to the door and spoke to a guard. She returned to Sarai, motioning to a low stool. When Sarai sat down, the servant took a shell comb and ran it through her mistress's hair.

Silence stretched on as she detangled Sarai's thick tresses. Sarai breathed in the heady scents of lotus and incense, fighting the calm they were meant to evoke.

"What is your name?" Sarai asked, her limbs growing sluggish, her mind struggling to focus.

"I am called Hagar."

Sarai turned in her seat and studied the girl, uncertain what such a name could mean. "How old are you, Hagar?"

Hagar's mouth twitched, but Sarai could not tell if she debated whether to answer or thought the question amusing. Before Sarai could ponder the action further, Hagar gave a slight bow. "My years are sixteen summers, my lady." She set the comb on the table and turned to light the lamps in the room. A servant arrived with fish, bread, and beer, and Hagar beckoned Sarai into the sitting room to serve her.

Music swirled around her, and she looked at the food, unable to summon her appetite. The scents and sounds of the place were meant to soothe and woo her, and she wanted none of it.

"You must eat, my lady." Hagar handed Sarai a golden goblet of beer.

Abram should be sharing this with her. She squeezed her eyes shut, seeing his stricken face in her mind's eye.

"Though most new wives choose only drink when they first arrive." Hagar's look held sympathy. "In time you will adjust." She coaxed the cup to Sarai's lips. "Drink."

Sarai stared at the liquid and recoiled. She shoved the stool back and stood, pacing from one end of the room to the other. She glanced at the servant, whose whole demeanor seemed too amused, not nearly subservient. Nevertheless, she was here and she knew this place.

"I will never adjust." She halted her pacing to face Hagar. "I want you to tell me all you know of the pharaoh. Help me find a way to convince him to release me."

Hagar lifted a brow but lost the haughty tilt of her chin. Something akin to fear flickered in her dark eyes for only a moment. She nodded. "It is impossible to leave, my lady." She lowered her gaze and dipped her head. "But I will tell you all I know of Pharaoh. Perhaps in the telling, you will find a way to help yourself."

Hagar awoke, missing her soft bed, and prayed to Bastet for an escape from this place. The new foreign wife Sarai had barely allowed her a moment's peace, pestering her with constant questions of what her father liked and didn't like, just as her mother would want her to do, only Hagar had chosen to speak truth to Sarai, disdaining her mother's wishes. Still, she had wearied of her servant's clothes and the restrictions the role placed on her. She missed the pool in her mother's apartments and Nitianu's kind smile.

Ra had yet to brighten the eastern sky as Hagar rose quietly and slipped from the servants' quarters. She listened for any sound of movement, paused briefly at Sarai's door, and was met only with the blessed sound of her heavy breathing. Holding her own breath, she moved to the door and stepped into the hall. She would send another servant to attend Sarai today, while she allowed herself one full day to take her rightful place as daughter to the king.

Once out of earshot, she hummed a soft tune, trying to mimic the melody the flute player had used a week ago as she'd dangled her feet in her mother's pool. Someday, when she had her own set of rooms, she would hire a whole cast of musicians to entertain as she ate and played. She smiled at the thought, but her joy quickly waned at the realization that at sixteen summers, she should have already wed a prince. Surely her mother and the pharaoh would recognize her maturity soon.

She turned at a bend in the hall. Distant groaning—or was it murmuring?—met her ear, and she paused, trying to discern from where the sound came. Somewhere in the apartment of one of the more favored concubines. Was someone hurt? But the sound faded, and Hagar continued through the Hall of Queens, past gardens and pools and twenty-seven apartments before she at last stopped before the carved image of Bastet, the cat goddess of protection, guarding her mother's rooms. Nabirye, her mother, remained the only one of Pharaoh's many concubines who had borne him five daughters, including two sets of twins. That feat, amazing though it was, had resulted in a loss of status in Pharaoh's eyes, since she had not produced sons.

Hagar stared at the glassy eyes of the bronze sculptured cat, wondering not for the first time how an inanimate object could protect them from anything. The goddess had done nothing to protect her from suffering the fate of least favored one, caught between two sets of twin sisters. If only she too had been a twin.

If only she had been beautiful like Jamila or outspoken like Kami-lah. She could not even measure up to soft-spoken Kakra or mimic Jendayi's enthusiasm for living. Her only good seemed to come from the information she could gather from her father's newest harem conquests to satisfy her mother's jealousies.

Hagar touched the latch and pushed open the ornate door. Cool air greeted her in the entryway, where running water poured through the mouth of an obsidian frog into a small pool. The rich, intoxi-cating scent of lotus and chamomile blossoms filled her nostrils, but silence met her ear. The normal strains of the single flute that came from the other side of a painted screen weren't there. Strange. Mother never went a moment without music unless she was ill . . .

She whisked off her confining wig, relieved of the servant's head-dress, as sudden fear taunted her. She hurried into the spacious sitting rooms. No sign of her mother or sisters. She raced down the hall to her own private chambers and stopped short at the sight of Jamila curled on her bed, moaning.

"What are you doing in my room?" Anger surged through her at the invasion of privacy. She had so little to call her own. But as she moved closer, her heart skipped a beat. "What's wrong?" She touched Jamila's forehead, then her cheek. "You're feverish." Fear turned a knot in her middle. "Why aren't you in your chamber? Where are the servants? Where's Mother?"

Jamila shivered and looked at Hagar with glassy eyes. "I'm cold."

Hagar stared at her, uncertain what to do. She snatched a thin covering from the end of her bed and placed it around Jamila's shoulders. "I'll be right back." She darted back the way she had come, her long legs nearly tripping over themselves in her haste.

There was no sign of life by the pool or in the courtyard beyond. Incense cones still burned before the shrine to Bastet, the one her mother kept near the gardens, but as Hagar moved through the cooking and feasting rooms, she found them eerily quiet.

Alarmed now, she ran down the halls to the sleeping chambers of her sisters. She opened the door without knocking and found Kakra and Kamilah both curled on their sides, moaning. She whirled on her heel and ran to the other side of the apartment to her mother's receiving chambers. The door stood ajar, and muffled chanted prayers came from the other side of the room. Hagar's feet were like clay, unwilling to obey her commands.

"Mother?" The word echoed too loud in the quiet room, but no one seemed to notice. A cloying, sour smell turned her stomach while the light from several oil lamps produced a gray smoke in the room. Desperate for fresh air, Hagar forced her feet to move and walked to the shuttered window, throwing it open. Light and cool air filtered in, and Hagar drew in a breath before turning to her mother's bed.

"Mother?" she said again as she approached a huddled form on the bed. No, not one form but two. Her mother lay with Hagar's youngest sister, Jendayi, tucked in her arms while trusted servant Nitianu placed a cool cloth on Jendayi's forehead.

"What's wrong? Why is everyone sick?" Had someone poisoned her family?

"Hagar? Is that you?" Her mother lifted her head for the slightest moment, then let it fall back among the cushions.

Hagar knelt at the side of the bed and touched Jendayi's arm. "Yes, Mama, it's me. What can I do? What has happened?"

"Tell your father—" Nabirye's face paled, and she jerked up suddenly and retched into a basin on the opposite side of the bed before falling back among the cushions.

Hagar held a hand to her nose, fearing she too would be ill if she stayed. Nitianu turned to clean the basin, but Hagar pointed to another servant to handle the task and motioned for Nitianu to follow.

Outside in the hall once more, Hagar turned to face the motherly servant. "Tell me what happened." She ran a hand through her short hair and forced her feet to stay still.

"It's as if someone has poisoned them all at once. They have had no relief since yesterday at midday."

"The servants are not affected?"

Nitianu shook her head.

"What of the other wives? What of my half sisters?"

Nitianu nodded. "There is talk among the servants that another god greater than our Bastet has placed a curse on the wives and daughters of Pharaoh."

A chill raced up Hagar's spine. "I must tell my father." Though the thought terrified her. She had never approached his presence without a summons. Perhaps she should send a servant . . .

"Are you not stricken as well, my lady?" Nitianu's arms fell to her sides, and her look held uncertainty. Or was it disapproval?

Hagar's mind whirled as she tried to comprehend how best to answer the question. Her stomach lurched, but not with illness. Why should she be singled out? Would they think *she* had poisoned the wives and daughters of Pharaoh?

"I have been dressed as a servant, caring for the needs of my father's newest wife for the past week. Perhaps the gods were fooled."

Nitianu bobbed her head, and Hagar breathed a relieved sigh as the servant suddenly embraced her. "Of course, of course. The servants—they have been untouched." She held Hagar at arm's length. "But do not let the gods know the truth. Do not go back to your rooms or dress as pharaoh's daughter lest the curse fall on you as well." She urged Hagar to the entryway. "You must go back to the new wife, my lady. Pretend until the curse is passed."

Hagar bristled at the thought. She had come home to rest by the pool, to be free of the confines of false servanthood. But her fear drove her forward. If someone had put a curse on her father's wives and daughters . . .

At the door of her mother's apartments, Hagar looked at the image of Bastet, then at Nitianu. "Whatever god did this, he is greater than Bastet, for Bastet did not protect my family as she is supposed to do." She touched the servant's arm and thanked the unknown god for sparing Nitianu. "Send someone to help Jamila and put an offering out to appease this god, whoever he is. Then send word to Osahar to meet me in the rooms of the new foreign wife. I will give him instructions on what to tell my father."

"It will be as you say, Mistress Hagar." Nitianu clung to her hand for the briefest moment. "Take care of yourself."

Hagar blinked back the sudden sting of tears, then turned and ran back through the Hall of Queens.

☀ 14 ☀

Sarai walked beneath the columns of an elaborate garden portico, her feet skirting the edges of a circular blue pool. White and blue lotus blossoms floated on the surface, and tall sconces filled the air with perfumed smoke. Palm trees lined one wall, a barrier to hide a brick wall beyond, keeping her from wandering too far from this Hall of Queens. Tears pricked her eyes as she rounded a corner, finding guards posted outside her doors and the halls strangely quiet. Even Hagar had deserted her this day, leaving her with no one to talk to, no one to comfort her.

She lifted a fist to her mouth, quelling the emotion, and headed back to the set of rooms reserved for her. She turned at the sound of running feet to see Hagar rushing toward her. The servant paused at a marble column, gripped it for support, and dragged in air. Fear filled her dark, kohl-rimmed eyes.

Her gaze moved over Sarai as though she had never seen her before. "You are well?"

"Of course I am well. What could possibly happen to me in the short time you were gone?" Though she wondered at her own choice of words. Much had happened to her in the past week, which seemed a lifetime ago.

Hagar fidgeted and nodded. "Perhaps it is a sign." She followed Sarai into the sitting room and paced, fluffing pillows and straightening cushions as she went. She stopped abruptly. "I will bring you something cool to drink."

She hurried away as though chased.

"Wait." Sarai's thoughts grew anxious, matching Hagar's mood. Hagar whirled about, hands clasped in front of her.

"What do you mean, perhaps it is a sign? What sign?" Sarai studied the dark eyes and plain features, wondering why the girl acted so skittish.

"All of the wives and daughters of pharaoh have been afflicted by a sudden illness. That you are spared . . . perhaps the gods do not yet know that you now belong to the king. They do not see everything or everyone, so it is possible . . ." She twisted the sash of her narrow white linen skirt. "If there is nothing else . . ."

"All of the wives and daughters of pharaoh?" *Impossible!*

Hagar nodded, then appeared to consider her words. "Almost all—more than should be. It is as though someone poisoned them at once."

Sarai drew in a tight breath. *Poisoned?* "Are they . . . will they live?" Fear coiled in her middle, mingling with the already overpowering sense of despair. Would she be next? Would she die in this place too, abandoned by both Abram and his God?

"They all still live . . . for now. I came to stay with you until the danger is past." She bowed then and did not wait for Sarai to dismiss her, but turned about and hurried from the room.

Sarai watched her go, wanting to call the girl back. Despite her strange and immodest dress, she was someone to talk to, someone who understood Sarai's Mesopotamian language, who could help her feel like she was not completely alone in this place. A chill worked through her, and she sank into a chair, wishing the cushions would swallow her whole. She needed to get out of here. There had to be a way.

✳✳✳

Hagar slowed her steps as she reached the storerooms of grain and wine. If her mother and sisters were dying . . . she should be with them. But she needed to speak to her father first. The thought stirred her blood, heating her skin. She alone had escaped the wrath of the gods. She and Sarai. But why?

The servant in charge of the wine casks returned with a painted jar and handed it to Hagar. She hefted the heavy clay vessel onto her shoulder and moved slowly back to the Hall of Queens. Would Pharaoh's overseers see her as singled out for blessings or curses? Would they notice her at all? Worry persisted, and her heart picked up its pace at the sight of Osahar waiting for her outside of Sarai's rooms.

"You called for me, my lady?" He bowed his head in respect.

"Yes, I did. Oh, Osahar!" She set the jug on the stone tiles and flung herself into his fatherly embrace, relieved when he held her, accepted her.

"There, there now, my lady." He patted her back, and for the briefest moment she felt loved, as she had when Nitianu held her. "Are you ill as well, Mistress Hagar?" At his gentle words, she pulled away and stepped back.

"No, no. I am well." She wrapped her arms about herself.

"How is that possible, my lady? The affliction—"

"You have heard of it?"

He nodded, his dark skin gleaming in the afternoon light, his brows furrowed with worry. "Pharaoh's household is in a panic."

She choked back the threat of tears. "Oh, Osahar, the gods have stopped protecting Pharaoh's wives and daughters."

"And his sons, my lady."

Shock sifted through her, and she teetered, nearly losing her balance. "All of the king's sons?"

Osahar nodded and folded his arms across his bare chest. Only a loincloth gave the servant covering, the sight of which Hagar had long ago become accustomed to. "The entire palace is in an uproar. Even the king suffers the malady, though he is not as ill as his sons. Ra has looked upon him with kindness . . . though it seems Ra has looked upon you with greater kindness than Pharaoh himself, Mistress Hagar."

"The new wife, Sarai, is also untouched." She met Osahar's gaze, noting the lift of his dark brow at the news.

"Indeed?"

Hagar shivered, suddenly chilled. "Perhaps I was spared because the gods thought I was a servant or because I was with the new wife?"

The ever-present fear throbbing within her sprang to life in Osahar's eyes. "This can only be the work of the foreigner's god. Their god must hold some power over our deities. It is the only explanation, for no evil plan of men could poison the king's entire household at once. It came on too suddenly and is too careful in its choosing, knowing the difference between royal and servant."

"What will we do?" Her voice sounded weak, and she felt like a child longing to crawl into a corner and hide from the world.

"I will go to the king and tell him my suspicions. You return to the new wife and find out what you can about her god. Perhaps she can explain what has happened." He turned to go, then looked back over his shoulder. "I will return with whatever news the king brings. Whatever you do, Mistress Hagar, take care not to offend the foreign wife. If her god is the cause of this, worse things could still come."

Hagar nodded. A deep shudder shook her thin frame, and for a moment she feared she had been stricken after all. But after several careful breaths, the feeling passed. Summoning her courage, she lifted the jug of wine to her shoulder again and walked to Sarai's rooms to find some answers.

※·※·※

Abram only half listened to Eliezer and the servants of Pharaoh Mentuhotep II, who inspected and chose donkeys and camels to add to the already burgeoning number of sheep and oxen that had been handed into Abram's care. The air in the stables, whose size seemed to stretch on forever, had grown warm and stifling, the scent overpowering. The amount of the pharaoh's gifts was staggering, but Abram could not look upon them without the constant weight of guilt in his gut. Sarai was worth so much more than this, and yet how could he approach the pharaoh and tell him the truth? He had already lived a week with the lie, and the anguish of losing her was killing him.

Oh, Adonai Elohim, how do I get her back? The prayer had played over in his mind as he imagined one rescue after another, only to discard each idea. He would risk his life and hers if he approached Pharaoh with the truth now. And yet he could not leave Egypt without her.

A commotion near the front of the stables caught his attention. He touched Eliezer's arm, motioning him from the middle stalls for a closer look.

A half-naked slave wearing only a loincloth bowed low before the overseer.

"Rise and speak," the overseer said. He straightened the jeweled collar at his neck and looked down at the darker-skinned slave.

"On order of Pharaoh Mentuhotep II, you must come at once!"

"What is this about that is so important?"

"A plague of illness has fallen on the king's sons, his wives, and his daughters. The king has sent for the priests and diviners to discern the cause. He has ordered every overseer to report to him at once." The slave bowed low again, and the overseer dismissed him.

Abram looked at Eliezer, tension and fear filling him. Eliezer leaned closer to Abram. "All of the wives?"

Abram's head throbbed. No reason for Sarai to be spared. He rubbed his neck and looked at Eliezer. "We must do something."

"Perhaps Sarai was not afflicted."

Abram moved to the doors, into the fresh air. "Adonai could have spared her." But would He? "We need a plan. We have to get her back." Abram lowered his voice at the sound of a donkey's clops on the dirt behind him.

A servant held the reins. "We will take the animals on barges to your camp at Succoth, my lord." He bowed to Abram and moved past while a line of servants leading nineteen more donkeys followed.

The overseer hurried to Abram's side as the servant started forward. "I must leave you. Other servants can complete the pharaoh's gift to you. Just follow the camel's scent around toward the back." He pointed behind him through the door and beyond, the opposite direction from where Abram wanted to go. "You will smell them before you see them." He inclined his head, then turned.

"Wait!" Abram called after him.

The man turned back, clearly annoyed.

"The wives of the pharaoh. My sister is among them. I must know how she fares."

The man's eyes widened at the rash comment. "No family members are allowed to visit the pharaoh's newest acquisitions. After she is established as a wife or concubine, then you may visit her. The process can take up to a year."

A year! Abram's insides melted. "But this illness . . . surely there would be an exception, to know whether she is well?" His heart beat heavy with dread as he read sympathy in the man's gaze.

"I am sorry. I cannot help you." He glanced behind him. "I cannot keep the pharaoh waiting." He rushed off without a backward glance.

Defeat settled over Abram. He turned at Eliezer's touch on his shoulder.

"Do not despair, Abram."

But he could not help the feeling that he was spiraling downward toward the yawning mouth of Sheol. If he could not get Sarai back, what good was his life?

Sarai accepted a golden goblet of spiced wine from Hagar's trembling hand. The girl had done nothing but fidget and mumble in the Egyptian tongue since she had returned from the storerooms, and her anxiety was seeping into Sarai's already worried thoughts. She held the drink to her lips, letting the tart tingle rest on her tongue, but the heady feeling she expected did not come, nor did the wine ease the tension in her heart.

Frustrated, she set the goblet aside and stood.

"Hagar, sit. You are making my head spin watching you fret so. You cannot help the king's wives and daughters with such anxious movement. If something is to be done, you must find a way to help them and act." She walked toward the girl and motioned for her to sit in the chair normally reserved for nobles, not servants. But propriety mattered little now.

When Hagar hesitated, Sarai gave her an encouraging smile. She walked to a window looking out on the courtyard garden, the only place that allowed her to breathe deeply, though none of it felt like home. "How can I help you, Hagar?"

How long should she keep up the pretense in this place? Was there yet a chance she could speak the truth to someone and have that truth reach Pharaoh's ears? Could she be spared marriage to the king?

"I . . . that is, there is talk . . ."

Sarai turned at the girl's halting words. Hagar tugged at her narrow shift, moving the wide straps to cover her exposed breasts. Sarai released a sigh, relieved that she could at last look upon the girl without discomfort.

"If you have something to tell me or a question to ask, do not fear to ask it."

Hagar crossed her arms over her chest and looked at the floor. "This malady . . . it has to have come from a god greater than the gods of Egypt, for our gods have not protected our people as they should." She lifted her gaze to Sarai's, her dark eyes filled with questions. "Is your god strong enough to overpower the ancient gods of my people?"

Sarai's heart skipped a beat at Hagar's haunted look. She took an involuntary step back, searching for a way to respond. Was Adonai Elohim more powerful than Egypt's gods? He had not kept her from being taken into Pharaoh's harem. Yet could He have afflicted Pharaoh's household?

"Why do you think this 'malady,' as you call it, is the work of a god? Perhaps the king's enemies are to blame for poisoning his household." Sarai turned, suddenly needing to walk, and moved from the sitting room through the latticed doors toward the pool.

Hagar slowly followed. "Only a god could do such a thing, my lady. My fa—the pharaoh has many guards who are loyal to him. No enemy could breach our walls. Not like this."

Sarai stopped at the edge of the pool and stooped to pluck one of the petals of the lotus flower. She fingered the smooth edges and held it to her nose, taking in the heady scent. Would they grow in Canaan? She shook herself. Canaan was lost to her.

As was Abram.

Sudden longing for her husband weakened her knees, and she swayed, grasping about for a place to sit. Hagar rushed forward and gently grabbed her arm. "Are you all right, my lady? Do you have the illness too?"

Sarai steadied with Hagar's hold on her. She closed her eyes, breathing deeply. "I am not sick. Only heartsick for my home." She met Hagar's concerned gaze, then tossed the broken lotus petal into the pool. She nodded toward the sitting room and moved there to perch on the edge of the cushioned couch.

"I will tell you, Hagar, that I do not know the God of my husband as well as he does, but I do know that He is the Creator Elohim, maker of heaven and earth. Abram would call Him all-powerful. As for me, I do not know, but I would like the chance to see if what Abram says is true." She clasped her hands in front of her.

"Your husband, my lady? The pharaoh's god is Ra, and the pharaoh embodies the deity. You will soon get to know him when he comes to you." She searched Sarai's gaze, but Sarai did not flinch or hide the truth in her expression. "You do speak of Pharaoh . . . do you not?"

Silence stood between them, a thick wall of uncertainty.

"I'm sorry, my lady. I did not mean to suggest . . . I did not mean to offend." She bowed low, and Sarai wondered if the girl feared that Abram's God was Sarai's to command, that she might have Him send the plague on her for questioning her mistress.

"No need to fear me, Hagar. I will not hurt you." She stood and walked to the window. "As to your question, I would prefer not to answer it, and yet if I do not tell someone, I fear I will go mad in this place." Even Melah's company was preferable to naked servants and this strange new world of solitude. She wanted to go home.

"Tell someone what, my lady?" Hagar picked up the goblet from the table and offered it again to Sarai, as though she needed something to do or she too would go mad. Had the plague brought with it a spirit of fear as well? The very air seemed oppressive now.

Sarai accepted the goblet and stared into the contents. "I do not speak of Pharaoh, Hagar. There is another husband of which I speak. Abram, the man who stood with me before Pharaoh Mentuhotep II, is indeed my brother, but he is only my half brother." She paused only a moment, though it could mean her death. "He is also my husband."

15

Hagar tiptoed over the inlaid mosaic tiles of Pharaoh's court, their familiar patterns of Egypt's gods imprisoned in artistic stone. Her head throbbed to the rhythm of the priests' anguished prayers, while a soothsayer raised a carved rod above his black wig, waving incantations about the room. Another blew his aged breath over tall cones of incense, waking the smoke to rise to the gods.

Hagar spied Osahar with the rest of the king's overseers in a huddled group near the king's gilded throne. She weaved her way through the crowd of servants until she reached his side. She touched his arm, standing on tiptoe to reach his ear. "I must speak with you."

He nodded, moving away from the group, and directed her to stand beneath a carved column along the wall. "You should not be here. If the king were to recognize you in servants' dress—"

"The king never notices me." She motioned him to lean closer. "I know the reason for the plague." She drew in a breath as though it could give her courage. "It is his new wife, Sarai. She is not . . . that is . . . she already has a husband. The man who is her brother is also her husband."

Osahar straightened, his broad shoulders glistening in the afternoon heat, his gaze clearly troubled. "You are sure of this?"

Hagar nodded. "Her god must be angry that my father—that Pharaoh took her as his wife when she already belongs to another man. This man, Abram, must be a prophet for a god to hold him or his wife in such high regard."

Fear filled Osahar's dark eyes. His gaze darted from her to the king to the priests and back again.

"You must tell him, Osahar. My father will not rest until he has an answer." The priests would start cutting themselves or someone would end up blamed and executed if one of them did not speak, and soon. "If you go, I will stand behind you, confirming your words. The king will listen better if there are two who agree."

He looked at her then and shook his head. "You should not go, Mistress Hagar. This is a servant's duty, not a princess's."

Before she could respond, he turned and strode to the table where the king's scribe sat, scratching words on papyrus with a long, thin reed. Hagar crept close to listen but stayed hidden behind a pillar.

"I have news for the king." Osahar bent low toward the table where the scribe sat.

The man looked at Osahar as though the whole affair bored him. "The king is occupied with important matters." He waved a hand toward the soothsayers and priests. "Surely you do not think he will interrupt their incantations and prayers." He looked Osahar over. "Even for you."

"This concerns those matters. I know the cause of the plague." His whispered words brought the scribe up short.

He rose halfway in his seat, leaning close to Osahar. "How do you know these things?"

"It doesn't matter how."

"Yes, it does. If you want an audience with Pharaoh, you will tell me at once."

Osahar straightened, his square chin jutting forward. "I will explain it to the king." He looked down his nose at the scribe. "Do you want to be rewarded for stopping this madness or not?"

Hagar watched doubt flicker beneath the scribe's outright disdain. She stepped forward. She couldn't let Osahar endanger himself. "The new wife is already married."

"What?" The scribe's voice rose to a thin squeal. Hagar jumped and glanced over her shoulder. The king's eyes rested on her.

"Come forward." Two loud hand claps stopped the clamor of soothsayers and priests as the large audience hall fell into silence. The king's tone held no kindness, and Hagar could not pull away from his stern gaze. "Step forward."

Osahar hurried forward and fell to his face before she could act, but her father's gaze did not leave her face.

"What is the meaning of this?" he said to Osahar. "I was speaking to the girl."

Hagar forced her feet to move, her breath growing thin. She stopped at the steps she used to play upon as a child and knelt with her face to the tiles.

"Why do you disturb my court? Are you blind to what is happening here? Speak quickly before I have you thrown to the crocodiles."

"Forgive me, my lord. If I may speak?" She waited, her heart thumping hard.

"Rise and speak."

She lifted her head but did not rise from her knees. "Forgive me, my lord, but I know the reason for the plague." The crook and flail did not move from her father's hands, and his regal look could have withered the sun. Did he recognize her?

"Tell me what you think you know." His eyes narrowed to slits, his mouth stretched taut.

"The new wife, Sarai, is the only wife of Pharaoh who remains unaffected by the strange fever and sickness."

"Not affected at all?" He turned the flail over in his hands.

Hagar shook her head. "No, my lord. I assumed her god must be keeping her from whatever is afflicting the rest of Pharaoh's household. When I asked her about her god, she confided to me that she does not know her husband's god as he does. I immediately thought she spoke of you, my king, but her words were too vague, and their meaning quickly became clear. She already has a husband, my lord."

"Impossible! Who would lie to Pharaoh, Lord of the Two Lands?" He leaned forward, his knuckles turning white where he gripped the crook and flail, the cobra in his crown seeming to breathe venom with his words.

Hagar swallowed, fear stealing her breath. If he recognized her now, he would know she had lied to him as well. "The man Abram is not her brother only, but also her husband."

"You do not speak as a slave girl. Where did you learn such cultured speech?"

Hagar's stomach twisted. What would happen if she told her father the truth?

"She has been in Pharaoh's house many moons, my lord. She has learned well from those she serves." Osahar's words made Hagar's heart beat faster. He should not have spoken. She could not bear to lose him!

She glanced at her father, whose silence unnerved her. At last he lifted the flail and waved it high. "Bring the foreigner Abram to me." The command jolted ten servants into action, and whispers broke out along the walls of the chamber. Pharaoh looked from Hagar to Osahar. "You will stand aside and wait. If I find you have spoken truth, you will live. If you have lied to your king, you will sleep with the crocodiles this night."

Hagar fell to the floor once more to pay her father homage, then rose swiftly and moved with Osahar to stand beneath the columns adorning Pharaoh's audience hall. Her fate would be decided soon enough. If the new wife had lied to her, she had just risked her life for nothing.

"After the camels are loaded with the rest of Pharaoh's gifts and settled on the barges, we can head back to camp." Eliezer came up beside Abram. "Or we can find a place in the city until you decide what to do."

Abram drew in a ragged breath. "I cannot leave her. How can you even suggest it?" He waved a hand toward the burgeoning mass of Pharaoh's gifts of animals and servants, carved leather saddles and finely woven blankets. "What good are such gifts without Sarai?" He fisted both hands, feeling the heat of the afternoon sun beneath his dark turban and wanting to sink under its strength.

The sound of marching feet jolted his painful thoughts. He turned at the sight of twenty Egyptian soldiers coming up the stone walk, clad in helmets and bearing shields and swords.

"Abram of Ur, you are to come with us immediately. Pharaoh Mentuhotep would have a word with you."

Abram stepped forward. "Do you have news of Sarai? Is she well? Tell me if you know."

The guard lifted a shoulder in a half shrug. "Pharaoh will tell you, if he has a mind to do so. You must come. Now." He placed a hand on the hilt of his sword.

"And I will come once you answer my question." Abram's fear rose, his thoughts spinning. If Sarai was stricken . . .

"You dare question Pharaoh's soldiers?" He withdrew the sword in one swift motion. Abram felt the tip of the blade beneath his chin. "You will come."

Eliezer stepped forward. "Forgive my father." He placed a hand on Abram's shoulder. "He spoke without thinking."

The guard gave Abram a stern look, then slowly lowered the blade. "You are to come at once. Defy me again and you will feel more than the tip of my blade."

Eliezer exchanged a look with Abram. Why would the king send soldiers when a single servant would have sufficed? Did he think Abram dangerous or fear he might flee? Abram stifled a derisive snort. As if he had a choice.

Abram bowed his head toward the soldier. "Lead the way," he said, and found himself quickly surrounded as he made the short, ominous trek back to Pharaoh's palace.

❋16❋

The staccato march of rushing feet brought Sarai out of a daze. She had spoken the truth to the maid Hagar, and now they were coming for her. What would become of her, of Abram? Fear tried to crush her, but she stiffened her back, resolved to die if she must. Better death than life in Pharaoh's gilded halls.

Oh, Adonai Elohim, have mercy on us.

Whether Abram's God heard such a prayer or not, she could not tell, but sharing her burden with the Unseen One steadied her nerves, calming her.

At the hard knock, she opened the door. One of Pharaoh's soldiers muttered Egyptian phrases she could not understand as he gestured for her to follow him along the tiled path. She reached for the shawl she had discarded when she arrived, glancing once more around this foreign room. Nothing here belonged to her, and she would be glad enough to leave it all behind. She draped the shawl over her head and walked with lifted chin and proud gait between the Egyptian soldiers.

The path was the same she had taken the week before, wide-pillared and winding, its carved images staring down at her, accusing. Foreign voices spoke in a cacophony of hurried babbling, and the smoke of heady incense made it hard to breathe. Homesickness and dread rose higher with each quickened step. She drew in a sharp breath when they stopped at the ornate double doors. A sleek black cat sauntered past and into the king's audience chamber as the doors swung open. She shivered. Such animals did not belong in king's palaces.

Trumpets blared, and the soldiers marched forward before and behind her, giving her little space of her own.

"There she is!"

"Send her away. Send them both away!"

"Throw them to the crocodiles!"

Voices of servants and nobles and priests came from the right and left as she approached the ornate throne. They knew. And they hated her presence here.

She caught sight of Abram standing near the steps, head bent, looking chagrined. He knew what she had done. The thought chilled her.

The soldiers stopped at a distance from Pharaoh and knelt. Following their lead, Sarai did the same. Silence fell over the chamber, broken only by the soldiers' heavy breathing.

"Abram of Ur, what have you done to me?" Pharaoh Mentuhotep's voice rang harsh in her ears. "Why did you not tell me this woman was your wife?" His crook moved in his arm with the fluid motion of one who wielded power with authority and ease, one who held the fate of kings in his hands. He pointed to his left toward a group of huddled servants. A woman stepped forward, and Sarai recognized the maid Hagar. "This maid tells me that the woman is not your sister but your wife. Is this the truth?"

Sarai glanced toward Abram, who stood with hands clasped in front of him. He looked at her and winced, then met Pharaoh's gaze. "It is the truth."

"Why then did you say, 'She is my sister,' so that I took her to be my wife?"

Abram's chest lifted in a heavy sigh. "Forgive me, my lord. I thought I could protect her better as her brother than as her husband. For in truth, she is my half sister. A brother has rights a husband does not."

Pharaoh's lips drew into a thin line, his gaze living fire. "You have brought the wrath of the gods down on us! Did you think you could escape the gods with your lie?"

"Only one God, my king. The Creator God, Adonai Elohim, is the one who brought this plague down on Pharaoh's house. He alone has power to do this. I am His servant." Abram's head lifted, and he met Sarai's gaze. She inclined her head, offering him a faint smile.

They looked back at Pharaoh. The fire in his eyes dimmed to embers, replaced swiftly by stark fear.

The king blinked, the fear masked. "Whether you speak truth now or not, I cannot tell. Here is your wife. Take her and go!"

Guards took hold of Sarai's arms and escorted her to Abram's side. Shock filtered through her at the pharaoh's sudden change of tone. She looked at Abram, seeing faith and strength in his now confident pose.

"Take this man and all that I have given to him," Pharaoh Mentuhotep said, his voice hardened stone, "and escort him out of my country. See to it that no one touches him or disturbs him."

Sarai lifted her head at that and met Pharaoh's gaze. She glimpsed Hagar standing near the steps of the throne, one knee bent forward and her head toward the floor. She hoped the girl would not be punished for telling what she knew. Would Pharaoh blame Hagar once she and Abram left?

As though he could read her thoughts, Pharaoh Mentuhotep looked at Hagar, his slanted brows narrowing further. "This servant was a gift to you," he said, now looking back at Sarai, his voice softening ever so slightly. "Take her and go." With that, he rose from his throne and slipped behind a thick embroidered curtain out of sight.

Surprise filtered through Sarai that the king should address her at all. His expression, though unreadable, had carried almost a hint of regret. As he slipped out of sight, Sarai glanced at Hagar. The girl's stricken expression as she watched the king depart touched a place deep in Sarai's heart. She knew what it felt like to leave all she held dear. A longing to comfort the girl rose within her, but before she could think to act, she felt Abram's firm grip on her elbow, urging her forward. Soldiers fell into step around them, leading them out of the glittering chamber, down the wide marble steps, and beneath the tall columned portico to the pier of Thebes, where servants waited to escort them onto the waiting barge.

Stars littered the blackness of night as the last tent peg stuck its claim in the ground on the other side of Egypt's borders. Sarai fluffed cushions in the corner of her tent, grateful for the mat she would sleep on this night, no matter how hard the ground beneath it. Her familiar goat's-hair tent rose above her head, and the chatter of Egyptian voices came from a tent made of Egyptian linen housing maidservants nearby. The young woman Hagar had remained silent throughout the trip, and her downcast eyes had glinted with the faintest sheen of tears.

"Thank you, Hagar, for helping bring me back to my true husband," Sarai had said, attempting to engage the girl a week after the barge had left Thebes. "I am sorry you are forced to leave your homeland, though. If you would prefer we leave you in some city where the pharaoh won't find you—"

Hagar shook her head. "There is no city where the pharaoh does not see." Though by her dejected look, Sarai wondered if the pharaoh had noticed Hagar as much as she had claimed. The thought troubled her, but now all she wanted was for Abram to join her, to hold her in his arms once more.

But as the voices around her drifted into the sounds of even breathing, he did not come. Disappointment stung, reviving the feelings of hurt and abandonment she had known throughout the days in Pharaoh's palace. Where was he?

She lifted the flap of her tent and stepped into moonlight. Embers from the hearth fire sparked upward, and she saw a huddled figure sitting on one of the large stones set nearby. She moved closer, wrapping her cloak tighter against the night air. At the edge of the campfire, she recognized her husband, his elbows on his knees, head in his hands. She approached slowly and sat by his side, saying nothing. At last she placed one hand on his arm.

"Come and take your rest at my side, beloved," she said, giving his arm a slight squeeze. "I need you."

He did not move or respond to her words.

"Abram?"

He straightened, looking at her, his gaze intense yet revealing nothing. What thoughts moved behind his dark eyes? Why would he not take her into his arms? She leaned closer, hoping to coax him with the scent of her perfume or the look of longing in her eyes.

He stood. Taking her hand, he pulled her to her feet and tucked her arm beneath his. His silence lingered as he led her back to her tent, but he did not follow past the threshold. She watched him take in the surroundings as though they were foreign to him. But nothing had changed save a few furnishings the king had sent along with the rest of his gifts. Still he stood, his look uncertain.

"Come," she said, taking his hand and tugging him toward her sleeping mat. "Please, my husband. Hold me in your arms."

He let her lead him to the mat and stretched out, hands clasped behind his head, his gaze toward the tent's wooden pole. "I don't deserve such a name." His pensive tone stirred her heart. How she loved this man!

"Well, deserving or not, you *are* my husband, and I want no one else." She folded her legs beneath her and traced a line along his arm.

He looked at her then, and she could sense him warming to her even while his gaze somehow still kept him withdrawn. He grasped her wrist and pulled her down beside him, wrapping strong arms about her. She breathed in the scent of his tunic and felt him stir next to her. As the clouds passed a hand over the moon, blocking the light from filtering through the slits in the goat's-hair walls, Abram's lips found hers. She was home again, and this time she would never let him go.

Part

2

Now Lot, who was moving about with Abram, also had flocks and herds and tents. But the land could not support them while they stayed together, for their possessions were so great that they were not able to stay together.

Genesis 13:5–6

So Lot chose for himself the whole plain of the Jordan and set out toward the east. The two men parted company: Abram lived in the land of Canaan, while Lot lived among the cities of the plain and pitched his tents near Sodom. Now the men of Sodom were wicked and were sinning greatly against the LORD.

Genesis 13:11–13

❊17❊

Eight Years Later

Sarai settled the head scarf over her face, blocking the wind. The voices of Lila and Melah mingled with the foreign tongue of Hagar and the other Egyptian maidservants. The combined chatter caused Sarai's head to throb. She moved away, head bent to the wind as she picked the path up the incline toward the stone altar. Abram stood nearby, his staff dug into the dirt, his back erect as he watched Eliezer and one of the younger shepherds maneuver the chosen lambs into place for the sacrifice.

At the sound of footsteps crunching the sandy gravel, she turned to see Melah trudging toward her. She stopped at Sarai's side.

"I've never understood the purpose of animal sacrifices." Melah flicked dust from her sleeve and lifted her chin, assessing Sarai with a glance. "I miss the formality, rhythm, and grace of temple worship. Tell me truly, can you possibly enjoy this crude altar over the beauty of the ziggurats?"

Sarai turned her gaze from Melah to Abram's altar. The stones were not cut or hewn from a quarry but picked from the earth, their sizes and shapes varied, not symmetrical or carved to fit perfectly on top of one another. The wood—sticks of many lengths, some thin, some thick—lay in a heap atop the stones, awaiting the sacrifice. Definitely not like the impressive ziggurats of Ur.

She glanced back at Melah. "There is beauty in both, only different." She would never admit it to her niece, but Abram's altars were crude and rough in comparison to the temples of their people.

"Do you ever wonder what it would have been like if we'd stayed in Egypt? I would have liked to have seen inside their temples. The images of their gods were everywhere, the artistry most impressive." Melah stepped closer until Sarai could feel her breath.

Sarai backed up a pace. "I do not care to revisit that place, even in my thoughts. Especially in my thoughts." She faced the altar again and closed her eyes. The memories had faded in the eight years since their ill-advised trip into Egypt, but the Egyptian servants they had acquired were a constant reminder.

"I was thinking . . . if you ever want to sell some of the Egyptians . . . I think they could bring a handsome price. And Hagar is one I would keep for myself." She shrugged one shoulder, her look telling Sarai she would be doing her a favor.

Sarai startled at that and lifted a brow, curious. "Why should Hagar be any different from the other maids?" If Melah wanted her, there was no way she would part with her.

Melah waved a hand as though brushing the thought away. "No reason."

"Then why did you bring it up?"

Melah gave a dramatic sigh. "All right, but if I tell you, you will just want to keep her."

Sarai stifled a groan. "Just tell me." The scent of burning flesh from the altar drew her gaze. Such a frivolous discussion at such a solemn occasion. Stepping back from the altar, she moved from the trees and walked down the hill.

Melah quickly followed. "She makes the most delicate pastries, and when she washes your feet, she works her hands over the skin so well that it makes your whole body want to melt."

Sarai came to an abrupt stop and faced her niece. "Lot bought you your own Egyptian slaves. You had no business engaging my maid to do the work of your servants." Anger flared at the thought that Hagar had not bothered to ask Sarai's permission for such a thing, and that neither Melah nor Hagar seemed to respect their place.

"My servants were busy. Hagar seemed willing enough. Besides, they're Egyptians. What does it matter whose needs they attend?"

"I should not have to remind you that it was I who endured the pharaoh's harem. I was the one torn from my husband, from all I love. The Egyptians came as my bride-price. Mine. They are not yours to command. Don't forget it." Sarai clenched her fists, trembling with each word.

"You didn't end up as the pharaoh's bride, though, did you? Seems like you came away the richer for your trouble. Perhaps you even enjoyed the luxury." She smirked at Sarai, then turned and hurried down the hill.

Sarai stood stunned, watching her go. Emotion rose within her at the unexpected barbs. How dare she! Melah had never spoken so rashly or so accusingly. She had no idea how awful that week apart from Abram had been, how abandoned and betrayed she had felt. How dare she!

A tremor shook her from head to toe, anger and hurt rushing through her. Such unkind words over a slave girl?

The scent of the sacrifice wafted to her as she looked down over the camp bustling with life. The Egyptian tents stood out, colorful among a sea of black goat's hair. She spotted Hagar emerging from one of them, a clay jug on her shoulder, a striped robe on her back.

Melah could admire her slaves all she wanted. But Sarai had earned the right to keep them, and as childish and petulant as it might seem, she did not intend on sharing.

❀✦❀

Lot sat with his feet propped on a small rock, watching the Egyptian slaves he'd recently purchased from passing Hittite merchants pound the last of the tent pegs into the ground. A female Egyptian slave came toward him carrying a skin of wine and a tray of sweetmeats. He paused, admiring her lack of dress, his heart beating faster. Melah would give him a dour tongue-lashing if she could read his thoughts. But he let his eyes feast on the girl just the same.

"Taking your ease already, Nephew?"

Lot started at Abram's tone. "I didn't see you there, Uncle." He quickly stood, offering Abram his seat. "Would you care to join me? The girl brought plenty for two."

Abram ran a hand over his beard, his gaze taking in the slave girl. "Go to Mistress Sarai and tell her I sent you for some proper attire."

The girl's eyes widened, looking from Abram to Lot.

"Go now!" Abram faced Lot as the girl hurried away. "I thought I made it clear from the start that the Egyptians are to dress as everyone else. There will be no distinction between them and us."

Lot crossed his arms over a slightly protruding middle, but he could not meet his uncle's gaze. "They have proper robes. Sometimes I ask them to wear the costumes of their homeland. You have to admit, the Egyptians' dress does hold a certain appeal." He grinned, glancing at Abram, but quickly sobered at his uncle's glower.

"Is this how you want to raise your daughters—to think such dress is appropriate?"

Lot felt heat rush to his face, suddenly ashamed. "I appreciated the view. Is that so wrong?" He drew in a breath, irritated with this intrusion into his personal affairs. "Besides, she is my slave. If I want my Egyptians to dress like Egyptians, what is that to you?"

Abram's brow lifted, his gaze never wavering. "This is my home.

We share the same campsite, the same meals. I will not have men and women exposing themselves for all to see, no matter what their culture dictates."

Lot shifted from foot to foot. His jaw clenched. "So as long as I live under your protection, we do things your way, no discussion?"

"Not when it concerns more than just you."

The slave girl returned, fully clothed in a striped robe like every other woman in the camp, her beauty no longer enticing. "Here is the wine and sweetmeats you requested, my lord."

Lot looked from the girl to Abram, anger settling where his appetite had been. "I'm not hungry." He dismissed her with a wave, then looked at his uncle once more. "I will accept what you say." He whirled about and stormed toward his tent, muttering, "This time."

❀ 18 ❀

Melah wrapped a thin scarf over her head, grabbed a basket from the floor, and stepped out of her tent. She glanced around at their servants, irritation rising at the sight of an Egyptian slave girl among the women grinding grain, while another shooed small children from the fire.

Since her confrontation with Sarai, which she admitted had not gone as she'd intended, her life had been in upheaval. She should have known better than to ask Sarai to give Hagar to her, especially not that way. But when she'd complained to Lot about it all, he'd seemed almost too eager to leave Abram's campsite.

Were these Egyptians why he was so happy to heed her suggestion? She had barely hinted, had not even worked herself into a whining pout yet at moving away from Sarai, when he jumped at the chance. Normally he never gave in without at least a small argument.

Heat burned her cheeks. Lot's gaze had lingered overlong on these women since leaving Abram's camp, especially when they wore their native clothing for him and he didn't know she was watching.

The thought made her blood pump fast. While she wanted to

live as mistress of her own estate, that did not mean she wanted to sacrifice her husband's affection. But did she even have his affection? He had vowed to never take another wife, and he could never legally divorce her, but what would stop him from having an illicit relationship with a slave?

"Where are you going, Mama?" Her oldest daughter, Kammani, hurried to her side, out of breath. Her younger sister trailed behind. "Can we come with you?"

Melah brushed a strand of hair from the girl's face and straightened her head scarf, which always seemed askew from the moment she left the tent each morning. She looked into the eager dark eyes so like her father's. "Of course. Only do not wander. We are going to the fields to see your father, and I do not want you waylaid by some fool rogue." Though the girl was only eleven, she was already showing signs of maturity. Soon enough—too soon—men would come seeking her hand. But not here. Not yet. Surely there were better men in the nearby towns than the ones in her husband's company.

"We won't wander, Mama."

Melah nodded once and set out walking again. Ku-aya, her younger daughter, skipped ahead while Kammani stayed at Melah's side.

"Are we taking food to Abi?"

"Yes." Melah quickened her pace, suddenly anxious to reach her husband.

"Can I stay with Abi in the fields? He said he would teach me to be a shepherdess."

Melah looked at her daughter, appalled at the thought. Though she knew many women tended sheep, her girls were not going to be among them. "There are other tasks you should be learning. Let your father worry about the sheep. That's why we have servants." She lifted her head, seeing a flock of sheep grazing just beyond them over the rise. "You are the daughter of a great man, Kammani. Daughters of great men do not stoop to such menial tasks meant for men."

"But I like animals. Sheep are so big and soft." She half ran to keep up with Melah's hurried pace.

"Then ask your father to give you one as a pet. But not now. I must speak with him first about more important matters." Perhaps bringing the girls was not as good an idea as she had first thought. But it was too late to send them back to camp alone.

Kammani opened her mouth as if to protest, but Melah silenced her with a lifted hand. "Don't cross me, Kammani." The girl flinched as though Melah had slapped her. Good. She had no intention of hitting the child, but letting her fear it brought swifter obedience.

Kammani ran ahead to join her sister picking wildflowers, and they chased each other through the grasses, laughing as they approached the sheep. Kammani spotted her father and reached his side before Melah could.

"Abi!" The girls cried his name in unison, jumping up and down. Lot bent to their level, scooped the youngest into his arms, and took the other by the hand.

"Abi, Mama said I could have a pet lamb. Can I pick her out now, Abi? Please?"

Melah bit back a scowl and an angry retort. The child was incorrigible, always pleading and prodding to get her own way. And her father was so easy to persuade. Not nearly strong enough when it came to his women.

Chagrin accompanied that thought. Would she want him any different? And yet she longed for something more.

She stifled the thought, unwilling to think too deeply about why she could not seem to be happy with her husband, her life. "I see the girls have already found you and taken advantage of your good graces." She offered him her most pleasant smile, lifting the basket for him to see. "I brought bread and cheese and some of the olives we picked last week."

Lot set Ku-aya on the ground, patted her on the back, and urged the girls to go and play.

"Can I pick a ewe, Abi? Please?"

He looked at Melah as if for permission. At her nod, he turned to face his daughter. "Pick a young one, but not so young that it still needs its mother."

The girls squealed and skipped off in the direction of Lot's flock.

"Let this lamb be a promise that you will not teach Kammani to be a shepherdess. We do not need our girls learning things the servants can do." She leveled him with a look, waiting.

"Knowing how to shepherd is a skill that would not hurt them to learn." He turned to watch the girls search the flock for the smallest ewes.

Melah shook her head. "I won't allow it."

His gaze swiveled from the girls to her. "You won't allow it? If I want to teach our daughters a skill, what business is it of yours?"

Melah's heart skipped a beat. She was not expecting such a tone from him. "That is to say, my lord," she amended, "I would not prefer it. The hills are dangerous for a young girl alone, and we have plenty of servants who can do the job equally well."

"I would never leave our child alone with the sheep. Not until she was well trained and fully grown, and even then, only if need afforded it." His scowl deepened as he turned his gaze fully upon her. "What kind of man do you think me to be?"

She lowered her eyes in a show of respect, surprised that she actually felt a twinge of emotion for him. He rarely crossed her, leaving her momentarily stunned now. This was not going at all how she had planned, and she must rectify the situation quickly before he stalked off and she ruined the reason she had come.

"Forgive me, my lord. I did not mean to imply . . ." She lifted her gaze to his. "I'm afraid I am not quite myself these days." She touched a hand to her middle. "I fear it is the babe that makes my words confused."

His brow lifted, and she could see his scrutiny in every line of his face. "The babe?" he said at last, as though the idea were impossible.

She nodded. "It is only a few months along. I feel certain this one is a boy." They had lost several boys already, so to say it this soon seemed almost rash, but she must turn his attention back to her purposes.

"A boy." His tone held a hint of hope. Would a son keep his attention on her instead of the slave girls?

"Shall we sit in the shade over there, my lord, and share the food I've brought?" She pointed to a copse of trees farther up the hill, one she knew overlooked the well-watered Jordan Valley.

He nodded, taking her arm, and gently guided her to sit among the soft grasses. The view was breathtaking, but it was the cities beyond the plain that shone like gold among the green, its many temples shimmering brighter than the sun.

"Do you ever miss Ur or Harran, my lord?" She lifted the basket's lid and handed him a thick slice of soft goat cheese and a fat loaf of raised bread.

He took the items from her hand and bit off a hunk of the cheese. "No." He looked from her to the view spread out before them. "The quiet of the hills is so peaceful." A wistful tone accompanied his words, and Melah worried that he might be harder to convince than she had first thought. She must tread carefully.

"Sometimes I would like to live close enough to visit the larger cities now and then." She swept a hand in Gomorrah's direction. "It sparkles like a jewel, and I can just imagine how exciting the place must be. I want to take our daughters there, to give them a taste for culture and art, to learn the ways of wealthy women, sophistication, and grace—something they will never learn living in tents." She nearly added "or tending sheep" but thought better of it. She gauged his mood as he bit into the bread and washed it down with the flask of water at his belt. "I am not suggesting we live in Sodom or Gomorrah, only that perhaps we could live closer on this beautiful plain, so that the girls and I could visit now and then." She smiled and touched his arm. "Perhaps I ask too much?"

He rubbed a hand over his beard. Looked out toward the valley. She hid a smile, knowing by his hesitation that she had triumphed.

"No," he said, making her heart skip a beat. She hadn't misread him. Had she? "You do not ask too much." He turned to her then, his dark eyes assessing, his smile almost unnerving. "You have not voiced anything more than I have already thought. But you forget my uncle's flocks and herds outnumber my own, and he is the patriarch of this group. Though we live in separate camps now, I must abide by his decisions." He touched her hands, grasping her fingers. "Be patient, my love. You already have wealth beyond anything we knew in Ur or Harran. What more could you want?"

What more did she want? She did not know, and his question brought back the restlessness she could never quite seem to shake. "I don't know. I only know I want more."

He looked at her, clearly puzzled, then released his grip and shrugged. "Be patient, Melah. Adonai has already blessed us with great abundance." His expression softened as he looked at her, and she hated the hint of pity in his eyes. "Perhaps when the babe comes, you will find peace."

He stood then, and she knew she had lost what she had hoped to gain. What did he know of peace?

"Thank you for the food," he said, then turned and headed back toward the sheep where the girls played.

She made no reply, her emotions swirling with a host of confusing thoughts. After tucking the remnants of the cheese and bread into the basket, she rose, dusted off the crumbs, and looked once more toward the cities of the plain. Somehow she must convince Lot to visit. Even once would be enough for her to show him how much better and cultured city life could be. There she could freely worship Ningal and push aside the nagging fear of Abram's God. Then she would know peace.

※ ✦ ※

Lot savored the fermented juice, then replaced the cap on the flask and let it hang from his belt. His tension eased only slightly as he took in the view of the lush Jordan Valley. Melah's comments of a few weeks before had taken root, and he could not shake the desire to move away from his uncle completely and live among the plains.

He ran a hand over his face, turning at the crunch of stones. "Thank you for coming, Uncle." He greeted Abram with a kiss to each cheek. He waved a hand toward the valley below. "Is it not beautiful?"

"Yes, Nephew, it is." He touched Lot's shoulder. "But beauty is not always a sign of good. The people of the plains—I have heard rumors."

Lot turned to face Abram. "Rumors mean nothing unless they are true. I have heard there is much good in the cities—culture, art, music, and much more." He ran a hand over his beard, choosing his words. "I am thinking of taking Melah for a visit."

Abram gave him a curious look as he glanced toward the plains once more. "Is Melah asking for such a thing?" He moved to the tree line and settled among the lush grass. The sun hung low in the west, the colors behind them casting an orange glow over the shaded cliff.

"She has mentioned it once or twice." Though in truth, it was the memory of her words and the silent pleading looks he had endured ever since that made the desire become his own. "But I agree with her." He settled beside his uncle, fingering the flask but ignoring the desire for more.

"If you have already decided, my son, then why did you call me here? You are not asking my advice, and you do not need my permission." Abram's expression held concern, his dark gaze unwavering.

Lot looked away, heat filling his face, whether from shame or anger he could not tell. "I thought . . . that is, you are the head of our households. I thought you should know." He lifted his chin in a show of confidence he did not feel and met his uncle's gaze. "You have no objection then?"

Abram stroked his beard, looking toward the darkening valley. "I do not think it wise. I think you will open yourself up to temptation you do not need and danger you need not fear. Has Egypt taught you nothing?"

The reprimand felt like a slap to the face, and Lot squirmed, pressing both hands to his knees. "Egypt made me wealthy. Egypt taught me that Adonai is indeed powerful. But Sodom is not Egypt. They do not steal men's wives, especially pregnant ones." He cringed at his petulant tone, hating the shadow he had caused to pass through Abram's eyes. "I'm sorry, Uncle. I didn't mean—"

Abram held up a hand. "Nothing to be sorry for, my son. I only hope you fear the right things." He stood then, leaning heavily on his walking stick. The years since Egypt had aged him, and Lot wondered at the foolishness of clinging to promises at Abram's age. Melah was right. Sarai should do more to give Abram a son.

"Perhaps it is time you took a maid as a second wife."

"What?" Abram's expression moved from concern to shock.

"I'm sorry, Uncle. I spoke without thinking." Had he sipped so often from the flask that it made his tongue loose?

"Yes, you did. Such things are not your concern." Abram moved away from the trees. The sun's fading glow illumined the sky as he turned in the direction of his tents.

Lot chewed his lower lip, kicking himself. He hurried after Abram. "I did not mean to offend. We come from different places, you and I. We just see things differently."

Abram did not pause in his trek down the hill, and Lot hurried to keep his uncle's pace. At the base of the hill, Abram stopped at last and turned to face him. "I do not know what is in your mind, my son, or why you can't seem to decide whether you want to ask my advice or give me your own. Perhaps in the future it would be best if you make your own decisions and leave mine to me." The slightest irritation flickered in his eyes, though his tone was controlled.

Lot studied the man for the briefest moment, a sense of sorrow filling him. There was a time when they had both tended smaller flocks back in Ur that they had talked of women and work and faith. He'd accepted Abram's counsel, even his rebukes, back when he had rashly taken Melah before they'd said their vows. But the man who stood before him now was not the man he was back then. Egypt had shown his uncle's weakness, and Lot suddenly realized that he no longer held his uncle in such high regard.

"You are right, Uncle. It is time I made my own choices." He lifted his chin, his confidence soaring. He would do what he wanted from now on. He bid Abram a brief nod of farewell, then proudly strode home.

Abram sat beneath the shade of his tent's awning, in desperate need of an afternoon's rest. Leaves in the great oaks above him whispered secrets from one to the next, and he closed his eyes, letting his body's tension slowly subside. The conversation with Lot the week before still troubled him, but bigger problems—bickering and arguing—had arisen between Lot's household and herdsmen and his, enhancing his sense of loss.

He drew in a breath, scents of smoke and roast lamb coming to him across the compound. The high-pitched chatter of women at the grindstones drifted over the short distance, and the laughter of playing children sent a pang of longing through him. He closed his eyes, listening to their young voices first calling to and then chasing after each other. If only one of the children belonged to him.

How long, Adonai Elohim? The waiting grew harder with each passing year. How easy it had been to believe the promise during his seventy-third summer when they set out from Ur. But eleven years had passed since then, and Sarai's age, though barely showing outwardly, had surely not helped their plight. How long before the way of women left her entirely, making the promised child truly impossible?

His gaze traveled to Sarai's tent at the thought, his eyes seeking a glimpse of the woman he had loved for so long. He'd been content in her love and in his roles as husband and brother and son. Adonai's call had changed all of that, making him long for more, making the promises given to him a thinly veiled hope.

When?

The question went unanswered.

He closed his eyes again, trying to blot out the sounds around him, but what seemed only a few moments later, male voices caused him to look up. He lifted a hand to shade the glare of the sun, spotting Eliezer and two of his chief herdsmen approaching. He reached for his staff and felt the stiffness in his bones as he stood. Gripping the staff for added support, he stretched his back, then moved to greet his men.

"What is it?" Abram settled a look on his chief steward. Eliezer did not usually interrupt his afternoon rest without good reason.

"There is trouble at the well." Eliezer glanced at the two men with him. "Between Lot's herdsmen and yours."

Abram bent to retrieve his turban from the ground and wound

it around his head. He stepped away from his tent and the shade of the trees. "Which well?"

"The one closest to Ai, toward the Jordan Valley."

"Nearest Lot's camp then."

"Yes." Eliezer fell into step beside Abram as the two walked ahead of the herdsmen. "Tensions have been rising in the past few years, but now, trying to share the land with the Canaanites and Perizzites has forced Lot's herds closer to ours." Eliezer met Abram's gaze. "Several of the men have come to blows."

Abram stopped at the edge of the camp. The distance to the fields was still nearly an hour's walk. He glanced at the two chief herdsmen, addressing the first. "Was anyone hurt?" He would never abide such a thing in his household, but Lot was not nearly as forceful with his men. And tempers were not always easily kept in hand.

"Several bruised jaws and ribs, but nothing that won't eventually heal," the man said, rubbing a hand along his square, bearded chin.

"The tensions are still simmering, though," Eliezer added. "I came as soon as the messenger reached me. Lot is apparently already there trying to keep the peace." His scowl reached his eyes.

"And not doing a good job of it?" Abram had come to read Eliezer's expressions with ease. It truly felt like the man could be his own son, lessening the worry that often nagged on days when he succumbed to faithless doubts. Hadn't God sent Eliezer when Abram needed him? Surely He would also send the child when the time was right.

"Lot is not you, my lord. He commands his own servants well enough, though sometimes I wonder if he isn't part of the problem."

Abram looked at the herdsmen as he started off again, picking a quicker pace. "Go on ahead of us and do your best to keep the peace. Tell them I am coming." He looked at Eliezer as the two took off at a fast jog. "I have no doubt Lot is some of the cause. He's a restless sort, and servants tend to follow the lead of the master."

Hadn't Abram learned that lesson long ago? Surely his many years had taught him something of value, though at times he wondered if he would ever learn enough.

"Then your servants are blessed. Their master is wise."

Abram chuckled. "I fear your memory is in short supply, Eliezer. Have you so quickly forgotten Egypt?" He used the staff to guide his way down a gentle slope, taking care to avoid rocks and bramble bushes in his path.

"I have not forgotten, my lord. But I fear perhaps you have remembered too well."

They approached the valley where numerous flocks of sheep and goats spread out before them, covering much of the grasslands. Beyond them, Abram knew, cattle would envelop even more of the open spaces.

"You fear I live with too many regrets?" Abram lifted a hand to shade his eyes, then continued on.

Eliezer kept pace with him. "You grow pensive at times, and Lila has noticed the effect your silence has had on Sarai. Sarai worries that you blame her."

Did he? Abram drew in a breath, slowly releasing it. "How could I blame her? For what? Her beauty? I might as well blame Adonai for making her so." He shook his head, stifling the unexpected irritation. "And if I blame Adonai for her beauty, might I also blame Him for her barrenness?" He glanced at his steward. "No. I cannot blame the Creator for what He has chosen to make. It is I who am unworthy."

Voices of angry, arguing men reached them before they saw the gathered crowd. Abram looked at Eliezer, reading in the other man's expression the same concern he felt. Had Lot done nothing to appease them? He straightened his shoulders and marched ahead, Eliezer parting the crowd before him.

"What is the meaning of this trouble?" Abram stopped near the center of the crowd, where Lot stood watching two men wrestling. "Put an end to this now!" His shout brought the jeers and jibes to a halt, though the two men did not stop. Abram nodded to Eliezer, who stepped forward, pointing at several of Abram's men.

"Stop this at once." They quickly obeyed, moving in to pull the men apart.

When at last the men stopped straining against those who held them, Abram approached Lot. "We are kinsmen, are we not?"

"Yes, my lord. Of course we are."

Abram nodded. "Then we must not let strife come between you and me, and between your herdsmen and my herdsmen." He clapped a hand across Lot's shoulders. "What can I do to settle the differences between us?"

Abram released his hold as Lot met his gaze, tilting his head, his eyes wide. "There is nothing to be done, Uncle. The land simply cannot hold all we have."

"Then we are not using the full extent of the land there is." He swept a hand toward the Jordan Valley he knew Lot favored.

Lot turned, a wistful look filling his expression. Silence passed between them. The voices of men were abuzz about them, Eliezer's calm, confident tone setting things right.

"Is not the whole land before you?" Abram said, moving his arm in an arc from the Jordan toward the west where the land was hillier and the water scarce.

Lot nodded. "You're right. There is much more land available than we are using now."

Abram came alongside Lot and placed an arm across his shoulders again. "Then separate yourself from me. If you take the left hand, then I will go to the right, or if you take the right hand, then I will go to the left."

Lot's eyes seemed to skim the west but clearly lingered on the well-watered Jordan Valley. "It's like the garden of the Lord, like Egypt."

Abram stifled a shudder at the comparison. Egypt's inundation was predictable, trustworthy, offering her inhabitants little reason to fear the barren land or lack of rainfall. Egypt was like Ur and Harran, whose rivers brought security and prosperity . . . and faithlessness. Like the Jordan Valley spread before them now.

"I will go east," Lot said after barely a moment's hesitation. He looked at Abram, rested his hands on both shoulders, and kissed each cheek in respect. "Thank you, Uncle. You are most gracious."

Abram kissed Lot's cheeks in return, his heart heavy. "Take care, my son."

Lot's gaze grew shuttered. He knew what Abram meant. But as he looked toward the valley, his countenance changed. A smile lit his face, turning the corners of his mustache upward. "Never fear, Uncle. Have I not servants aplenty to protect me? Do not worry about me."

He kissed Abram and thanked him once more, then turned to his men, ordering them to gather his flocks and move east toward the valley floor. Abram joined Eliezer and headed back the way he had come, feeling suddenly older than he had earlier that day. Concern for Lot and his family weighed heavily on him, and yet as they came closer to his camp near Bethel, a greater peace accompanied each step. Had not God commanded him to leave his family and go to the land He would show him? Parting company with Lot would finally allow him to do as Adonai had commanded. Perhaps now that he had fully obeyed, Adonai might fully give as He had promised.

❊ 19 ❊

Melah watched the campfire sparks flying upward toward the black of night and shivered. She pressed her hands, palms down, closer to the flames, knowing she should be huddled beside her children in the tent rather than standing here waiting, fearing for Lot's safety. Where was he?

She cinched her scarf closer to her neck and glanced once more at the sparkling city lights winking like so many distant stars across the plain. Two months living on the plains had done little to still her restless spirit. If Lot cared about her at all, he would have listened to her pleas and given her a house of stone inside the city, with bars to shut them in and keep them safe. What kind of protection did he expect from a tent?

Her fear turned to anger and mingled with deeper dread as she left the fire and strode the short distance to the thin-walled shelter. The girls' even breathing met her ear. Moonlight bathed the entryway, casting grotesque shadows over the baskets and cushions and cooking utensils. She removed her sandals and crept along the wall, letting the flap close behind her.

She stilled, cocking her head to listen. Male voices drew close.

Too close. Her heart beat faster, her breath growing thin. Lot's men were usually more considerate coming into camp late at night.

She pressed a hand to her middle to cradle the babe, easing her way back toward the opening. A man's shadow filled the entrance. She scooted back a pace, nearly tripping in her rush, fear clogging her throat.

He stepped into the room. She drew in a breath, but a hand clamped over her mouth, blocking her cries. "Hush. Don't scream." Lot's voice in her ear made her legs lose their strength. His arms came around her, holding her steady. "It's all right. It's me." He pulled her close until she could feel the beat of his heart against her ear. She drew back enough to meet his troubled gaze.

"Where were you? What happened?" She reached for his hand and drew him further into the tent on the other side of the partition to her own sleeping quarters. "Tell me everything."

He drew in several breaths, then sank onto her cushions. "We escaped bandits by the space of an arrow's shot, perhaps less. They were waiting for us as we led the sheep to the rock pens. My men fought them off, and those we didn't kill barely escaped. They did not flee in pairs, but alone and wounded." He squeezed her hand. "I fear my uncle was right. It is not safe in the plains."

"I have thought the same myself. Surely now you will listen to reason and move us to the city to a house of stone with doors that bar." She knelt beside him and skimmed his lips with hers. "Please, my lord. Think of your children, of the babe." She lowered her chin, letting his beard brush her face, then reached to stroke his cheek with one gentle hand.

He covered her hand with his. "You do know how to get your way with me." His smile made her respond with a playful pout, but rather than the passion she hoped would come, he planted a chaste kiss on her forehead. "I will listen to reason," he said, his breath on her ear. "We will move at first light."

※ ☀ ※

Abram awoke to the sound of birds chirping before the voices of the rising women could drown them out. He rose quickly in the darkness of his tent, alone. Sarai's uncleanness had kept her in her own tent—again. A sigh escaped him, bringing with it a sense of resignation. Nothing could be done but to wait on Adonai, and though Sarai grew impatient, he knew that fretting would do them no good.

He thrust his arms through the sleeves of his tunic and robe, reminding himself once again that Adonai could be trusted. Hadn't He rescued Sarai from Pharaoh's clutches? Hadn't He given them peace with their neighbors and a land of promise? Why should he doubt? Yet the nagging uncertainty of *when* remained.

Setting aside the disconcerting thoughts, he donned his sandals, lifted the tent flap, and stepped into the stillness, ready to greet the dawn. Pink-hued skies blanketed the earth, beckoning him to climb the hill toward the altar he had built when he first arrived in Canaan. A sacrifice would be needed soon. Though Adonai had not commanded it, Abram sensed deep within him that he owed Him as much and more.

As he reached the summit of the low hill, Abram paused, glancing again at the lightening sky, marveling at the beauty, the splash of color and light beckoning sleepers to wake. *You are great, Adonai. Your creation speaks of Your glory.*

He could not observe a sunrise without a stirring in his soul. Surely God was with him, knew him by name. He could not imagine it otherwise or imagine life apart from knowing the Creator.

The last vestige of color crossed the threshold of the horizon, fully embracing the sky's expanse, when suddenly the air grew thick around him, cocooning him in gentle warmth. He looked about him, sensing a presence, feeling the softest brush of wind on his cheek. But nothing moved in the stillness, the only sound his own breath.

He stood still, waiting, his heart beating faster, an inexplicable joy filling him. The breeze caressed his face now, and he turned to watch it weave through the branches of the adjacent trees.

Abram.

He felt his name more than heard it, his whole being yearning heavenward.

Yes, Lord, I am here.

The response seemed nonsensical. Surely God knew where he was. He waited again, tilting his head, but the sound seemed to come from every direction at once, echoing in the ground beneath and the air above.

Lift up your eyes and look from the place where you are, north-ward and southward and eastward and westward, for all the land that you see I will give to you and to your offspring forever. I will make your offspring as the dust of the earth, so that if one can count the dust of the earth, your offspring also can be counted. Arise, walk through the length and the breadth of the land, for I will give it to you.

The words ended. Slowly Abram turned, sensing the presence had gone as unexpectedly as it had come. He lowered his body to the grasses and pressed his face to the earth. "Your servant is unworthy." The very ground seemed set apart, as if the dust itself belonged to God. "I will do as you say, Adonai."

When he lifted his head, the sun had barely moved, suspended in the exact spot it had been when he first arrived at the altar. He must find Eliezer and quickly offer a sacrifice, then set out to inspect the length and breadth of the land God had promised.

Melah sank onto a plush couch in the sitting room of her new home, barely able to enjoy the luxury. Exhaustion came over her in waves, and she tilted her head to listen. Could she hear Assam's cries from here? Oh, but she needed to rest! Surely he would sleep for a while.

She closed her eyes, faintly aware of the chatter of her servants and the scraping of the millstone in the courtyard beyond. In the three months since Assam's birth, she had done nothing but attempt to feed and care for him. She would allow no one else to interfere. Let the servants do the daily tasks.

The thought pleased her as her mind drifted in a half sleep to the shores of the Euphrates where Lot had first wooed her. Their love had meant something then. Surely he had loved her. And she had at last given him a son.

Tinny, high-pitched shrieks and squeals jolted her. Where was she? She blinked hard, anger flaring. What were they arguing about now?

Her limbs protested movement, but she forced herself up, her temper rising with her daughters' bickering voices. She stomped down the hall toward the chamber they shared. They would wake Assam if they kept up this racket. She stopped at his door, her heart plummeting at his soft cries. She would punish them but good this time! Could he not sleep even an hour?

Assam's cries grew louder, as if he thought to drown out his sisters' shouts. She closed her eyes, drew in a breath, and whirled about to storm into her daughters' room.

"What is wrong with you?" She yanked Ku-aya's hair until the girl's screams grew real, then shoved her away. Rage lashed her. She turned on Kammani, raised a hand, and struck her across the mouth. "Your brother never sleeps! When at last he does, you can't keep quiet for even an hour?" Her whole body shook. "I will lock you out in the street to sleep with the wayward ones tonight. Don't think I won't!"

Melah stared down at her daughters, not really seeing them,

barely hearing their cries, now quiet whimpers. Assam's wails pierced the air, and the girls fell silent.

He couldn't possibly be hungry again. Her milk let down at the thought, her instincts alert. She could not still the trembling as she hurried to his side. Hadn't his sisters been half again as big?

Her touch silenced his pitiful cries, and she settled into a cushioned chair, guiding his small mouth to her breast. She felt his tug, but her milk came too fast and he nearly choked, pulling back. She cursed, grabbing a cloth from beside his bed to stop the flow.

"There, there. It's all right." She drew in several breaths, but she could not relax. Weariness and fear had dogged her since his birth. And now, with each effort, only a little milk found its way into his stomach. "Come now, sweet child, if you are not hungry, why do you cry? Why will you not grow?" Had she somehow offended Ningal? Or was this the work of Abram's God?

A door opened and slammed from across the house, and heavy footfalls hurried in her direction. Lot's anxious voice called to her until he stopped at the threshold of her room.

"There you are." He drew in a labored breath. "Does he eat?"

She shook her head and could not stop the tears. "I don't know what to do for him."

He regarded her, then stepped closer to her side. "There is trouble." He touched the babe's head and stroked the fine, dark hairs. "King Bera and his allies have rebelled against the heavy taxes Chedorlaomer has placed on us. They are gathering to war against Chedorlaomer and his allies in the Valley of Siddim."

She pulled her baby tighter against her chest. What did she care of war? "So let them go. The king takes too much from us as it is."

A snort of disgust came from Lot's lips, and he knelt at her side. "Melah, I don't think you understand. This is a foolish act on the part of the king. Sodom and Gomorrah and their small-town allies are no match for Chedorlaomer and his forces. They've already defeated the Rephaim, the Zuzim, the Emim, and the Horites in their hill country as far as their border of the wilderness. Then they turned back and defeated all the country of the Amalekites and the Amorites. There is no stopping them."

A shiver of fear worked through her, not only at Lot's words, but at the intense anguish in his dark eyes. "But what can we do? You cannot stop the king. You barely know him yet."

He nodded and stood, running a hand over his beard. "There is nothing to do but leave."

"What?" Her heart fluttered at his meaning as her gaze traveled to look at their son. "Where do you propose we go? We cannot travel with Assam."

"We must. I have already told the servants to begin packing. We must leave Sodom and escape to my uncle's until the danger is past. There is no other way for me to keep you safe."

"I cannot go." She stood, clutching Assam to her breast, her breath agitated even as she tried to still her racing heart. "Have you not seen the way Assam seems to grow hungry every time the flutes play at Ningal's temple? It is as though Ningal is waking him to remind him to eat. If we leave, Assam will not hear the flutes and then he will not eat at all." She was crying now and barely felt Lot's arms as they attempted to pull her close.

She broke free of him, her mind hurrying ahead of her pacing feet. "Surely Ningal will protect us from any silly war. You don't really think, after all of my sacrifices to her, after how faithful I have been, that she would abandon me now, do you?" Was that her voice rising in pitch and volume? The sound seemed so far away.

Another cry pierced her consciousness as Lot's hands gripped her shoulders. "Melah, stop! You are scaring Assam."

His tone snapped her thoughts into submission. She looked at

Lot, though his face seemed distorted before her eyes. "I'm not scaring Assam." She stroked the baby's cheek, then lifted him to her shoulder and patted his back. His cries settled again, and the room grew still, broken only by the distant chatter of servants. Even the girls' bickering had ended.

"Melah, listen to me. We cannot stay here if we expect to survive the coming invasion. Chedorlaomer will defeat Sodom. You can count on it."

A laugh escaped before she could stop it. "And what else should I count, dear husband?" She touched his face. "The new worry lines along your brow? Surely if King Bera has decided to go to war with this Chedor fellow—"

"Chedorlaomer, and he is not someone to take lightly."

"Well, then King Bera won't take him lightly if that's the case." She sank back onto the cushioned seat, her energy drained. There was no reasoning with Lot when his mind was so set.

"King Bera is taking this war far too carelessly, and I can see that my wife is no different!"

"How will I ever get Assam to nurse if you keep fussing at me! You know how many nights he has kept me awake? How hard it is to calm him then?" She lowered her voice to a mere whisper and patted Assam's back, rocking back and forth.

Lot looked at her as though he did not know her, his gaze finally resting on their son. What was wrong with him today? So much worry over a little war. She had far more to worry over with the child. If he did not start to eat better soon . . . She could not think about that now. She had already lost so much.

"All right, Melah. I know I will live to regret this, but if you think the babe is too weak to travel—"

"He is. He most definitely is." At last he was listening to her! And giving in as he always did. Such a good husband he was to give her whatever she asked of him. A sigh escaped her, and she turned her attention to the babe, pulling him from her shoulder and trying once again to coax him to eat. When she looked up, she saw no sign of Lot.

"Come on, sweet child. A little more milk and you will be strong like your father."

20

The steady vibration grew, its pulse matching the rapid pounding of Lot's heart. He stood on his roof, taking in the sight from a home that no longer felt safe, his wife and daughters sleeping below. Torches dotted the Valley of Siddim, moving fast, headed toward Sodom. The battle could not have gone well. A sinking feeling turned to stone in his gut.

He should never have listened to Melah. Though there had been only a few days to travel, they could have reached his uncle's camp by now, safe from the marauding invaders whose swift horses and iron chariots would weave around the tar pits and across the plain to Sodom's gates long before morning light. He must do something. But the very movement of light coming toward them held his feet to the roof, weighting his legs.

Oh, Adonai, what have I done? He glanced at the stars, sensing the truth his uncle had tried to teach him. The Creator God was the only true God, the only real Savior. If ever he needed to be rescued . . . But would Melah heed his words? Even now, would she follow him if he readied his household to flee? How far would they get before the chariots would swoop down on them?

The thought spurred him from his sluggish inaction, and he

turned toward the stairs, grasping the railing in his hurried flight. He nearly bumped into his steward, dressed in his night tunic.

"My lord, I thought I heard a noise."

"Undoubtedly you did." Lot grabbed the torch from the outer courtyard wall and motioned the servant to follow. "You must dress quickly and run to my uncle. Tell him that Sodom has been captured and we are all prisoners." He pointed to the servant's room. "Take your robe and staff and go!"

The servant blinked, his groggy gaze quickly replaced by fear. "But . . . we are not prisoners. Sodom is not captive." It wasn't like his servants to argue, but the man's fatigue seemed to be slow in leaving, probably exacerbated by too much drink.

"Can you not hear the chariots and the racing hoofbeats? Listen, man!" He cocked his head toward the direction of the sound. They were approaching faster than he had anticipated.

The servant shook himself as though coming out of a stupor, his eyes growing wide as the sound grew closer. Shouts and an accompanying war drum suddenly burst the thin night air, and in the next instant, the clatter of wheels over cobbled stone streets drew near.

"Do as I say!" Lot swore at the man, then left him, rushing down the halls toward his wife and children. How could he possibly protect them? To surrender . . . Was there another choice, another way to escape?

Fear filled him as he stood at the threshold of Melah's room, the babe nestled against her breast, her exhaustion evident in the dim torchlight. Should he wake her? But how could he not?

He rushed into the room, setting the torch in its stand. "Melah, wake up!" He shook her rougher than he'd intended. She startled and cried out.

"What is it?" She shifted to face him. "I just got him to sleep." She sounded angry and near tears.

"I'm sorry, dear wife, but you must rise. The city is being invaded. We must flee. It may already be too late."

She looked at him as though his words did not register. "Where would we go?" She lifted up on one elbow and glanced at their son, still sleeping and peaceful, though even in this light he lacked a healthy glow.

"To the hills, to my uncle." He gripped her arm to tug her out of bed, but she pulled back and lifted the child like a shield between them.

"I cannot go. Assam is not well."

The shouts from the street did not seem to penetrate her stupor. He wanted to shake her, to make her see, but there was no talking to her like this. "Stay then. I'm taking the girls and going." Perhaps that would rouse her. He left her side and grabbed the torch from the wall.

"You can't leave me!" Her screeched words drew him to a quick halt, the sound like that of a trapped and wounded animal.

He stood, indecision thickening his blood, making him suddenly weary and helpless. He slowly turned at the sound of her weeping. How had it come to this? In the early days, he had known how to charm her, but after he wed her, he couldn't bring himself to care. At first. When at last she meant something to him, the child had come between them. He didn't know her anymore.

The squeal of iron wheels clattered against the stone streets until the pounding of horses' hooves died away, replaced by the screams of his nearest neighbors. Banging against the outer door sent a jolt through him. Footsteps of servants rushed down the halls. The cries of his daughters restored life to his blood.

But the splintering sounds of the doors and windows caving in nearly paralyzed him. He rushed to his daughters' room, snatched them both from their beds, and dragged them to Melah's room. A prayer died on his lips as Chedorlaomer's soldiers barged through the door.

✳✳✳

Sarai stood over the pot of sheep's milk and stirred the mixture with a fig branch, being careful not to let it burn. She darted an anxious look at the sky. The wind had picked up in the last few moments, threatening to extinguish the flames beneath the pot. A storm was surely coming.

"Perhaps we should have the servants bring an awning to protect us." Lila called to her from close by, where she stirred her goat's milk with an equally anxious gaze. "A little protection might keep the fires from going out."

Sarai agreed. "Hagar!" The girl lifted her bent head from the millstone. "Find a tent to put over us. Get some help if you need it." She looked over at Lila as Hagar bowed low and hurried to do Sarai's bidding. "I didn't expect a storm today."

"Nor I." Lila's smile warmed Sarai. "I hope Abram and Eliezer are not caught in it unawares."

Lila's gaze moved beyond Sarai to the group of children in the field nearby gathering flowers for dye and twigs for the fire. Lila and Eliezer's young sons were with Eliezer now, helping in the fields, but their daughters were nearby, one just beginning to help her mother while the other still nursed at her breast. Sarai followed Lila's gaze. Lila's children were like grandchildren to her. If not for Adonai's promised child, she might have contented herself to adopt Lila and Eliezer and never long for more.

She stirred the milk, noting the soft bubbles rising in the creamy liquid, as Egyptian servants hurried to where she worked, carrying the goat's hair canopy. She glimpsed Hagar again as she settled once more over the millstone, grinding the endless grains beneath the hard surfaces. She was a plain girl, and her foreign looks hadn't captured any of the male servants' notice.

The curds slowly separated as Sarai turned her attention back to the boiling milk, wishing she could rush the process. She could smell the storm on the wind.

Distant male shouts made her look up. She glanced at Lila, whose concern matched her own, but she could not leave the cheese until she squeezed it through the cloth.

"Shall I run to see what has happened, my lady?" Hagar stood at her side as if sensing her thoughts.

Sarai gave her a curious look. The girl said little, and despite the nine years she'd lived with them in Canaan, Sarai knew almost less about her than she had during their short stay in Egypt.

The shouts increased in the distance—men calling Abram's name. Whatever it was sounded urgent. "Go, and be quick to return." She clenched her jaw, silently cursing her own lack of agility as she watched the girl sprint away, slim brown legs peeking beneath her lifted tunic as she ran. The young woman had no modesty, but then Egyptians were a barbaric people.

Sarai looked at Lila. "I hope the Canaanites aren't stirring up trouble with the wells."

"It's probably nothing." Lila's reassuring words did not match the lines across her brow. She called to her girls, her voice carrying on the wind.

"Of course, I'm sure it's nothing." But worry swirled inside Sarai just the same.

Abram dug his staff into the dark earth, bracing against the steady wind. Eliezer stood nearby conferring with the camel herder while Abram spoke with the merchant who had just returned from the east with his goods. From the field just over the rise, the sounds of his captains barking orders during training exercises carried to him. Though he had made alliances with the Amorites Mamre,

Eshcol, and Aner, he could not risk attack by others who did not view his presence here so kindly.

"The prices from Damascus were higher than those from Ebla and Kadesh. Their king has imposed higher taxes, so I thought it wise to spend the gold in the other cities," the merchant said. He opened up his leather bags.

Abram inspected the wares and nodded. "A wise choice. Damascus has had its struggles of late." Though he would always be grateful to the place for giving him Eliezer.

"Master Abram! Master Abram!"

He turned to see a man come to an abrupt halt and fall to his face at Abram's feet. "Master Abram, let your servant speak a word with you."

"Catch your breath, then, and speak." Abram summoned Eliezer to join him. "Bring the man some water."

The messenger sat back on his heels, hands to his knees, sucking in great gulps of air. A servant handed him a skin of water. He sipped slowly, his breath returning.

"I have come from Sodom, where Chedorlaomer has been at war with Bera, King of Sodom, and his allies. Sodom is defeated, and Chedorlaomer has swept down and taken all that belongs to Sodom, including its people. Your nephew Lot was also taken captive along with his family. I alone escaped to tell you."

Abram drew a long breath. Hadn't he warned Lot of what living in such a place might mean? Anger stirred within him, but he held it in check. "When were they taken?"

"Early this morning, my lord. Before dawn." The man sipped again and slowly stood. "Lot did not sleep for fear of them. If he had not spotted them from the roof coming toward Sodom, he would not have sent me to tell you in time. I would have been swept away with the rest. Please, my lord. You must come to rescue them."

Abram nodded once, then glanced at Eliezer, the grim set to his jaw telling Abram he did not like the odds. Chedorlaomer's exploits were well-known, his contests without defeat. "Find the captains and send messengers to Mamre and his brothers," Abram said. "We will meet in my tent at dusk to plan and then leave at first light."

He glanced at the man, then glimpsed another lone figure hurrying toward him from the direction of the camp. A woman alone? What now?

He dismissed the man and went to meet the servant, recognizing Sarai's Egyptian maid. "Is your mistress all right?"

The girl nodded. "She is fine, my lord. We heard the shouts calling your name and—"

"She sent you to find out?"

"Yes, my lord."

Abram regarded the slave for a moment, then shook his head. "I will explain the news to Sarai myself. Tell her we will have guests for dinner." He turned then, making his way back toward Lot's messenger.

21

Sarai glanced at the darkening sky, grateful that the threat of a storm had passed, then lifted the lid on the stew pot once more. The cheeses were done, the bread baked, yet still Abram and the guests Hagar had told her to plan on had not come. Where was he?

That he had refused to explain the news to a slave and wanted to tell her himself both worried and pleased her. She had no intention of giving up her rights as Abram's wife to know his plans, especially to a slave girl—and a young one at that—but in the anxiety of the moment, it had seemed the prudent thing to do. Now she almost wished Abram had given a hint to what he was planning. Yet a part of her feared knowing. If the news was good, might not Abram have already hurried home to share it?

Foreboding settled around her with each passing breath as dusk turned to darkness and the fires dimmed.

"Any sign of them yet?" Lila appeared at her side, holding her youngest daughter on her hip. The girl would wean soon, and they would hold a celebration among the women, much smaller than the kind given Lila's sons.

"None. I'm sure nothing is wrong." She looked into Lila's dark eyes, assessing. "Do you think something is wrong?"

Lila shook her head. "You know how men are." She laughed, the sound lighter than the look in her eyes. "Perhaps these guests have not yet arrived, and they are waiting by the road."

"Perhaps." But the worry would not leave.

Sarai bent over the pot and stirred the stew once more. Voices drifted on the gentle wind, their sound growing louder. Abram had returned! Relief filled her. She laid the stirring branch aside and moved from under the canopy to where torches lit the path to the central fires. Abram and Eliezer approached with three men following behind. She recognized Mamre, Eshcol, and Aner, the three Amorite brothers who had allied themselves with Abram, before they settled near the large oaks.

"My lord," she said, bowing to Abram.

He bent to kiss her cheek. "I am sorry we are so late, my love. When the food is served, you may wait in your tent."

He passed her then, moving toward the circle where a low fire glowed. She would not learn more from him until he came to her that night. Whatever business he had with these men, the women were not welcome to witness it. The earlier foreboding returned in full force as she hurried to serve Abram and his guests.

Darkness crept far into the night, but Sarai could not sleep. Surely the men would end their conversation and Abram would come soon. She stifled a yawn, picked up her mending, and dipped the bone needle and wool thread into the tear of one of Abram's tunics, barely able to see the stitches by the light of the clay oil lamp. The flap of the tent rustled, and Abram came inside, his expression grim. He removed his robe and sat down on the sleeping mat beside her.

"What is it, my lord? You have made me wait these many hours, and I fear I will burst with the need to know." She took his hand between both of her own and clutched it to her heart. "Why were Mamre and his brothers here? Why couldn't I listen as you spoke?"

He placed a finger to her lips. "Sarai, Sarai, you are speaking faster than I can think! I know you are curious, which is why I will tell you now." He stroked her cheek, his gaze turning somber. "Sodom has been invaded, and Lot and his family captured. I must go to rescue them."

She leaned away from him, stunned. "No! That is, you can't. Surely there is someone else who can go."

"Sarai." His look held reproach. "You know there is no one else, and Lot is kin. I must rescue him."

She stared at him as silence filled the space between them. "When do you leave?" She hated giving in so easily.

"My men are ready to leave at first light. Mamre and his tribe will join us. Adonai will make a way for us to rescue Lot." He reached for her then and pulled her to him. "Don't worry over me, Sarai. Adonai will protect us. Not one of us will be harmed."

"How can you know such a thing?"

"I just know." He kissed her forehead and rubbed her shoulders. "I will be back in a month, perhaps sooner." He held her at arm's length and looked into her eyes. "Do not worry, my love." He kissed her as though his words were enough to allay her fears.

"How can I not worry? You are a foolish old man to think I won't!"

He chuckled, making light of her comment, then kissed her again to silence her protests. But she meant what she said, and only wished she had the strength to fight him.

Sarai stood on the hill overlooking the plain, watching Abram head for Sodom, the distance between them a wide chasm. She drew her shawl across her neck, the pale light of dawn lifting like a mist. But even the brightening sky could not lift the veil over her heart.

If Lot had not foolishly chosen to live in such a wicked city, he would not be in danger now. She folded her arms, clutching them to her chest. Melah was surely to blame for such a move. Lot didn't have the strength to stand up to his wife. She would be his ruin—Sarai knew it deep down. Yet the thought pricked her conscience in its stark criticism, filling her with guilt.

She felt Lila's presence beside her, the silence between them comforting. They stood watching until the men disappeared beyond a ridge, the height of a hill obscuring them from view.

"A month." Sarai looked at Lila, unable to keep a shiver at bay. "Do you think that's all it will take? Abram suggested as much."

Lila placed a comforting hand on Sarai's arm, her gaze drifting to the plain once more. "Eliezer thought it could take two. With the time it takes to travel to Chedorlaomer's land, rescue the people, return them to Sodom, and then come home again, it could be at least that long. He said not to worry if it took that long, or even half again as much."

Sarai moved away, irritated that her husband had not bothered to reveal the truth, choosing to let her believe the impossible. Much like he believed the impossible about the child, telling her to trust.

"Let's go home. We have work to do." She hurried, reminding herself that Abram, above all men, could be trusted. If he said he would return safely in a month or so, then she would believe it. She didn't have any other choice.

Melah slumped in a corner of the cave, Chedorlaomer's temporary prison in the hills, and clutched Assam to her breast, weeping. The forced move, along with a shortage of food and water, had weakened the boy. Now they were huddled in a cave like animals.

Her milk had slowed to a trickle, and what little remained barely made it past her son's throat.

He would die soon.

She closed her eyes, tasting the salt of her tears. The weight of Assam's small body pressed in on her as her daughters rested against her shoulders, smothering yet comforting her. Lot's heavy snores were a stone's throw from where she sat.

She glanced once more at the babe in her arms. She could barely distinguish his features in the darkness, but alarm shot through her when she realized that what she had assumed was his even breathing was in fact her own.

She shook him. Gently at first. But a hand to his cheek and forehead told her what her heart already knew. His last breath had already come. Had she known it all along yet simply refused to accept it? How long had she held him thus, weeping? By the cool touch of his skin, she sensed that his spirit had left him some time ago. When had he stopped his soft mewling?

A soft cry escaped her as she stared into his light, unseeing eyes. She must wake Lot before the barbarians returned. A sacrifice must be offered . . . but she had no way to reach Ningal's temple, and they had no lambs to sacrifice to Abram's God in this forsaken cave. She looked into the child's serene face, her tears dampening his soft tunic. Lot stirred, shifted on the hard ground, and rolled onto his side, unaware of her pain.

She must wake him, and then together they would gather stones and build a small altar. Lot could steal a torch from the enemy, and they would offer their son's body for the protection of those who remained. She drew in a shuddering breath and slowly released it. Surely Ningal would be pleased with such sacrifice.

She twisted, freeing herself from the grip of her daughters, and rose to her knees, then crawled with the boy the short distance to Lot's side. She touched his arm. He jerked upright, instantly alert.

"What is it?" He glanced around, then rested a concerned gaze on her. "What's wrong, Melah?" Why did he look at her so strangely?

She brushed the tears from her damp cheeks and clutched the baby to her breast. "You must help me. We cannot let the barbarians touch him."

"Why would the—" He stopped, looked at her. "Is he . . . ?"

She nodded. "I just now realized he had stopped breathing some time ago, while you slept. We must quickly build an altar and sacrifice his body to the gods. I will not have him left in this desolate cave."

Lot squeezed his eyes, then rubbed a hand over his face as if he were trying to awaken from a dream. She tried to read his expression in the pale light coming from the lone lamp they were allowed.

"How do you expect us to build an altar? And how can you even suggest such a thing to do to our son?" His whispered words carried rebuke and anger.

"I . . ." She looked at him, suddenly uncertain. "We can't bury him here. We will never see him again." She choked on a sob and clutched the boy tighter.

He touched the blanket-clad body of their son. "I will take care of him." He held out his arms, but she could not release him. "No one will harm him, Melah, and you can rest here with the girls, protect them." He cupped her cheek, coaxing her to meet his gaze. "Trust me."

"You can't take him from me. I will go with you."

"Then who will stay with the girls?" He wrapped his hands around the boy's body and gently tugged. "We cannot build a fire or others will notice." He bent forward to kiss her cheek. "Please, trust me."

Melah felt her son's body slip away, her hands useless limbs at her side. Lot wrapped the boy in the crook of his arm and picked his way further into the cave. Melah collapsed in a heap, begging the earth to swallow her, wishing she could die with her son.

❄ 22 ❄

Lot turned a corner, taking another corridor in this labyrinth of caves, praying he would be able to find his way out again. Darkness settled around him, dispelled only by tiny slits of moonlight seeping through cracks in the cave's ceiling above him. Oppressive silence heightened his labored breathing. At least he was hidden from the watchful eyes of Chedorlaomer's men. He paused, dragging in stale air, feeling the weight of his lifeless son pressed in his arms. Grief pierced him, and he stumbled to his knees against the uneven rock wall.

He would not build the altar Melah had suggested. A troubled sigh escaped at the thought. Where did she get such an idea? Even in death he would never think to offer a child in sacrifice. Adonai would not be pleased with such a thing. She could only have gotten the notion from the foreign goddesses she worshiped.

Sweat broke out on his brow. Distant voices carried faintly to him. He paused to listen, then satisfied that they were not growing closer, he set the boy gently against the wall. He crawled on hands and knees, feeling for rocks of any size, gathering a pile large enough to cover the boy's small body. When at last the pile would suffice to keep animals from discovering his remains, Lot looked one last time at his son's ashen face, then wrapped the blanket securely around any exposed skin and tucked him beneath the stones to take his final rest.

The job done, Lot leaned back on his heels, overcome, his hands pressed against his knees. He had little strength to stand or the will to return to Melah and the future that awaited them as captives to Chedorlaomer. How could he protect her or his daughters from such a large army of unscrupulous men? He should never have brought them to Sodom.

Uneasiness mingled with sudden, overpowering grief as he stared at the mound he could barely see. Tears filled his throat not only for his son but for his own ineptness and foolish choices.

Adonai, if You will see fit to rescue us, I will do all in my power to obey You as Abram does.

The prayer surged from a place deep within him, but even as the words left his heart, he wondered if he could keep them. He had never been strong like Abram. If Adonai asked the things of him that He had asked of Abram, could he obey?

He searched his heart, found it wanting. Abruptly casting the thoughts aside, he stood on shaky legs and brushed the dirt from his robe. Somehow they had to get away from their captors and return to the life they knew. If that meant leaving Sodom and living in tents again to please Adonai, despite Melah's protests, he would do it.

Abram stood at the crest of the hill looking down on the valley just north of Damascus, where tents spread out like a sea of black locusts. Torches dotted the camp, but Chedorlaomer's men did not appear to move. At the crunch of stones, he turned, spotting Eliezer in the moon's dim glow.

"The men are ready at your command, my lord." Eliezer stopped at Abram's side, his haggard gaze matching Abram's own. The trek from Hebron had taken longer than they expected, though he could be thankful they had yet to come upon the rainy season. They were able to avoid floods in the wadis and cross the unpredictable streambeds on dry ground.

"We will divide the men into two groups. One will go this way," Abram said, waving a hand to indicate they should circle around behind the camp. "The other will attack from the front. I will take the lead group." With Adonai's help, they would see victory long before morning light.

"What signal shall I give when we are in place?" Eliezer looked from Abram to the sleeping camp below.

"Flash your torch once, then hide it behind a shield. Flash it a second and third time. On the third flash, attack from behind, and we will attack from before. May Adonai give us quick success."

"It will be as you have said." Eliezer dipped his head, then turned and crept down the hill.

Abram waited until Eliezer's footsteps faded, then studied the outline of the camp once more. He lowered himself to his knees and put his face to the rocky earth.

In You, Adonai, I put my trust. Give us command over these people that have kidnapped Lot, and help us to rescue all.

He lay there a moment, his heart attuned to the night sounds of insects and wind rustling in the trees dotting the hills. No voice responded to his prayer, no inner sense of guidance, only a quiet assurance and a measured peace. He stood and descended the hill, his staff keeping time with his determined feet, and went to lead his men to victory.

Battle cries woke Melah from a restless sleep. She startled, her heart thudding swift and sharp as the memory, the fear of Sodom's invasion, surfaced. She blinked twice, her eyes adjusting to the cave's dark walls. The sounds came clearer now, swords clanging and men screaming, guttural wails and angry outcries. She sat up, fully awake, and disentangled herself from her daughters' sleeping arms. Lot stood nearby and turned, offering her a hand to help her rise.

"What is it?"

"A battle."

"Of course it's a battle. But whose?" She drew close into his embrace and breathed in his earthy scent. None of them had bathed in days, weeks even, but the smell reminded her of his years in the fields with the sheep. The thought was somehow comforting.

"If I knew that, I would have already told you."

"Have you tried to get close to the entrance to see?" If he wouldn't do so, she would.

"I thought protecting you and the girls might be a better choice. I have no weapon, so what good would it do to venture into the fray?" He released her and moved forward several paces. "Never mind. Don't bother to answer. I'll go."

She lifted a hand toward him to stop him, but he had already slipped into darkness. She wrapped both arms over her chest. A touch on her arm made her jump, and the sounds of others in their group rousing brought her fear to the surface once more.

"What is it, Mama?" Kammani slid her hand into the crook of Melah's arms. "Where is Abi going? And what is all that noise?"

Melah glanced at the corner where Ku-aya still lay sleeping. "Keep your voice down. I don't know. Your father went to go see."

"It sounds like men fighting." Her voice sounded small. "Will they hurt us?"

Melah put an arm around her and squeezed, wishing with the pain of loss that she was still holding her son.

"We will not let them hurt us." Melah hoped her tone held more conviction than she felt. "We will fight them with all of our strength."

"But if we fight them, won't they hurt us?"

Melah's stomach tightened, and the dread she had known since the moment of their capture quickly returned. She had used Assam as a shield to protect herself from the men who eyed her, and Lot had thus far been able to keep the barbarians from touching the girls. But what if something happened to Lot? Assam was gone, and she had only herself to offer in her daughters' place. A shiver worked through her, and she pulled Kammani close, resting her chin on the girl's head.

"We will stay away from them and we will pray." She turned, taking Kammani's chin into her hand. "We will give them whatever we must to stay alive so we can go back home again." She wondered if Kammani knew what she was suggesting, praying to whatever god was listening that her daughter did not understand the implications. She would wash the feet of their lowest slave before giving her daughters to those men.

The battle sounds grew distant and faint as she stood there watching her neighbors crowd near the cave's entrance, still waiting for Lot to return with news. Kammani left her side and settled against her sister. As dawn broke a path through the cracks in the cave's ceiling, Lot returned with several men following behind. Melah squinted, her heart squeezing in recognition.

"Abram." She rushed forward and fell at his feet. "You are a prisoner too? Oh, how can this be?"

At his touch on her head, she looked up. "Rise, Melah." He offered his hand. "Come out of the cave. We are going home."

She placed her hand in his, disbelieving. Then all at once, her limbs quivered, weak as a newborn lamb's. Lot caught her as she stumbled.

"We're going home?" She choked on a breath. "Truly?"

"We're going home."

As the men gathered her daughters, Melah wept in her husband's arms.

23

Sarai lay among the cushions in her tent, refusing to rise. The sun had already found its path toward midday, but she did not care. She had already turned several servants away, unwilling to share her pain.

The tent flap rustled, light from the day disturbing her self-imposed darkness. She closed her eyes, praying whoever stood in the entry would think her asleep and leave. She did not want their sympathy. Her body had betrayed her, had dried up and shriveled, and nothing anyone could say would restore what had been lost. Even Adonai could not give her body life. All chance of bearing the promised seed of Abram had disappeared with the proof of a dead womb.

"Sarai?" Lila's voice cut into her thoughts, only adding to her pain. Tears stung unbidden, and she rolled onto her back once more, flinging her arm over her eyes.

"Go away." The words were choked, filling her with dismay. She didn't want Lila to see her like this. The woman had everything Sarai wanted, and yet Sarai could not fault her for it. She loved Lila like a daughter, more than she had ever expected possible.

Footsteps drew closer, and Sarai sensed Lila had knelt at her side. "Please, Sarai, tell me what is wrong. Everyone is worried about you."

"Why should they worry? I am of no consequence to them." How bitter she sounded! And yet she could not bring herself to care what Lila thought of her.

"Of course you are! Everyone loves you." She touched Sarai's arm. "Please, tell me what has happened. What if Abram returns this day and finds you curled on your mat? He will worry you are ill." She paused, and Sarai pulled her arm from her face. "Are you ill?"

Sarai forced her weary limbs into a sitting position and wrapped her arms around her knees. "I am ill. I am weary of life. There, I have told you, now go." Though she prayed she wouldn't.

"Can I get you some herbs, some broth?" Lila placed both hands on her knees, her round face wreathed in concern.

"You cannot help me." Her voice dropped to a whisper, and she looked away, unwilling to see the pity in Lila's gaze. "I have discovered . . . the way of women has left me. There will be no promised son from me." She swallowed hard but could not stop the thin stream of tears from spilling down her cheeks. She swiped them away, angry at their intrusion.

Lila sat in silence until at last Sarai looked at her. The pity she expected was not there, only the slightest wrinkling of her brow.

"What will you do?" Lila placed a comforting hand on Sarai's and squeezed.

"There is only one thing to do." Everyone knew the laws, the expectations put on a wife. Her father's command rang fresh in her ears.

Sarai, daughter of Terah, I hold you to your promise to give Abram, son of Terah, a son. If you do not fulfill your vow to my son, his vow to you never to take another wife is null.

"I must find a suitable maid and give her to my husband to

wife. She will bear him the promised one." The words grew gritty on her tongue, and she longed to spit them out. But she refrained, knowing with a growing conviction that they were true.

Lila slowly nodded. "Do you have a maid in mind?" She leaned closer, her gaze full of sympathy.

Sarai shook her head. She had gone over the list of her maids all through the night, even during the past weeks when the realization had settled over her. She'd spent days watching the younger unmarried girls, discarding those who were beautiful, yet not wanting to send one to Abram whom he could not wed with pride. His son would need a strong woman, one with good features, an intelligent maid, yet not one who might usurp Sarai's own authority. Sarai would be the child's true mother, after all. The promised son would still be hers.

"I am not sure," she said at last. "Someone young and strong enough to bear a child, but not someone who might turn my husband's head too often in her direction." The very thought sent a stab of pain to her heart. She lifted a hand to her mouth to stifle a sob and turned to Lila. "Oh, Lila, I can't bear to share him!"

Lila scooted closer and wrapped one arm around Sarai's shoulders. "I know."

"But I must. There is no other way he will have a son. I certainly cannot give it to him." She tasted bitterness like bile on her tongue.

"Which women have you considered?" There were many servants they had acquired, but most had been given in marriage to other servants. Sarai's own handmaids were the most logical choices, of whom Lila had once been part.

"Hagar comes often to mind." Sarai drew in a slow breath. She'd dreamed of Hagar and could not seem to shake the servant's image from her thoughts during the night. And though she was neither beautiful nor hard to look upon, Sarai loathed the thought of offering such a one to Abram. Abram rarely paid attention to her, and part of Sarai still felt sorry for the woman, yanked so swiftly from her homeland and never quite finding a place of belonging here. Though she now looked like one of them in dress, her manner still reflected the Egyptians' in the tilt of her head, and her onyx eyes reminded Sarai of one of the Egyptian statues she'd seen nearly every step she'd walked in the Hall of Queens.

"Hagar could be a wise choice." Lila offered Sarai a smile that did not quite reach her eyes. "She is foreign, so chances are Abram will never take to her the way he has to you."

Sarai balked at the comment. "Do not even suggest such a thing! Of course he will not take to her. He will do his duty, and she will bear him a son. I will not abide him making her a full wife."

"I am sorry. I didn't mean—"

Sarai waved a hand, stopping the apology. "No. You are right. Though a foreign wife . . . Do you think Adonai meant for the promised child to be born of mixed blood? Could he have meant to bring Ur and Egypt together in one common bond?"

"I do not know. I suppose that is possible. But I had always thought Adonai meant for you to bear the promised one. As Abram has so long agreed." Lila picked up one of the cushions that made up Sarai's bed and smoothed the wrinkles.

Sarai's heart pricked again, the pain familiar and unrelenting. "I thought so too," she whispered. She sat for the space of many breaths, then finally pushed up from the ground and stretched the kinks from her back. "Obviously we were wrong. Not even Abram gets everything right every time. Our stay in Egypt should have taught us that."

But perhaps something useful had come out of Egypt. Could Adonai have allowed her to be taken in order to meet and acquire Hagar as her maid? Did the Creator God have in mind Hagar for this purpose? She turned the new thought over in her mind, testing it, viewing it from different angles. She could give Hagar to Abram with restrictions. She was still the first wife here, and Hagar a mere slave woman. Giving her to Abram would change Hagar's status, but if anything went wrong, Sarai could easily convince Abram to do right by her. Couldn't she?

Worry niggled the back of Sarai's neck, and she suddenly wondered if she had lost all perspective. But as she joined Lila outside the tent, working among the women for the day's meals, she watched the young Egyptian and the thoughts grew stronger. Hagar could be the solution to her barrenness. The woman was kind and often gracious, quick to serve, and despite a certain Egyptian stubbornness, she seemed content with her lot. So why not choose her to carry Abram's seed? Their age difference alone would ensure Abram would never truly bond with the woman.

Sarai blinked back tears, reminding herself that if she did this, she would no longer have Abram exclusively to herself. He would share intimacy with another—a woman she was not even sure she liked, a woman she would never consider an equal. But as she bent to stir the lentils and felt the stiffness in her joints, she was reminded with harsh clarity that she was no longer young, and her last chance at conceiving a child had left before Abram ever took off to rescue Lot. When Abram returned, if in fact he did return, she must offer him another way to bring the promise to pass, before his body grew as shriveled as her own and hope was lost for good.

Abram rode beside Eliezer, his whole being longing for home. The Valley of Shaveh spread out before him as they neared the city of Salem, the rich green of the land soft beneath the camels' feet. He adjusted the head cloth away from his mouth, the dust no longer kicking up as it had during the trek across the sands. Glancing at Eliezer, he smiled.

"Soon. I will be pleased to sit in the shade of my own tent again."

His smile widened as he imagined Sarai's relieved expression and could almost feel the strength of her arms clinging to him. How he missed her!

"It can't come fast enough." Eliezer nodded and shifted in the camel's saddle. "Ariel has probably learned to grind grain, and Jael has surely weaned by now. Eran and Nahum have probably grown as tall as I am. I won't recognize them."

"A few months cannot make such a difference."

"To you and I, no. But to a child . . ." He stopped the words and met Abram's gaze.

"It's all right, Eliezer. Do not be afraid to speak of your children to me. Someday I will need your advice when I hold a son of my own."

They rode in comfortable silence a little longer, Abram's thoughts turning to Adonai. How long it had been since the promise had been given. Twelve years since he had left Ur. Sarai had aged more than he had, despite her youthful appearance. She rarely spoke of it, but he knew she feared her time was running short when it came to any chance of motherhood. *How much longer, Adonai?*

The sound of horses thundered toward them across the valley. Eliezer reined in his mount, and Abram followed his example.

"Can you tell who it is?" Abram asked. Eliezer's eyesight was keener than Abram's, though he could see clearly enough once the objects were within a bow's shot.

"They're still too far off, though the flags bear the colors of Sodom." Eliezer glanced at Abram. "It could be Bera, their king."

Abram pondered the thought a moment, then lifted his hand heavenward. "As Adonai Elohim, Creator of heaven and earth, lives, I will take nothing that belongs to him, not even a thread or a sandal's thong, lest he be able to say, 'I have made Abram rich.'" He lowered his hand and looked again at Eliezer.

"What of the men or Mamre and his brothers?"

"They can take their share. The oath applies only to me." How could Lot return to live in such a city and overlook what everyone within walking distance knew of Sodom and its neighboring city-states? But there was no reasoning with Melah after the loss of their son, and Lot's initial relief at being rescued and determination to obey Adonai had faded the closer they drew to Sodom.

Adonai, have mercy on them. Turn their hearts to You.

They moved forward again, slowing as they reached the walled city of Salem. The place sat like a precious stone near Mount Moriah's crest, and Abram's heart felt a strange warmth at the sight of it. A trumpet sounded, and he drew in his mount, turning his attention to Salem's gates, where a procession of priests, flag bearers, and trumpeters approached in a kingly parade.

"Now what?"

Something stirred within Abram as he watched the high priest, his office evident by his resplendent robes decorated with pomegranates, tinkling golden bells along the hem, and a jeweled ephod worn over his chest. He carried a flask in one hand and what could only be a loaf of round flat bread in the other. At his approach, Abram commanded the camel to kneel and dismounted the beast.

A priest, or a king? A band of thick gold encrusted with small, sparkling jewels circled the man's hoary head. Abram bowed low and waited until the man stopped in front of him.

"Rise, Abram, son of Terah." He waited, and Abram did as commanded. How did the man know his name? Yet one look into the king's fathomless eyes gave Abram the sense that this man knew him well.

"I am Melchizedek, king of Salem, priest of El Elyon, God Most High." The king/priest dipped his head to acknowledge Abram. "Come and break bread with me." The man turned and led Abram to a large boulder and bade him sit.

Melchizedek handed the flask to a servant, then broke the bread and gave some to Abram, keeping the other half for himself. "Eat all of it," he said, doing the same.

When Abram had finished the last swallow, the priest poured wine into two golden goblets the servant held out for him. He handed one to Abram. "Drink." Abram again did as he was commanded while Melchizedek drank from his cup. When they had finished, Melchizedek stepped closer to Abram and placed both hands on his head. He stood still for a moment, saying nothing, but Abram could feel his heart constrict at the man's simple touch. He felt suddenly weak and exposed, yet at the same time enveloped and loved.

"Blessed be Abram by El Elyon Elohim, God Most High, Creator of heaven and earth," Melchizedek said, "and blessed be God Most High, who delivered your enemies into your hand."

He lifted his hands from Abram's head and grasped Abram's arm, pulling him to his feet. The man's strength surprised him, and yet it didn't. He met Melchizedek's gaze once more.

"Thank you, my lord. Let me bless you now as well. I give you a tenth of all we have recovered."

The priest kissed Abram on each cheek, then moved back a step. "Let it be as you have said."

Abram nodded, then turned, waving Eliezer closer. "Of the spoils of Sodom, I will not take a thread or a sandal's thong, but a tenth of all we have shall be given to this king."

Eliezer looked at Abram, his gaze holding awe and approval. "Yes, my lord."

Abram turned his attention back to Melchizedek. "Will I see you again?" Somehow he did not want to leave the man's presence, yet knew he must.

Melchizedek's smile warmed him, his eyes bright with unspoken mystery. "I must now return to my city." His gaze lifted heavenward for the slightest moment, then he turned to walk back toward the gates of Salem. "You will see me again, my son Abram."

Abram watched him go, unable to deny the sudden loss he felt, yet his hope in the blessing remained. He turned back to his men to speak with Eliezer while the gifts were still being dispersed and caught sight of the contingent from Sodom, King Bera at their head, coming his way. Eliezer joined him as the man approached.

King Bera stopped, leaving a lengthy space between them, his guards flanking his sides. His expression carried none of the arrogance Abram had heard about, only uncertainty about the outcome of his fortune. He raised a hand in supplication.

"You have done me a great service in rescuing my people from Chedorlaomer." He bowed low, paying Abram homage.

"You owe me nothing. You need not bow to me."

"Give me the people then, and keep the goods for yourself."

Abram shook his head and lifted his right hand toward the heavens. "I have raised my hand to Adonai El Elyon Elohim, the Lord God Most High, Creator of heaven and earth, and have taken an oath that I will accept nothing belonging to you, not even a thread or the thong of a sandal, so that you will never be able to say, 'I made Abram rich.' I will accept nothing but what my men have eaten and the share that belongs to the men who went with me—to Aner, Eshcol, and Mamre. Let them have their share."

King Bera's brows drew close together for the briefest moment, as if he could not decide whether to take offense or feel relief at Abram's words. "Take what is yours and go in peace."

The joy he had felt in Melchizedek's presence had swiftly dissipated in the short moments with this king, as though light and darkness had both met with Abram, and the one could not abide the other.

Now Sarai, Abram's wife, had borne him no children. But she had an Egyptian maidservant named Hagar; so she said to Abram, "The LORD has kept me from having children. Go, sleep with my maidservant; perhaps I can build a family through her." Abram agreed to what Sarai said.

Genesis 16:1–2

So Hagar bore Abram a son, and Abram gave the name Ishmael to the son she had borne. Abram was eighty-six years old when Hagar bore him Ishmael.

Genesis 16:15–16

❋ 24 ❋

Sarai's hands shook as she attempted to pour wine from a goatskin flask into the new silver chalice Abram had purchased on his return from rescuing Lot. To know Lot and Melah were safe brought her a measure of comfort, though her real comfort came in knowing Abram was home with her. She glanced at him where he sat across the fire. So handsome his features in the flickering firelight. Age had only distinguished the lines of his face, and the gray strands in his hair were few. How could she bear to share him?

She glanced at Hagar, who stood awaiting Sarai's next order. What would she say when Sarai told her to go into her husband's tent and give herself to him? The wine sloshed over the side of the chalice, and she nearly dropped the flask. Hagar hurried to her side.

"Let me help you, my lady." The girl's strong brown fingers curled around the base of the flask, steadying it.

Sarai's defenses rose. She was not helpless yet! But she refrained from jerking the flask away from the girl. If she treated her poorly, she might not agree to her request.

"Thank you," she said, realizing the awkward silence as she released the flask into Hagar's hands. "I don't know why I am so clumsy tonight." She shrugged as if the problem was of no consequence.

"Perhaps you are just relieved to have the master safely home. If you would sit, I can serve both of you." Hagar's soft smile almost made her pretty. Abram would find her comely enough.

Sarai nodded. "Thank you, Hagar. I believe I will." She picked up the goblets and carried them to Abram, then sat beside him. Hagar soon followed carrying a tray of meat and an assortment of roasted vegetables.

"How are you feeling, my love?" Abram's deep timbre soothed Sarai's frayed nerves. She must tell him her decision, but she couldn't bring herself to put voice to her words.

"I am well now that you are home." She slipped her arm through his and leaned against his shoulder. "Tell me you won't leave me again."

He chuckled. "Ah, Sarai, you know I cannot promise such a thing. But I am here now." He laid one arm across her shoulders and squeezed.

Silence settled between them as Hagar served the meal. Sarai watched her move with lithe grace, glancing from the girl to Abram. Did he notice her? Yet he seemed unaware of the woman's presence, his attention on the food. She sighed, the sound loud in her ears.

Abram looked up from his plate to search her face. He swallowed and wiped the sticky meat from his hands with a linen towel Hagar quickly handed to him. Observant, she was. A good quality for an inferior wife. If indeed Abram would agree to take her as such. But Sarai must make her plan carefully. He had only just returned. She must give him the idea in small amounts.

"Something troubles you, Sarai. Tell me." He took a long swig from his cup.

She looked down at her own plate, stirring the food with a golden-pronged utensil. "I have something I must tell you. I fear you will not like it." She looked up then and met wariness in his eyes.

"Whether I like it or not matters little. If it concerns you, I want to know." He took her hand in his and patted it.

She drew in a shaky breath and looked from their clasped hands to the concern in his dark eyes. One quick glance around her told her the servants, Hagar included, were far enough from where they sat not to overhear. And Eliezer and Lila had already moved from the campfire to Eliezer's tent. She looked again at Abram's comforting gaze.

"While you were away . . ." She lowered her voice further and leaned in close to him. "I discovered . . . I am no longer . . . that is . . ." Her words came to a halt, and she choked on an unexpected sob.

He tipped her chin up with a gentle hand. "Tell me." He stroked her cheek with a finger. The action made her lip quiver, and she feared she would weep.

She swallowed once, twice, then tried again. "The way of women no longer visits me, my lord. I will never bear the promised child." The words came out rushed, and she released a sigh as she finished. The rest of her plan would wait. She must give him time to absorb this information.

He cupped his palm to her cheek, then drew her close to his heart. "And you are quite sure of this?" His question hung between them, and she wondered if he would jump ahead of her plan and suggest another wife before she had the chance.

"Yes, my lord." Shame suddenly enveloped her. "I have failed you."

He rubbed circles over her back in silence for more heartbeats than she could count until she realized she had dampened his tunic with her tears.

"Adonai has promised us a son, beloved. You must not think you have failed. His timing is just not ours."

"His timing is past for me. How can a woman bear a child when there is no life left within her?" She leaned away from him, searching his face for something, anything to indicate his thoughts. But his clear gaze told her another wife was the furthest thing from his mind.

"Believe, dear one. Trust Adonai to keep His word. If He could create all of this"—his hand moved in an arc over the area now darkened with night, then pointed heavenward where the stars glowed down on them—"then He can do something so small as to give us a child, can He not?"

Could He? She wrestled with the thought, testing and discarding it. "I do not know. Perhaps He has a different plan in mind."

He tilted his head to look into her eyes. "A different plan? What do you mean?"

She glanced beyond him, spotting Hagar, then quickly looked back at him. "Eliezer is our heir. He might be all we were ever meant to have."

His gaze turned thoughtful, but a moment later he gave his head a stubborn shake. "No. I did not misunderstand the promise." He stood and pulled her up with him. "Let us speak of this no more. When the time is right, you will bear a son, no matter how impossible that seems now."

She slipped her hand into his as he led her toward his tent. She would not argue with him. Now was not the time, though she knew she must say something soon. If she was going to raise a slave woman's son, she must give her husband a slave woman to bear the child.

Abram lay on the mat in his own tent several nights later, Sarai's words still ringing in his ears. He sensed she had wanted to say more but was glad she held her tongue. He knew she carried the burden for the child far more than he did. It was a wife's place to provide her husband an heir, and if she failed, it was also her place to offer him a maid as a wife to fulfill what she could not. Was Sarai contemplating such a thing? The thought carried a lack of faith, and he dismissed it as quickly as it came.

But as his eyes grew heavy, Sarai's worried look floated in his thoughts. If only he could reassure her. And yet her words had sparked his own sense of fear, his faith wobbling like a calf on newborn legs. A sigh lifted his chest, and he breathed deeply the familiar scents of the campfire and listened to the soft breeze rustling the leaves in the oaks nearby, lulling him deeper into sleep.

Do not be afraid, Abram. I am your shield, your very great reward.

Abram heard the voice, but his limbs would not move, his eyelids weighted against an inescapable light. "O Sovereign Lord," he said, though his voice sounded as if it came from a distance, "what can you give me since I remain childless, and the one who will inherit my estate is Eliezer of Damascus? You have given me no children, so a servant in my household will be my heir."

This man will not be your heir, but a son coming from your own body will be your heir.

The light grew shadowed, and Abram awoke. Had he slept at all? The presence remained, and he stood up and wrapped his cloak about him, sensing an urging to step out of his tent. He obeyed, standing in moonlight.

Look up at the heavens and count the stars—if indeed you can count them. There was a pause, as though the voice wanted to be sure he looked from one end of the heavens to another, taking in every star. *So shall your offspring be.*

I believe You, Adonai. His heart warmed to a sense of deep approval. He stepped further from the tent so his gaze of the heavens was unhindered by the trees.

I am Adonai, who brought you out of Ur of the Chaldeans to give you this land to take possession of it.

Thoughts of his foreign neighbors and their many fighting forces swept through him. "O Sovereign Adonai, how can I know that I will gain possession of it?"

Bring Me a heifer, a goat, and a ram, each three years old, along with a dove and a young pigeon.

Abram waited but a moment. "Yes, Lord. I will seek them at first light and bring them here to you."

No words came, but his heart sensed affirmation. He waited, feeling the breeze caress his face and lift the hair from his forehead. He would visit the flocks and choose the choicest animals for the sacrifice. Then he would see what God would do.

The following afternoon, Abram had his servants tie the animals to the nearby trees while the birds remained caged in baskets on the ground. Dismissing his servants, he prepared the animals for sacrifice, arranging the halves of the heifer, goat, and ram to face each other with the birds whole beside them.

Hours passed. Abram moved between and around the dead animals, driving off the eagles, hawks, and vultures that swooped low, determined to steal the flesh from the bones. Abram's muscles ached from the butchering and the running, his movements slowing as the sun descended below the hills to the west. His body spent, he settled on the ground beneath one of the large oaks as a deep sleep fell over him. But even in sleep he sensed a thick, dreadful darkness holding him, pinning his limbs to the earth. His heart beat slow and heavy as though his blood forgot how to pump through his veins. Stillness held the air captive, and he sensed even in sleep that his breath had stopped.

Know for certain that your descendants will be strangers in a country not their own, and they will be enslaved and mistreated four hundred years.

The whispered words terrified him.

But I will punish the nation they serve as slaves, and afterward they will come out with great possessions. You, however, will go to your fathers in peace and be buried at a good old age. In the fourth generation your descendants will come back here, for the sin of the Amorites has not yet reached its full measure.

A smoking firepot with a blazing torch appeared before Abram's vision, passing between the pieces of animal flesh.

To your descendants I give this land, from the river of Egypt to the great river, the Euphrates—the land of the Kenites, Kenizzites, Kadmonites, Hittites, Perizzites, Rephaites, Amorites, Canaanites, Girgashites, and Jebusites.

The firepot rose and disappeared from his sight, taking the voice with it. The dreadful darkness lifted, and the night sounds returned. Abram awoke, the sign of Adonai's covenant still clear in his mind's eye. The covenant had been one-sided, not at all what Abram had expected. Adonai's only requirement of Abram had been to offer the sacrifice. Adonai had walked between the pieces alone.

Awe settled over him where he sat among the trees, unable to do more than lift his face toward the heavens. He *would* have a son, and his descendants would outnumber the stars. He closed his eyes briefly, then opened them again. Brilliant jewels of light covered the blackness so thoroughly he could count them no easier than he could the sea's grains of sand.

Oh, Adonai, You are so faithful, and I am so undeserving.

He forced his limbs up from the ground and stretched, his gaze taking in the camp. He could not see far in the moonlight, but he had walked the length and breadth of the land months before. He looked to the starry night once more. "Thank you," he whispered, knowing that though God had left him, He could still hear.

Heart stirring with joy, he returned to the camp, washed the blood from his arms and legs, and went to find Sarai.

25

Sarai leaned on Abram's arm as she walked with him in the fields the following week, the vision Abram had seen of Adonai still fresh in her thoughts. But the promises held little comfort for her, and it was time she told Abram what she needed to say, despite the pain such thoughts evoked.

"If you look far enough, you can almost make out the edge of the sea." Abram pointed westward toward the Great Sea, where merchant ships landed at Gaza and Joppa and brought goods toward Beersheba and Hebron, goods she could not help but appreciate. "Our descendants will inherit this land, Sarai. They will outnumber the stars in the heavens, the sands on the seashore."

"Your vision is clouded, my husband. Surely it is a mirage you see rather than the waters of the Great Sea." She lifted a hand to her eyes and strained a look from the perch of the hill where they stood, but all she could see were grasslands and trees. The bluish haze in the distance could have been sky as easily as it was sea—impossible to tell from here.

He placed a hand on her shoulder. "Whether my vision is clouded or clear, our descendants will possess all of this land one day." He turned her to face him. "You will bear me a son and our son will bear more children, and from us there will come a great nation."

Sarai looked at him, moved by his sincerity, hating to force the truth on him but knowing she must. She pulled away from his embrace and walked a few steps nearer the edge of the cliff. Wind whipped her clothes, forcing her robe tight against her body and lifting her scarf away from her face. She turned back into the shelter of the overhanging terebinth tree.

"My lord, there is something I have considered every day since your vision, and I think you should pay it heed as well."

He took her hand and pressed her fingers to his lips. "What troubles you, Sarai?"

She looked beyond his scrutinizing gaze and worried her lower lip. At last she faced him and stiffened her back, determined to go through with her plan. "The promise Adonai made to you said nothing of me. It named only you, my husband. Since it is quite obvious that I am too old to possibly bear a child, it is my right and my duty to provide you an heir from another source." She paused, drawing a deep breath for support. "I am giving you my maidservant Hagar the Egyptian."

Abram released his hold on her but did not move. "Have you heard nothing of what I have told you? Adonai promised us a son."

She shook her head. "No. He promised *you* a son. Why do you find this so hard to accept?"

"I do not want another wife. You are all I need."

"She would be only a seed-bearer, a secondary wife. Any child born of her would be mine to claim."

He looked at her for the longest time, until at last he turned and strode to the edge of the cliff where she had just stood. The sight of him there, staff in hand, facing the wind as it pushed against him, made Sarai's heart ache with her decision. Why couldn't she have

Abram's faith? But she was right, whether he wanted to believe her or not. And somehow she must convince him of it.

She tucked the scarf closer to her neck and wrapped both arms about her, though the breeze was far from chilly. Slowly, each step weighted with indecision and dread, she moved to his side and slipped her arm beneath his.

"Adonai has kept me from having children," she said, leaning close to his ear. When at last he looked at her, she offered him a reassuring smile. "Go, sleep with my maidservant. Perhaps I can build a family through her."

He held her gaze until she thought she might break under the strain of trying to assure him. "I love you, Sarai. I don't want another."

His words thrilled her, but the truth remained. "And I you, my husband. Can't you see how hard this is for me?"

He nodded, at last seemingly satisfied. "Send her to my tent tonight."

❋❋❋

Hagar sat at the grindstone, the rhythmic scraping of grain against stone droning in her ear. How strange life had become, how long ago her life as Pharaoh's daughter. Sometimes at night when the wind blew a certain way, she could almost smell the waterfront along the Nile. Her sisters had probably married foreign princes by now, if they lived.

A sigh worked through her, and she straightened, rolling the kinks from her shoulders. Wistful longing filled her for the briefest moment. She missed Nitianu and Osahar the most, and often prayed to Abram's unseen God to keep them safe. They had been truer parents to her than Nabirye and Pharaoh had ever been. Emotion rose within her, but she shoved it down to a place deep within her as she always did—as she had done in her mother's household and continued to do since coming to serve under Sarai in Abram's camp. She could not go back. There was no use dwelling on what she could not change.

She bent over the grindstone again but looked up at the sound of footsteps approaching, surprised to see her mistress coming toward her. Normally she was summoned, not approached. She laid the grindstone aside, brushed the flour from her hands, and stood, bowing low.

"How may I serve you, my lady?"

"You may rise and follow me to my tent. There we will speak." Sarai abruptly turned, her steps hurried, and moved far from Hagar before her maid realized what had been said. She scrambled to catch up, keeping a respectful distance behind.

At Sarai's tent, her mistress lifted the flap and bid Hagar enter ahead of her. Hagar looked at Sarai, unused to such treatment, but hurried to obey.

"Come, sit among the cushions. I brewed some herbs for tea. Let me pour you a cup." Before Hagar could think to protest, Sarai busied herself in one corner of the spacious tent and returned to the area where Hagar still stood, dumbstruck.

"Sit," Sarai said again. "Here, tell me what you think of it." She handed the clay cup to Hagar and motioned her to the cushions again, her smile congenial. She lowered herself to the plush ornamented cushions opposite Hagar and rested both hands on her knees.

Hagar folded her legs beneath her and held the cup in both hands, putting it slowly to her lips. The brew tasted sharp yet sweet, a combination she had not enjoyed since her life in Egypt.

"It is a taste of my homeland. Like the lotus blossom."

Sarai nodded. "The merchants brought the dried blossoms from Thebes. I thought you might find it to your liking."

Hagar sipped again, her gaze never leaving Sarai's drawn face.

The woman had something on her mind, and her features were tense, almost rigid. But Hagar held her tongue, unable to give voice to the questions filling her.

"Hagar."

Hagar stiffened, waiting for whatever strange reprimand must be forthcoming.

"Yes, my lady. How may I serve you?" She lowered her gaze to the mat at her feet, adopting her familiar servant expression.

A sigh escaped Sarai's lips, causing Hagar to look up again. "Hagar, it is not me you are to serve this night."

Sarai looked away, avoiding eye contact. Strange. A moment passed. Hagar's hands shook at the tension in the room, sloshing the tea in her cup. Fearing she would spill it onto Sarai's expensive cushions, she took a long drink, nearly burning her throat in her haste to be done with it.

"Hagar, I want you to serve my husband this night."

"Of course, my lady, I will do whatever you wish." She downed the last of the liquid and set the cup on the mat, clasping her hands in her lap to still their unease.

Sarai shook her head. "I don't think you understand my meaning."

Hagar looked up again. As she held the older woman's steady gaze, something shifted inside of Hagar. She couldn't possibly mean . . . "Perhaps you should help me to understand, my lady. How would you like me to serve the master?"

Sarai kneaded the sash at her waist, looking down at it as though she could draw her response from the soft fabric. When she lifted her gaze again, there was a hardening in her dark eyes. "Adonai has promised to give my husband a son, and it is up to me as his wife to do the providing. But as we all know, God has kept me from bearing children."

Her gaze flitted beyond Hagar toward the tent's door. The voices of women working nearby drifted through the closed flap, and a steady wind ruffled the walls of the tent. The breeze would be welcome right now, and Hagar almost opened her mouth to suggest lifting the sides of the tent to let it in, but she knew that to say such a thing would be utter foolishness. She sat perfectly still instead, waiting, ignoring the sweat trickling down her back.

"It is also within my right and power to give my husband a maid, to procure sons through her. The child would be mine, but the maid would give him birth." Sarai cleared her throat and leveled a look at Hagar. "Do you understand what I am saying?"

Hagar clasped her hands tighter until she could feel her nails dig into her palms. "I think so, my lady." Was she suggesting Hagar bear Abram's son? The thought chilled and warmed her, at once repulsive and enticing.

"You are the maid I have chosen for this privilege. I am taking you from the status of slave to concubine of my master Abram. When you bear him a son, you will do so on my knees. I will raise the child as my own, giving Abram his son of promise." A deep sigh lifted her chest, but no more words came from her lips.

Hagar sat in stunned silence, staring at Sarai, her thoughts tumbling within her like chaff in a windstorm. She was to be married, but not married? Would Sarai truly share her husband so easily? Yet by the look on the woman's face, Hagar could see her decision had not come to her lightly. Even now the pain of her words etched twin lines across her brow. Age had done little to mar Sarai's beauty, but this decision had surely cost her.

But thoughts of Sarai quickly dissipated as she let the woman's words register in her heart. This night? Her pulse quickened, and a flutter of unease settled in her middle. She had never been with a man. But she could hardly tell that to Sarai, who sat looking at her now as though she expected some response.

Hagar shifted among the cushions, longing to stand but afraid to move without permission. "I don't know what to say, my lady.

You do me great honor." The words tasted like dust on her tongue. She had dreamed of marriage once, but never as a secondary wife or a concubine. Her dreams had been far grander back when she was Pharaoh's daughter and dreams seemed possible.

She looked at her feet, uncertainty warring within. Abram was an old man. What if she went to him and no son came about? Would she be put out of the house then? Would they banish her from Canaan, return her to Egypt? She would have nowhere to go if they did.

But what if she did give Abram a son? Despite Sarai's claims that the child would be hers, Hagar would never let her son forget who it was who had borne him. A seed of pride sprouted within her. She lifted her chin but masked her true thoughts.

"I will do as you say, my lady. Only . . . I do not know what is required of me." She swallowed her embarrassment, knowing the comment was only half true. She had heard the women as they drew water at the well or ground grain together. There were few secrets of what to expect when a man took a woman to his bed. Still, she didn't know from experience.

"Abram will make it clear enough. Now come. You will go to the river to bathe and dress in the robes I have chosen for you. Then Lila will take you to Abram's tent." Sarai stood, her back straight, her bearing stiff. She marched to the tent's door and lifted the flap without waiting to see if Hagar followed.

Hagar rose slowly, the impact of what had been said making her teeter on unsteady feet. She stood still, drawing in a breath, then another, until at last she could move without stumbling. She hurried after Sarai, heart pounding with anticipation and dread.

❧ 26 ❧

The sun dipped low into the west, taking Hagar's courage with it. As the light fully faded, replaced by torches at the camp's perimeter and a fire in the central pit, Lila slipped her arm through Hagar's and guided her toward Abram's tent.

"It will be all right," Lila whispered, patting Hagar's arm in a gesture that was surely meant to reassure. "Abram is a kind man."

Was he? But of course that was true. Though he had never paid her any mind, Hagar had seen the way he acted with Sarai and Eliezer. But Abram loved Sarai and set great store by Eliezer. She was nothing more than a slave. Would he talk to her? A moment of panic came over her that she would have nothing to say to him. Did men care if a woman spoke or did they just do what was required and send them away?

She stopped at the door, her heart skipping several beats. He sat beneath the awning of the tent. Was he waiting for her? He stood, stepping aside, and nodded once to Lila.

Lila gave a quick bow, then ushered Hagar inside. Clay lamps illumined Abram's sleeping quarters, where a thick wool mat topped with soft linen sheets took up most of the area. Near the pillows at the head sat a lidded chest, probably housing Abram's extra robes and tunics or maybe even some of his gold, though Hagar did not know where Abram's wealth was stored.

Her gaze moved quickly from the ornately carved chest to focus on the rest of the room. Cushions for sitting lined one corner, and a small table sat nearby. The room was awash in rare blues and purples, a sign of Abram's great wealth—and Sarai's handiwork, no doubt.

Another wave of fear washed over her. She was an intruder here, a woman who had no place in the private quarters of such a man. Her throat grew dry, and her feet would not cross the threshold into that part of the tent.

"You must come, Hagar," Lila whispered. "You must prepare to meet your husband."

Husband? The word seemed disconnected from the truth. Abram was Sarai's husband, not hers. She didn't belong here.

"I can't." The words came out choked, and she looked at Lila, knowing the other woman could see the fear she could not hide. "The master . . . he is Sarai's, not mine."

"And Sarai has given him to you to give her a son. You must do this."

Of course she must.

"Perhaps if you leave us, Lila, I can be of some encouragement." Abram's voice from behind took her breath. She placed a hand to her middle to still the uneasiness and looked to Lila for support, begging her with a look not to leave.

"Yes, my lord." Lila glanced at Hagar, offering her a reassuring smile. "It will be all right," she said again, then turned and hurried from the tent.

Hagar stood still, unable to move, though Abram remained at her back. She felt him draw closer, the scent of rare spikenard wafting from his clothes. Had he bathed and perfumed himself just for her? She slowly turned but could not bring herself to meet his gaze.

"Won't you come and sit among the cushions, Hagar?" He motioned to the corner where the embroidered pillows made up a seating area.

She reluctantly obeyed, sinking into them, suddenly wishing she had such plush comfort in her own tent. But of course, such things belonged to princes, not to slave girls.

"Would you like some wine?" He moved to an area just out of her line of sight and bent to retrieve a flask from the ground. He lifted the lid on the chest and removed two silver goblets, then proceeded to pour the wine, though she had yet to respond to his question. He stepped closer and offered it to her. When she took it, their fingers touched, and she instinctively pulled back before realizing his touch was not something she should want to avoid.

"It's all right, Hagar." His tone was meant to soothe, and he smiled as he sat opposite her, his gaze penetrating and frank in its perusal. "So Sarai has chosen you to bear our son."

She nodded, her cheeks heating.

"Do you know how to speak, or am I to expect only gestures from you?"

She lifted her gaze at his unexpected words and released a breath when she saw only kindness in his eyes. "I can speak, my lord. It is just . . . I am nervous."

"Understandable," he said, sipping from his cup. "And do you approve of Sarai's choice? Can you give your body, your life, to this old man in the hopes of giving him a son?" His wistful tone made her heart constrict, and when she looked at him this time, she did not turn away.

She searched his face, reading hope in his eyes, suddenly wanting to please him, to give him what Sarai could not. "I can," she said at last, clutching the cup with both hands. "But I do not—"

"I will teach you what you need to know."

Sarai met Lila as she emerged from Abram's tent, tears clogging her throat. "It is done then," she said.

Lila clutched her arm, and the two walked the perimeter of the camp, picking their way along the rocky ground.

"Yes. At least she is with him. Time will tell if she conceives." Lila led them toward the cooking fires, empty now with the heavy darkness.

"How many days should I give them?" She choked on the words, and Lila bade her sit on one of the stone benches.

"Several weeks at least. A month before we can know anything."

"Of course." She knew that. Had counted the cycles of the moon for nearly all her life. *Please, Adonai, do not let the girl take long. I cannot bear this to last for months.*

"If it takes her more than two months, I will find a different maid." Hagar could go back to Egypt.

She checked herself. How could she allow such feelings against the woman she had carefully chosen for this task?

"That is your right, of course."

She looked into Lila's eyes, barely visible in the firelight. "You think me impatient."

Lila shook her head. "No. Just . . . I know it must be hard to share him. But you must accept the fact that Hagar could be the mother of Abram's child before the year is out—your adopted son."

A tremor swept through her, bringing with it a strange mixture of pain and hope. "Abram would be pleased to have a son."

"Yes, he would. And you would have the pleasure of raising him." She smiled, her look thoughtful. "Though raising children is not always so easy a task."

Sarai turned her hands over in her lap, trying to imagine what Abram's son would be like. "A son will be a good thing." She had to believe it.

Lila draped an arm over Sarai's shoulders. "Yes, and you will be a good mother."

❧ 27 ❧

Hagar let her hips sway as she moved from delivering Abram a plate of flat bread and cheese and a mug of spiced wine, a favorite of her people. She tossed a glance over her shoulder to see his reaction to her, and hid a smile that his gaze followed her with obvious interest. Though far older than she, the man looked twenty years younger than his actual age. His skin was not mottled or thin as some of the ancient ones in Egypt had been. His step held vigor, and in the short week sharing his bed, she had come to care for him.

She moved to the campfire, her shoulders straight, a lightness to her walk she had not felt in years. Tonight she would show Abram an Egyptian dance she'd been perfecting in the privacy of her tent, to perhaps endear herself to him in ways Sarai could not.

She smiled as she bent to stir the fire. Sarai had not shown her face at the morning meal, and though the first week of Hagar's new marriage was over, she knew Abram would not so easily set her aside until she had conceived. If Abram's God smiled on her, she could remain the favored wife for months to come.

She looked up at the sound of voices, spotting Sarai and Lila talking together. She tensed at sight of her mistress. But no. Sarai was no longer her mistress. In giving her to Abram, Sarai had forfeited her right to rule over her. Abram was her master now, as well as her husband. The thought lifted her chin, though it did little to ease the tension as Sarai moved gracefully toward Abram and settled on a rough-hewn bench beside him.

Sarai's head bent toward Abram's, and the two were caught up in a familiar camaraderie Hagar had witnessed many times during her years with them in Canaan. She looked away, feeling like a jealous wretch and an unwanted intruder.

"You can't expect to take her place." Hagar's hand jerked at the sound of Lila's voice, causing the fire stick to send burning embers out of the protective stone circle. She hurried to stomp them out with a sandaled foot before turning to see Lila watching her.

"I would never expect such a thing." That she'd had those same thoughts only irritated her more. Her expressions were surely not so easy to read. She'd spent years masking her true thoughts.

Lila shrugged. "You're in a difficult place. Once you conceive, he won't need you anymore. Sarai will make sure of it." Lila's smile was less than reassuring. "I just wanted to warn you not to let yourself grow proud around here. Jealousy is a cruel thing." She turned and walked away before Hagar could offer a word of protest.

She watched Lila leave, then glanced across the fire to Abram and Sarai once more. He stood, offered Sarai his hand, and tucked it beneath his arm as they walked away from the tents toward the fields. His head tipped back, and he laughed at something Sarai said, the two of them lost in each other's company.

Hagar's gaze followed them until they disappeared beyond the trees, a sinking feeling settling deep within her. She could not join them. She was not welcome near Abram when Sarai was at his side, and it went without saying that Sarai was not happy with her decision to send Hagar into Abram's arms.

But hadn't that been her decision in the first place? How could she now shun Hagar when she was the one giving herself to save their future?

Anger rose within her, swift and hot as the fire fanning her face. She tossed the stick to the side and grabbed her skirt in both hands, lifting it as she stormed off. She walked on toward the open spaces past Abram's tent, where the altar of God stood. Abram had offered many lambs on this spot, to what purpose she could not imagine. If he had done everything as his God intended, why did they need her? Sarai should have already borne his child.

Her long legs led her past the altar toward the cliffs looking down over the valley below, toward Sodom, where Lot and his family and servants had gone. Would she have been better off with them?

Wind tugged at her scarf and cooled the heat still pouring into her face. She brushed the hair from her mouth, surprised at the hint of moisture on her cheeks. But she could not deny the emotion that surged through her, even admitting to a handful of tears.

Life was so completely unjust. And the gods of her people had long since failed her. Did Abram's God care that Sarai had put her in this situation? Did Abram care for her at all? Or was she just an object, a tool for them both to get what they wanted?

She tilted her gaze toward the blue expanse of sky, wishing she knew how to entreat the Creator to give her a home with a husband as well as a son. Was that too much for a daughter of Pharaoh to wish for? But no, she was a daughter no longer.

She brushed the drying dampness from her cheeks and turned back toward the camp, her anger only slightly appeased. She would practice the dance of her people until she had perfected it, and tonight, if Abram called for her, she would make him want her for herself, not just what she could do for him. If she could endear herself to him, she could wedge herself between him and Sarai and ensure a place for herself and her child in the future.

✸✸✸

Abram kissed Sarai good night, defeat settling in on him like a sodden cloak. He did not look back as he slipped from her tent, all too aware that she would spend the night in misery, probably weeping into her pillow. He should never have agreed to her plan to take another wife, even a secondary one. But the deed was done now, and he couldn't just send Hagar away. Not without giving the woman a chance to conceive.

The thought caused a slight quickening of his step, but his heart still carried the weight of Sarai's pain. He'd spent the day trying to console her, and the action had wearied him. Now she expected him to take Hagar to his tent without thought of Sarai's emotions or the frustration such actions caused? He was a man, not a god.

He kicked a stone a short distance from Sarai's tent, bruising his toe, and cursed softly. Hagar's tent had not been moved from the servants' quarters, a situation he should remedy but had no strength to tackle. In truth, he had no desire to walk in that direction, but Sarai would question him on the morrow, and dealing with her frustration would stretch the limits of his patience, which was already too thin.

He spotted Eliezer and Lila across the compound. Eliezer had their youngest daughter perched against his shoulder, fast asleep, while Lila had hold of the hand of the other girl, their two sons racing circles around them. Something akin to heartache pierced him. Such a contented man Eliezer was—such a family to be proud of.

Abram turned about quickly, unable to bear the scene despite the fact that he had watched the man with his wife and children every night for years. What had changed?

He drew in a deep sigh and set out for Hagar's tent. Perhaps Sarai was right. Maybe Hagar could give them the son they craved. Unless . . . what if he was somehow to blame? Could his body be as dead as Sarai's womb? He had never taken another wife to prove otherwise. Doubt filled him, slowing his step. If Hagar did not conceive soon, it would make the promise completely impossible.

Quickening his pace, he crossed the compound to the servants' quarters. He needed Hagar tonight. Not only for the promise but for his own vindication. Otherwise, fatherhood for him was truly too late.

✳ 28 ✳

Hagar bent over a clay pot in her tent and emptied what little remained within her from the night before. Sweat beaded her brow and her stomach rumbled, though how she could feel hunger after repeated mornings of illness, she did not know. She sat back and collapsed against the cushions, plush replacements of the type she was used to—gifts from Abram. She'd been more than grateful for his kindness to her, and half certain she had begun to win his affection, if not away from Sarai, at least in part toward her. Would that favor increase when she told him about the babe?

She had yet to confirm her suspicions with the camp midwife, but she knew as every woman knows deep within her. There had been no need to sleep apart from him the first month, and now as her cycle should have approached again, the morning sickness had come upon her. She would have no need of separation this month either.

Sounds of the women calling to their children amid the normal daily chatter filtered to her through the thick curtains of her new tent, another gift from Abram. She no longer slept in the servants' area but had her tent pitched not many paces down the row from

Sarai's—enough to show Sarai's status as first wife, yet affording her a measure of respect just the same.

She fingered the cushioned fabric, telling herself to rise. It was time to break her fast, and if she could manage it, today was the day she would tell Abram her news. She closed her eyes, envisioning the scene. She would take food to him in the fields and share their joy beneath the shade of one of Mamre's great oaks. He would surely embrace her and set her at his side publicly during the evening repast. And in days to come, when her son was born, he would give her the full status of wife, not just concubine. Was it too much to ask? Too much to hope for?

Her stomach rumbled again, and she forced herself up from the cushions, chiding herself for her foolish girlhood dreams. She was married to a prince, but the man would never give her the recognition or affection he gave Sarai. The thought threatened to churn her stomach again, so she shoved it aside. She donned a fresh tunic and stood before a bronzed looking glass, fearing she might appear listless, her skin sallow from the illness. Pleased that she didn't look as bad as she feared, she rubbed red ochre into her cheeks and darkened her eyelids with kohl, something she had not done since coming to live with Abram and Sarai in Canaan.

At last satisfied that she looked presentable, she lifted her chin and walked, head held high, to join the women. She passed Lila setting a jar of water in a hole made to keep it from tipping, and thought momentarily about stopping to ask her opinion about the babe. But Lila was not the camp midwife, and Hagar did not want Lila to tell Sarai her news before she had a chance to tell Abram.

She moved on with a silent nod when Lila looked her way, then paused where the servants were making griddle cakes, no longer able to keep her hunger at bay. She snatched one from a plate and bit off an end, feeling a sense of remoteness toward the life she had once lived at these women's sides. The soft grains nearly melted in her mouth, relieving the hunger. She grabbed two more from the plate, along with a square of goat cheese, and walked toward the central fire where Abram sat eating with Eliezer.

Hope sprang to Hagar's heart at the smile he offered her as she drew near. The lines around his eyes softened as she took the seat he motioned to—the one Sarai normally occupied. She sat on the edge, listening, as he resumed his conversation with Eliezer.

"Word has it things have not improved in Sodom, though Lot's servants have indicated he has no plans to move away. Apparently, his wife will not think of returning to a life living in tents." Eliezer's voice droned on, and Hagar only half heard his words. She had long ago accepted the nomadic life, though most people would prefer living in houses of stone in walled, protected cities. She could hardly blame Melah for her choice, though she would not want the violence she heard went on in Sodom and its neighboring cities.

She chewed slowly, her thoughts wandering, and glanced up at the sound of footsteps. Sarai stood near Abram, her back straight, her gaze brittle.

"What is she doing here?" Sarai did not point or even look Hagar's way, her tone matching the anger in her eyes.

Silence followed the remark, and Eliezer stood, excusing himself. Hagar thought to do the same but was stricken to the spot.

"Are you going to answer me, husband?"

Hagar sucked in a breath, surprised at Sarai's accusing tone. It was bold for a wife to publicly chastise her husband, and Hagar suddenly did not want to be in the middle of this marital quarrel. She stood, ready to flee, but Abram stayed her with a hand on her arm.

"She is here because I invited her." He looked at Hagar. "But perhaps she would sit here instead." He motioned to the seat Eliezer had just left, his tone pleasant but cool. Hagar's heart thumped faster as she moved to do his bidding. She glanced at Sarai, but the woman did not meet her gaze.

"Please tell your concubine not to sit in my place again." Sarai lifted her chin, gave Abram a stern look, then turned abruptly and stormed across the compound toward her tent.

Abram would go after Sarai. Surely he would go.

But as the moments passed and the rising sun cast better light over the dusky camp, he did not move. At last he turned to her, his jaw working as though struggling with what to say.

"Did you seek something from me, Hagar?" Of course, he would expect she wanted him for a purpose or had some important news to tell him. Why else would she have sought him out before the dawn fully crested the sky?

She looked quickly around her, determining who might be listening. "Could we walk a short way, my lord?" Sudden shyness came over her, and she could not meet his gaze.

He paused but a moment. "Of course." He stood and extended his hand.

She placed her smaller one in his, a blush creeping up her neck as she finally looked into his eyes. "Thank you."

They walked past the circle of tents toward the fields where Abram's many flocks grazed. He stopped near the first set of sheep pens and turned to face her. He grasped one of her hands and lifted her chin.

"What is it you wish to tell me, Hagar?" A dim sense of what she could only surmise as hope flickered in his dark brown eyes.

She swallowed, then smiled. "I am with child." She quickly lowered her gaze, feeling the heat creep from her neck to her cheeks. "I have not confirmed it with the midwife yet, but I am certain . . . There are signs." She looked up again and suddenly realized he had never experienced a pregnant wife. The shock on his face made her laugh for joy.

"I am without words." A broad smile lit his face, brightening his eyes. "And yet there is so much to ask you. You must see the midwife at once, of course. Sarai will be most pleased."

She masked the pain Sarai's name brought to her heart, reminding herself that Sarai would adopt this child and claim it as her own. She was still but a slave in Sarai's estimation, after all. No matter what Abram thought of her, she could never undo that fact.

"I understand, of course. But I wanted you to know first." She squeezed Abram's hand still holding hers. "It is a blessing of your God, is it not? He has smiled on us." She was not sure why she pressed him, but a part of her begged him to notice her for who she was, not to see her simply as Sarai's maid.

He glanced beyond her for too long, and she knew she had asked the wrong question. When he looked at her again, he smiled, then pulled her close until her head rested against his chest. "You have done us a great favor, Hagar, and Adonai has surely smiled on us. This child will be destined for great things and blessed of Adonai."

She felt his kiss on the top of her head as he hugged her, but though she sensed his desire to comfort her, the attempt failed. She meant nothing to him other than a woman to carry his child. He did not love her. Perhaps he was not capable of loving more than one woman.

"Great things, yes." She choked on the words.

He held her at arm's length and searched her face. "I am sorry, Hagar. This will not be easy for you, giving your son to another woman to raise—"

"Our son, my lord." That she dared interrupt him startled them both, but after a pause, he merely nodded.

"Our son, yes." His smile grew broad again. "You have filled my heart with gladness today, Hagar." He bent his lips to hers and gave her a chaste kiss.

His action stirred something in her, and despite the risk, she threw her arms around his neck and returned his kiss with a passionate one of her own. A little thrill passed through her that he responded in kind. When he finally released her, he laughed, the spark returning to his eyes.

"My own little temptress," he whispered, slipping an arm around her waist. "Come, I will walk with you to the tent of the midwife, then you must make sure of your suspicions before I tell Sarai." He moved ahead, guiding her to follow. "I will spare you that difficulty."

Her heart lightened, losing the sharp pain of before. Perhaps he cared for her at least a small amount. Enough to protect her from Sarai's jealousies, which were already evident from the first night she'd spent in Abram's arms. He would protect her and perhaps in time learn to love her. For the sake of their son.

Their son. Not Sarai's.

❄✛❄

Abram lifted the flap and stepped into the lamplight of Sarai's tent. The midwife had confirmed Hagar's suspicions, filling Abram with a mingled sense of joy and uncertainty. The news should ease Sarai's misery and bring her some measure of happiness. She had planned this thing, and Adonai had answered her prayers. The thought made him pause. Had this been Adonai's plan? Abram had always thought Sarai would be the one to bear the promised child, that God meant the promises for both of them. But surely Sarai had a point. Perhaps Hagar's son would indeed be the one to fulfill all that God had said would come.

Bolstered by that thought, he smiled as he came upon Sarai, where she sat with her mending. She looked up, but her expression remained stoic, withdrawn.

"Why are you here? Shouldn't you be with *her*?"

The sentiment in her tone cooled Abram's blood. All previous assumptions that she would be pleased with his forthcoming news vanished.

"Is that any way to greet your husband?" He moved closer into the room and sat at her side. He took the mending from her, set it aside, and enfolded her hand in his. "Would it not be better to tell me how glad you are to see me? Even a gentle lie would please me more than knowing my wife prefers her own company to mine." He smiled again, lifting her chin until her eyes held his.

"I'm sorry, my lord." This time she returned his smile. "I always enjoy your company to my own." Her gaze skittered beyond him. "I only thought . . . that is . . ." She met his gaze again. "Until she conceives, you should be with her, not me." He felt her tense beside him even as he drew a line along her jaw.

"Well, you no longer have to worry about that, dear wife. Hagar is already with child, so you can no longer be rid of me so easily." He wanted to laugh, longing to see his joy mirrored in her eyes, but held himself in check when her expression did not share his emotion.

"Already?" She pulled away from him and wrapped both arms over her chest, a self-protective gesture he'd seen her use many times over the years. "Why did she not come to me at once? She told you first?" Her incredulous tone held a hint of anger, matching the spark now evident in her dark eyes.

"She senses you are not pleased with her, Sarai. She has done nothing but what you asked, yet you seem to resent her intrusion into our marriage."

"Only because she has tried to take you from me. I see the way she walks, swaying her hips in full light of day, and looking at you as though she has a right to usurp my authority. You invited her to my place during the meal! What else am I to think of her but an intruder? She is that and more." Sarai's words flew at him like sharp barbs.

"You invited her to my bed."

She startled at that, and tears filled her eyes. His heart constricted at the sight. Sarai was not a woman given to frequent tears, so whenever they surfaced, they moved him to pity. Of course, it had not been easy to share him, the man she had known all her life. He was a fool to think otherwise.

"I'm sorry, beloved. I will never again put her in your place, at a meal or anywhere else." He reached for her and pulled her into his arms, letting her weep. Was this how it was going to be then? One wife sorely jealous of the maid who carried his child—the child they had longed for, waited for, prayed for?

Had he prayed for this child?

A check in his spirit made him suddenly uncomfortable, but he brushed it aside. Of course they had prayed. Years had passed and their prayers had seldom ceased.

He patted Sarai's back, wishing he had words with which he could comfort her. At last she quieted and leaned away from him.

"I'm happy for you, my lord. The child proves what I had feared all along. Adonai meant the promises for you and your children. He said nothing about including me in that promise. At least now we know." She looked at him, her eyes so full of pain he felt his heart constrict again.

He cupped her cheek with his palm, smoothing his thumb along her jaw. "I'm sorry it had to be this way, beloved. You know the child will still be yours. Hagar is but a maid, after all."

She nodded, then swiped at her eyes, her expression changing from sorrow to something akin to hope. "I will be there for his birth. I will hold him on my knees." She smiled, but her lower lip trembled as though she was trying valiantly to warm to the thought. "We will need to begin sewing garments for him at once. Only wool from the best of your flocks, Abram. Nothing too harsh. And Hagar must share my tent in the early days until he is weaned, so I can be there for the feedings . . . for everything."

Abram studied her, seeing in her the resolve he'd grown so accustomed to, relieved to see the pain slowly slip from her, replaced by something resembling his joy. He squeezed her hand in his and bent to kiss her.

"We will have a son, Sarai. A child of my flesh at last!" He knew the last words were probably best left unsaid, but he could not keep from her the pride he felt. A father. As Eliezer was. As his father had been. And one day, a father of a nation.

"We will have a son," she echoed, and he knew her light tone was meant to appease him.

"Now come. Let us get Hagar and call the men and women together. It is time to celebrate." He pushed to his feet and offered her his hand, pulling her to him.

"Should we not wait until morning? Dusk has settled, and some of the men may already sleep."

He read her uncertainty, saw the puffiness around her eyes. "Of course, you are right. We will celebrate tomorrow morning when the day is fresh." He took her in his arms and kissed her again. "In the meantime, get some wine and perfume your bed. Tonight will be ours alone."

Her chest lifted in a sigh, and she nodded, turning from him to do his bidding. But as she left his side, he could not help but wonder what would become of their marriage in the days to come.

❈ 29 ❈

Hagar awoke with the familiar nausea, barely making it to the clay urn before losing what remained of last night's supper. She leaned back, sweat beading her brow. Her heart skipped a beat at the sound of voices approaching her tent.

"Hagar?" Abram's tentative tone sent a little thrill through her, reinforcing what she had sensed, had hoped the day before. He cared for her. At least he cared for the child she carried.

She pushed aside what that thought suggested, wiped her mouth on a piece of soft linen, and rose from the floor, then took slow steps toward the tent's door. Hunger gnawed at her, ravenous now. She lifted the flap and looked into Abram's concerned face.

"I'm here, my lord." She bowed her head, then looked beyond him to the sounds of many voices coming from the central meeting area.

"Good. You must put on your best robes and come with me at once. Today we will announce our good news." His voice sounded light, like a little boy who has found a buried treasure.

She met his gaze and smiled, briefly touching his arm. "Give me but a moment." She ducked back into her tent, heart pounding. *Our good news.* He had included her in this! Or had he? By *our*, did he mean Sarai as well?

She tucked the thought into a hidden place, unwilling to let it dampen her spirits. She walked over to the Egyptian chest she had saved from her days in the king's palace and pulled out the striped red, black, and yellow robe Abram had given her. She quickly donned a tan tunic and wrapped the robe over it. He would grow impatient if she took too long with kohl and hair adornments, so she pulled her hair back with a large comb and draped a blue scarf over her head. Eyeing the mineral pots with a longing to make herself beautiful, she merely dabbed her finger into one and rubbed a small amount of ochre into her cheeks.

She glanced at the herbs tied to the ceiling poles above her head, snatched a bit of fresh parsley, and chewed briefly, then spit the remnants into the clay urn. She would need to send a maid to wash out the urn before the tent grew rank, but there was no time to waste. Hurrying now, she emerged from her tent, relieved to see Abram still waiting for her—alone.

His gaze took her in, and she blushed at the appreciative smile just showing at the corners of his beard. "Do I look all right, my lord?" She gave him a sideways glance, her satisfaction sure when his dark complexion took on a ruddy glow.

He cleared his throat. "You look very nice as always, Hagar." He shook himself as if her appearance had distracted him, and placed a hand on the small of her back. "They are waiting for us."

He ushered her toward the camp, which now overflowed with the leaders of Abram's tribe, along with their wives and children. Hagar looked around for Sarai, spotting her sitting in Abram's reserved spot like a princess among princes. Hagar's heart thumped faster the closer they came to Sarai. Did Abram mean to announce the child at Sarai's side? But of course he did. She swallowed her disappointment and lifted her chin as they at last came to stop in front of Sarai.

Abram extended a hand to his wife while Hagar stayed two steps behind him. Sarai rested her hand in his and rose with grace.

Hagar lowered her gaze at the other woman's stark perusal, but not before she glimpsed the royal clothes she wore—clothes much finer than her own, as though Abram had intended to make sure everyone there remembered the distinction between them.

But a moment later, Abram's other arm came around her waist, keeping one woman on each side of him, nearly claiming them as equals. Well, perhaps not equals, but surely he held Hagar in honor. She raised her chin again, taking care to keep any edge of defiance from her face, while Abram called the men to order.

"I have good news to announce to you this day."

Abram's voice rang out over the compound while Hagar's stomach rumbled, her hunger still waiting to be abated. She rested a hand on her middle to quell the feeling.

"Adonai has blessed my house. I am to be a father!"

A cheer erupted, and Abram laughed as Eliezer came forward. Abram released his hold on Hagar and Sarai and embraced his overseer as Eliezer kissed each of his cheeks.

"Wonderful news, Abram! May the child be blessed of Adonai."

More men came forward, echoing Eliezer's blessing, while the women rushed to congratulate Sarai, barely noticing Hagar. Her stomach twisted with more than hunger. She glanced around for a stone bench and sank down on it. She sensed movement and saw one of the Egyptian servants approach with a plate of flat bread, goat cheese, and thick dates.

"You did not come as usual to snatch the bread." The woman smiled, handing Hagar the plate. "I know what it's like during those first months. First you are sick. Then you feel as though you will never get enough to eat."

Hagar took the food, grateful that someone had seen and cared for her plight. "Thank you." She bit off a hunk of bread and chewed, her stomach slowly settling.

She had finished her food by the time the crowd dissipated,

leaving Abram and Sarai alone again, the company going about their daily routine. They would know soon enough that Hagar carried Abram's child, though she knew both Abram and Sarai would have told the well wishers. It was not her place as a lowly concubine to share their joy. Her son would, after all, be theirs by right.

A sense of loss filled her that she would never have a child that she could claim solely as hers.

"Thank you, Hagar." Abram's voice cut through her self-pity, and she looked up from where she sat, feeling his hand on her shoulder. "We owe you much." He turned to Sarai, who stood staring down at her. Hagar met the older woman's gaze, trying to read the myriad emotions flitting over her beautiful face. The woman never seemed to age, though her body obviously had or they would never have needed use of Hagar's younger one.

"Yes," Sarai said at last, her eyes suddenly filming with a thin sheen of tears. She visibly swallowed. "Thank you." She turned quickly away and kissed Abram's cheek. "I must see to the weaving. The little one will need many linens." She moved away, but Abram stayed her with a touch on her arm. A look passed between them that Hagar could not read, but a moment later Sarai turned back to her. "You may join me, Hagar. It will take more than my skills to complete all that needs to be done by the time the babe is born."

She whirled about as though the words scorched her and headed toward the tent of weaving. Hagar rose and brushed the crumbs from her robe. She nodded to Abram and moved to follow Sarai, though every part of her being screamed against the thought of spending the day in the woman's company. Why couldn't she be more civil? Hagar was doing her a great favor, yet Sarai acted as though she was animal dung.

Abram touched her shoulder, stopping her. His smiled warmed her, easing some of the tension Sarai's presence had evoked. "She needs time," he said, as though Hagar should understand perfectly.

"Yes, my lord. I suppose we all do." She walked away, certain that given any conflict, Abram would side with Sarai over Hagar. She would have to be careful to watch her words. Her jaw clenched along with her fists as she trudged to do as Sarai had bid her.

The afternoon wore on, the sun heating the goat's-hair tent above their heads where Sarai sat with Lila working the weaver's loom, while Hagar turned the spindle, spinning the previously dyed wool into thread. Three months had passed since Abram's announcement, each day showing a greater pile of material to be sewn into garments for the coming child.

The child. A tightness settled along Sarai's shoulders, and she lifted them several times, trying to ease the tension. She glanced at Hagar, the source of her irritation. At first she had noticed only the tilt of her chin—beyond what was acceptable for a servant, as though she thought a concubine deserved some sort of respect. Then the looks had taken on an air of arrogance, though the words coming from her lips dripped with appeasement. Was the woman mocking her?

Sarai's hand slipped on the lease rod, loosening the warp line. Lila held the slashing stick from pushing the weft into position until Sarai regained her grip. She nodded to Lila to continue, silently cursing herself and the anger bubbling inside her. She should send Hagar to work with the dyes. Let her bend over the hot liquid in the blazing heat.

But no. The woman should be protected—for the sake of the babe.

"Excuse me." Hagar interrupted Sarai's musings and stood. "Nature calls."

The woman took more breaks than Lila ever did. Could it be she was trying to get out of her share of the work? Or did she prefer to be away from Sarai? As she left the tent, Sarai waited but a moment.

"Is it my imagination, or does she run off to relieve herself every hour?" Sarai stretched, rubbing her back where stiffness had set in. She looked at Lila, whose hands had stilled as she obviously waited for Sarai to continue.

. "It is different for some women than for others."

Lila's smile seemed to hold too much pity. Sarai clenched and released her shoulder muscles, trying to ignore the ache in her middle. Would she never outlive the stigma of her barrenness? It would help if Hagar did not seem to flaunt the swell in her belly.

"Perhaps," Sarai said, trying to mask the sudden disquiet that had settled over them. "But I don't like the way she looks at me. She is a servant, yet her arrogance makes it seem like she is the master and I am the slave!" She lifted a hand to her mouth, realizing the words were louder than she intended. "Forgive me. I am simply out of sorts today." She stood and walked to where the tent's roof stopped and the open sun began.

Female laughter drifted toward her, and she moved away from the weaver's tent to investigate the sound. She paused as she neared a group of Egyptian servants surrounding Hagar. She moved to the side, ducked behind the low-hanging branches of a willow tree, and strained to listen.

"Did you see the strut in Abram's step when he left the campfire to work in the fields?" Hagar's unmistakable foreign lilt carried to Sarai, cinching her already taut nerves. "I have given him what Sarai never could. In the end he will respect me for it. And when our son is grown and takes Abram's place as head of the tribe, I will be held in great honor." She laughed, and the Egyptian maids laughed with her. But the sound held scorn more than mirth, and Sarai could not stop the surge of anger rushing through her.

She gripped a branch for support. Her stomach clenched, and her heart beat like a thing gone wild. She drew in a breath, barely able to get it past her thickened throat. The nerve! She tried again, breathing deeper this time, and moved further behind the tree as Hagar and the maids passed. The maids moved on, depositing Hagar back at the weaver's tent.

Sarai watched Hagar pick up the spindle and say something to Lila before she emerged from the tree's shade and set out across the compound. Her feet crunched stones and small twigs, their sound hardly heard above the steady pumping of her heart. Abram. She would go to Abram and tell him everything. It was time the man decided just whose side he would take. The Egyptian's or hers.

The heat of the midday sun drew beads of sweat beneath the head scarf she wore to protect her skin, but Sarai pressed on, shading her eyes against its glare. He had said he would be in the farthest pasture today, and she questioned her own good judgment at coming to him at this hour alone. What if a wild beast assaulted her? The area was safe enough as far as bandits were concerned. Abram's men kept watch over each of the many fields where Abram's flocks of sheep, goats, and cattle grazed. But they could not control the actions of lions and jackals and bears that prowled these hills.

A shiver passed through her, and she tightened the scarf at her neck as she quickened her pace. Hagar's words singed her thoughts, spurring her anger. She curled her hands into fists. Wild beasts had nothing on her.

She paused for breath as she neared the rise overlooking a dip in the land that led to a meandering stream. Tall terebinth and willow trees dug deep roots beside its banks, where a line of sheep lowered their heads to drink. Others were sprawled on the rich grasses, resting. She looked over the spot, searching. She found Abram under one of the trees, leaning against the bark, his eyes closed.

His posture did not surprise her. Most of the camp rested during the hottest part of the day. Hagar and Lila would set aside the weaving and spinning and return to their tents in short order, which was exactly where Sarai would be if not for that woman! She ground her teeth and hurried down the rise toward the spot where Abram slept.

He stirred as she approached. "Sarai? What are you doing here— and in this heat?"

She drew in a breath and released it, wishing she'd thought to bring a skin of water. She touched a hand to her forehead, feeling the dampness, then lowered herself to Abram's side. She swallowed.

"Have you come all this way alone? Where are your servants and your water skin? Is something wrong? Is it the babe?" He rose, sat upright, and untied the goatskin at his side, offering it to her. "Drink and then tell me everything."

She obeyed, though his instant concern for the child made her anger rise another notch. "The babe is fine," she said after several deep swallows of water. "It is the mother you should be concerned with."

She searched his face, watching his silver brows draw together. His strong jaw stiffened, and his dark eyes held an expression of confusion. "Explain yourself, Sarai."

She rested a hand over the opening in the skin, then clamped it over the neck. "The Egyptian thinks she will be held in honor after her son is born. She sees the way you strut about, proud of your parenthood. She thinks to usurp my authority and my place." She strengthened her grip on the skin to still the sudden trembling of her limbs. She should never have given Hagar into Abram's arms, and he should not have accepted the gift! "May the wrong done to me be on you! I gave my servant to your embrace, and when she saw that she had conceived, she looked on me with contempt. May Adonai judge between you and me!" She held his gaze, daring him to contradict her but silently begging him to intervene, to do something to make Hagar remember who she was.

Abram stroked a hand over his beard, once dark, now woven in shades of gray. He studied her, but she did not falter, her anger never abating, even beneath the concern in his eyes. A sigh lifted his chest, and he glanced beyond her, then held her gaze once more. "Your servant is in your power. Do to her as you please."

She startled, not expecting such a quick decision, and yet it was not a decision at all. "You will not speak to her?" She was his concubine. Yet no. In that one statement he had returned Hagar to Sarai's possession.

"She is yours to deal with." He leaned back against the tree and closed his eyes, the discussion at an end.

"Promise me you will not call her to your bed again." If Abram would not touch her, Hagar would truly be Sarai's servant alone.

"I will not bed her again." Weariness held his tone, and she knew she could not press him further. He had given her what she asked. It was up to her now to make Hagar see that she was not so honorable after all. Her son would be Abram's heir, but only if Sarai agreed to adopt him as hers. Hagar would remain as she had always been. A slave. Not a wife.

"Thank you, my lord." She took another drink, then rose to return to camp.

"Stay until the sun moves from its high point." Abram opened one arm, silently bidding her to rest against his chest. "I will have a servant return with you then."

She lowered herself back to the earth and searched for a comfortable position beside him. Her racing heart slowed its pace as it kept time with Abram's breathing. His arm came around her, and she tried to relax, but all she could think about was returning to camp and giving Hagar a severe tongue-lashing. Then they would see just how arrogant the girl would remain.

30

Hagar rose from her pallet, the afternoon shadows along her Egyptian linen tent telling her that she had slept far later than she planned. She had retired to rest after returning to the weaver's tent to find Sarai gone. Lila had agreed that the heat was too great to continue to work, and since Sarai had undoubtedly done the same, sleep seemed a good choice.

But the babe had made her stay abed too long. She blinked twice and rubbed her eyes, careful not to smudge the kohl, then rose to a sitting position. A flutter in her middle made her pause. She placed a hand over the spot, but the feeling did not return. Had the babe moved? Three moons had passed since she had told Abram her news. Surely soon. She lay down again, willing the feeling to return, barely daring to breathe. Such confirmation would be a balm and a relief to the inadequate sense she carried with her every step in Sarai's presence.

She waited, counting the rise and fall of her chest. There. Another flutter. And another. With gentle fingers she slid her hand over the spot again and felt her heart give a little kick when the movement came once more. Were these the first signs of her baby's life? Tears pricked her eyes. Her babe. Hers and Abram's. And someday the camp would realize the truth. She would see to it.

The flutters fell silent after a time, and Hagar rose slowly, a sense of satisfaction settling deep within. She donned her robe and cinched the belt, though not too tight, and stepped into the cooler warmth of the afternoon light.

"Just how long did you think it appropriate to rest, Hagar? A servant should be about her master's work, and you have grown sorely lax in yours of late." Sarai stood in the path, a long, thin branch from a willow tree flexing in her hand.

Hagar blinked, startled at the sight. "I . . . I don't know what you mean, my lady. I took a rest at midday, as we all do—"

"The rest of us have been up for hours. Preparations for the evening meal began long ago. I should whip you for your tardiness." A gleam in Sarai's deep blue eyes told Hagar that Sarai meant her words. But why? What had she done?

"If not for that babe you carry . . ." Sarai let the words drift off, her gaze never leaving Hagar's. "Don't think I'm unaware of your interest in my husband. Don't think I don't know that you seek to take my place."

"No! I never—"

"Ha! You never what, Hagar? I heard you talking with your Egyptian friends, those maids who have served you since my husband took you to his bed. Well, no more. You will serve me as you ought. You will not sleep with my husband again, and your son, if it is indeed a son, will be mine, not yours. Do you understand?" Heat spilled from Sarai, her bearing pure anger.

Hagar took an involuntary step back while raising her hands in supplication. "I meant no harm, mistress. I merely did as you asked of me." She could not believe Abram would allow his wife to treat her this way. She carried his child! The child he had longed for all his life. The child Sarai could not give him. What was wrong with her?

"You are an ungrateful, selfish wretch." Sarai lifted the branch as though to strike.

Hagar covered her face and crouched lower. "Please, don't hurt me! I felt your babe move today." She waited but a moment, peeking through half-closed eyes.

Sarai let the branch fall to her side. When she said nothing more, Hagar slowly stood.

"I thought you should know. About the babe, I mean." Her heart beat fast, and she couldn't stop the sudden thickening in her throat. She could not cry. Not here. Yet she could not seem to help herself.

Sarai still did not move or speak, and Hagar lowered her gaze, emotions warring within her. Sarai wanted a servant? All right then. She would be the servant even her mother had thought her to be. The thought brought with it seeds of despair, and she covered her face with her hands, looking away to hide her tears.

"Don't cry about it. So the babe moved. Good. At least that means it lives. Too many do not." She moved the dirt in her path with the toe of her sandal. "Now go. Help grind the grain for the evening meal."

Hagar turned to obey, glancing back to see if Sarai watched her. When the woman moved in the other direction, Hagar let out a breath and hurried away, desperate to get hold of her racing emotions. Had Sarai truly overheard her comments to her Egyptian friends? She had not meant to sound superior to Sarai, had she? But a check in her spirit told her that was not the whole truth.

She needed Abram to come to her aid, to intervene, to give her back her rightful place that Sarai had so quickly stripped from her. But as the evening waned and she saw Abram with Sarai, saw the way he no longer looked in her direction, she knew she had lost him. He had given in to Sarai's complaints without notice or thought to her feelings. She was nothing to him. As she had always been.

Tears filled her eyes, and her stomach turned to stone. She put a hand to her mouth and ran toward the trees. Grief won as she found a spot among them, bent to the ground, and lost what little her stomach had left in it.

Sarai stood at the entrance to her tent a week later, her ears attuned to the sounds of the bustling camp. Abram had long since headed for the fields, and the servants had cleared away the remnants of the morning repast. She had ordered the Egyptian maids dispersed throughout the camp, far from where they could mingle and plot ways to side with Hagar. The less strength Hagar derived from the outsiders, the better.

She crossed both arms over her chest as the breeze fanned her face, her stomach a mass of tangled knots. Why had it come to this? She had liked Hagar when they'd met in the pharaoh's palace nine years before. And choosing her to carry the son she could not bear had made perfect sense back when she had made her decision. Hadn't Adonai given her this woman to be their second chance at having an heir? But oh, she had not realized, had not imagined how hard it would be to share Abram with another. And she had not expected Hagar to lift her chin in such arrogance against her.

She walked from the tent's opening, her jaw clenched as tight as her fists. She spotted Hagar talking with Lila, her head bent as though sharing some secret. Anger surged through her at the sight, her loathing for the woman a tangible force. Her feet carried her like wings.

"What are you doing here, Hagar? My pallet needs airing and my pots need cleaning. Get to work." She felt a twinge of triumph at the woman's shocked expression, then turned to face Lila, dismissing Hagar without another look.

"Yes, mistress." The brittle tone in Hagar's voice made Sarai whirl about and strike Hagar's cheek.

"You will address me with respect!" Her blood poured hot through her veins, and she could not slow her racing breath. How dare Hagar flaunt her sarcastic arrogance! Seething, Sarai took a step closer until Hagar cowered and slipped to her knees.

"Forgive me, my lady." Hagar lifted a hand over her head as though to ward off a blow.

Sarai looked down at the woman, but even her subservient posture brought little satisfaction. "Get busy. And don't let me catch you resting until every last chore is done."

"Yes, mistress." Hagar scooted backward, then rushed off before Sarai could say another word.

"She did not mean to offend you, Sarai." Lila spoke softly at her side, and Sarai turned to face her again.

"Will you side with her too? Is there no one here who understands my plight, who sees the way she disdains me, the way she plots to take what is mine?" She searched Lila's expression, reading a mixture of concern and pity in her gaze. "I gave her my husband, and she would take all I have. Has she taken you as well, Lila?" She hated the sudden hurt in her tone, wishing she could mask the pain.

Lila touched her arm and squeezed. "Never! You know you are like a mother to me, Sarai. Hagar could never take your place."

Sarai's heart twisted yet again at the word *mother*, knowing it was a kindness she did not deserve and an honor she would never truly know. She swallowed, longing to pull Lila close. "Do you care for Hagar?" She couldn't bear to know, and yet somehow she must.

"Hagar is lonely. She does not know her place, and she misses the other maids from her homeland. I thought only to befriend her." Lila turned at the sound of her daughter running toward her, calling her name. Jael bounded closer, and Lila scooped her into her arms.

"She might have stayed in my good graces and kept her Egyptian friends close by if she had not despised me for something I can do nothing to change." If only she could.

"And yet do you not despise Hagar for something she cannot change as well?"

Lila's pointed question brought Sarai up short. She took a step back and crossed her arms. "I don't know what you are talking about." Though in truth, she did. Hagar could not change her status as slave or her pregnancy or anything about her life if Sarai did not allow it. Did she despise the woman for being a slave, or for wanting to rise above it now that it seemed within her rights to do so?

"I only mean that Hagar wants to belong, Sarai. Perhaps she looked down on you in hopes that she would be accepted. Her ideas were misguided and misplaced, but perhaps they were not with ill intent." Lila shifted her daughter to the other hip. "If you would excuse me, I must see to Jael's needs. Come to my tent, and we can talk more if you like."

Sarai regarded her but a moment, feeling rebuffed and dismissed, emotions she neither expected nor embraced. Had the whole camp turned against her for her dealings with Hagar? The thought stung.

"No. You go ahead. Your family needs you." She turned and hurried across the compound toward her tent. She did not stop until she reached the opening, then realized too late that Hagar would be inside cleaning—the last person she cared to see. She would go to the weaver's tent and work alone if she must, but the basket of new threads was inside her tent.

Thinking only to grab it and hurry off, she steeled herself for another encounter with Hagar, however brief. She lifted the flap and ducked inside, but the rooms were deceptively quiet. "Hagar?" She tilted her head, but no one responded. Had the girl disobeyed a direct command?

She searched each side of the partition, which divided the

sleeping quarters from the living area, but there was no sign of Hagar. Sarai's pallet remained as she had left it, and one whiff told her that the nighttime pots still needed emptying. Where was the woman?

Anger surged within her again, mingled with the slightest twinge of fear. Would she have gone to Abram to report all that Sarai had said to her? But Abram would not care. He had given Hagar into Sarai's keeping to do as she wished with her. Still, where else would she be?

She moved out of the tent into the compound again and headed for Hagar's tent. When she found that place empty as well, her fear kicked up a notch. She had to be around somewhere. But the girl would regret the work it would take to find her. When Sarai got hold of her this time, she had better have a good excuse, or Sarai would have little mercy.

🌟31🌟

Abram strode into camp wearier than he had been in months. In moments when he allowed himself to ponder the cause, he could trace his lack of energy to the day Sarai had visited him in the fields and blamed him for her own problems with Hagar. There was no pleasing the woman, and the thought drained him. With Hagar he had begun to feel young again, and when his seed had quickened within her, even he had noticed the new spring in his step.

But now he put greater force on the walking stick and took slower steps over the rocky, uneven ground. Age had caught up with him, and despite the coming child, he was feeling it deep in his bones. Would he live long enough to see the child raised to manhood? He shook the useless thoughts aside. There was no sense guessing the future. Adonai alone knew what was to come.

The sounds of women and children greeted him as he drew closer to the campfire, and he smiled at the sight of Eliezer scooping his little ones into his waiting arms. A twinge of wistfulness filled him, accompanied by a small spot of joy in knowing that in a few months, he too would hold a babe on his knee.

He turned from the sight a moment later and headed for his tent. There was still time to rest before the evening meal, and his persistent fatigue needed respite. A short rest before he was forced to watch the growing animosity between Sarai and Hagar. A sigh escaped him, but as he approached his tent, he tensed at the sight of Sarai standing beneath the awning, waiting for him. Now what?

He drew in a breath, silently praying for strength. She came to meet him before he reached the tent's door.

"She is gone, my lord. The Egyptian is gone." One look at Sarai's frantic gaze told him this was no ruse.

"She has a name, Sarai. 'Hagar.' And what do you mean she is gone?" He leaned heavier on the staff with one hand and used the other to rub the growing ache at the back of his neck.

"I mean, I looked for her—the whole camp has been looking for hours. I sent servants to search the fields, thinking perhaps she had come to you to complain, but there has been no sign of her. Did she come to you? Have you sent her away somewhere?"

As her words sank deep, alarm rushed through him, his exhaustion gone. He shook his head. "I have not seen her since this morning's meal." He looked beyond her, then briefly took in the camp, making a quick attempt at his own lame search. "Where could she be?" He looked back at Sarai. "Has some harm come to her? So help me, woman, if you have done something to make her run away . . ." He stopped himself at the look of shame flickering in her eyes.

She averted her gaze and took a quick step back.

"What have you done?" Anger surged through him. He knew her well enough to know she was hiding her guilt. "The woman is carrying our child, Sarai. If you don't know where she is . . . at least tell me why. What happened?" He tried in vain to gentle his tone, knowing she always responded better when he soothed her like he did his smallest lambs. But a part of him simply did not care anymore. The life of his son—surely it was a son—could be in danger if Hagar had run off and fallen among thieves. The thought brought a sharp, knife-like pain to his gut.

"I . . ." Her tone faltered, and for a moment he feared she would weep, but in the next breath she lifted her gaze to meet his, crossing both arms across her chest. "I yelled at her . . . and I struck her cheek." Her own cheeks flushed crimson at the admission. "I only did so because she disrespected my orders. If she had given a proper servant's attitude, none of this would have happened."

"So the blame rests solely with Hagar?" He took a step closer. He had never hit a woman in his life, but for a brief blinding moment he was tempted to do so now. "You gave the girl into my arms and then have mistreated her since she gave us the very thing we craved. And now, because of your actions, you admit that we have lost her." He turned, pounding the earth with the staff, then looked back at his wife, the woman he had loved since his youth. "Go to your tent, Sarai, and pray to Adonai that we find her. You had better hope no ill has come to my son."

He stalked off then, too angry to look back or to soften the words that had caused the stricken look to come over Sarai's beautiful face. She would survive his wrath. Hagar, on the other hand, might not survive whatever fate she had chosen. Had she run away from his protection?

A bitter laugh escaped him. He had done nothing to protect her.

He walked on until he reached Eliezer's tent. "Eliezer!"

Eliezer lifted the flap and hurried to his side. "Yes, my lord? What's wrong?"

"Hagar is missing."

Eliezer nodded. "Lila told me. The camp has been in upheaval all afternoon looking for her. They have questioned the Egyptian servants thoroughly, along with the other servants, but there is no sign of her."

"There is only one place she would choose to return."

"Egypt."

Abram lifted a hand to his neck again, the ache becoming a

relentless throb. "Send ten men toward Shur, along the road to Egypt. But to be safe, send ten others north toward Damascus. Leave no stone unturned."

Eliezer touched Abram's shoulder. "We'll find her. Don't fear." He hurried off to do Abram's bidding while Abram went to the place of the altar to pray.

The sun beat down on Hagar, and her feet tingled with the scorch of the hot desert sand. Sweat rolled down her back, and her tongue tasted thick, her thirst unquenched. The days since she had left Abram's camp stretched behind her, nearing a week. How far had she come? How much longer until she reached one of the branches of the Nile? Longing for her homeland spurred her feet to continue. But the ache in her belly and her growing thirst made her stumble. If she didn't eat soon, she would die in this forsaken land.

She pressed a hand to her middle and forced herself upright, cupping her other hand to shade her eyes from the glare of the midday sun. Up ahead, the outline of trees beckoned. Could she have come upon water at last? Tears filmed her vision even as hope surged within her. She quickened her pace, barely mindful of the stinging sand creeping in between her toes. Palm branches swayed high in the trees as though bending to greet her approach. A spring's bubbling waters drew her attention, and she moved toward it.

At last, at the water's edge, she sank to her knees and scooped water into her mouth. Over and over again her hands poured the cool liquid onto her parched tongue. Her thirst finally quenched, she filled the empty skin she had snatched before she left Abram's camp, then crawled toward the shade of the cluster of date palms. After she rested, she would find a way up the tree to pluck the ripe dates from the sagging clusters.

Her eyes closed of their own accord. She was so tired. But the ache in her stomach would not be ignored. She opened her eyes and glanced at the fruit high above her head. She had little strength left to climb the trunk. Despair threatened. Would she die here so close to food? Why had she not thought to take a satchel of dates and nuts with her along with the skin of water? But she knew why. There had been no time and little thought to her running. Sarai would have stopped her if she'd known of her plans. Sarai would beat her if she ever found her now.

The woman had no right to treat her that way! She had done everything Sarai had ever asked of her, even when she did not have to in Pharaoh's palace. If only she had stayed with her family that day. If only she had never met Abram and Sarai.

Bitterness nearly suffocated her as the spring danced nearby over rocks on its way toward the sea. What was this place? She glanced up again at the bulging trees. Surely someone would come to harvest them soon. Could she wait that long for food if she offered to help? Would her help be accepted?

"Hagar, servant of Sarai."

A deep voice startled her, and she jumped up. Backing up a pace, she lost her balance, then quickly righted herself. She cinched her robe close, entwining her arms over her chest.

"Who's there?" Trembling shook her, but she forced her feet to hold steady, looking about to find the source of the voice. She spotted a tall, handsome man who stepped closer, a cluster of dates resting in his palm. He extended it toward her. She eyed him warily, transfixed by the light in his dark eyes. "Who are you?"

He placed the dates in her hand, giving her no choice but to accept them. "Hagar, servant of Sarai," he said again, "where have you come from, and where are you going?"

You know me? The trembling increased, her senses suddenly sharper, her heart racing with each breath.

"I'm running away from my mistress, Sarai." There was no

reason to lie to the man, though she realized the stark truth of the fact that she could not have lied if she'd tried. The words would not form in her mind or on her tongue.

"Go back to your mistress and submit to her."

I can't! She staggered, nearly losing her footing again. She fingered the dates in her hand but was no longer hungry. Silent protests sprang within her, but she could not voice them. Nor could she glance at the man who seemed much more than a man, or meet his steady, penetrating gaze.

"I will so increase your descendants that they will be too numerous to count."

Her breath caught, and despite her fear, despite all she had been taught, she boldly looked his way. Suddenly her fear dissolved in the kindness of his smile. Relief spilled over her like showers after a drought, filling her with hope. "My descendants?"

His smiled broadened, its warmth soothing. "You are now with child, and you will have a son. You shall name him Ishmael, for Adonai has heard of your misery."

Tears filled her eyes at his words. Adonai cared about a slave? He saw her? He knew?

The man's expression changed, compassion in his eyes along with something she could not define. "He will be a wild donkey of a man; his hand will be against everyone and everyone's hand against him, and he will live in hostility toward all his brothers."

The words only skirted the surface of her mind. All his brothers? Which meant either she or Abram would have more sons. Or did he mean brothers in a more general family sense? As it stood, there were no others that could even be named relatives. Abram's brothers lived far from Canaan.

Canaan. Not Egypt. Where Sarai still lived to torment her. *Go back to your mistress and submit to her . . . You will have a son . . . You shall name him Ishmael.*

Ishmael. *God will hear.* And God had heard, had seen her misery. She lifted her head and looked again at the man who was not really a man. "You are the God who sees me. I have now seen the One who sees me."

His piercing look told her she had surmised the truth, and the realization sent her to her knees. She planted her face in the dust at his feet, her heart humbled yet filled with overwhelming joy. Though her father, the pharaoh of Egypt, had never noticed her, and her own mother had barely acknowledged her existence, and Abram, the only man she might call husband, had also turned his face from her, there was One who had not only heard but seen.

He had not only seen, but He knew her misery and had promised to bless her and the child in her womb. As though the thought of Him awakened both the child and her hunger, she felt her stomach rumble and kick all at once. She lifted her head, about to ask the man if He wished to share the dates He had offered to her, but He was gone.

Thank you, El Roi, O God who sees me. For though He had gone from her, she knew He watched her still.

❄❄❄

Sarai stood near the edge of the camp between the road leading south toward Egypt and the path heading west where Abram had gone to pray each morning in the ten days since Hagar had disappeared. Worry gnawed her middle, the image of Abram's wrath playing over and over again in her mind. He'd been angry at her before, but never like this, and never before involving another woman to rival her affections in his heart. The breeze teased the hair away from her face, its cloying warmth oppressive. Would the men find Hagar alive?

A chill worked through her despite the heat, and she toyed with indecision. Abram had sent her to her tent. Lila, in her kindness, had told her that first night that Abram had gone in the direction of the altar and that Eliezer had sent men to look for Hagar. Shame heated her face. The news should have come from her husband, but he clearly had nothing more to say to her until news of Hagar could be found.

She tugged the corners of her robe more tightly against her body and turned back toward the camp. The stones crunched beneath her leather sandals, and children's laughter grated on her already heightened nerves. She glanced at a group of boys taunting a younger son of one of Abram's servants. She quickened her pace, marching closer.

"What do you think you're doing?" Her voice came out harsh, as she intended, snagging the boys' attention.

They jerked their heads toward her, looking chagrined.

"Go on, off with the lot of you. Go back to your mothers and obey, or I'll see to it you are put to work cleaning the waste pots!" They scampered away from her, even the boy who had been taunted, leaving Sarai alone again despite the hum of voices nearby.

The thought depressed her. What kind of a mother would she have been? One who protected her child against boys who would hurt him? Absolutely! One who would make sure such children were kept far from her son. She would have done all in her power to keep him safe.

But there was no son to keep safe, not even the son of a maidservant she might adopt. Her shoulders sagged, and she turned toward her tent. Perhaps today would be a good day to work on her more intricate weaving. She no longer had a desire to sew the lengths of cloth they had made into clothes for the coming babe.

A rush of excited voices drew her attention back toward the road she had come from, the road leading out of camp toward Egypt. Moments later, she heard Abram's voice above the din.

"She is found! Hagar has returned to us." The joy in his tone sent her spirits spiraling downward. She would give anything to return to her tent and stay there until Abram came to tell her the news. If he would come. Doubt added to the worry twisting inside of her. She would have to face the woman sometime.

She moved in the direction of the growing crowd, grateful that they parted at her approach. She lifted her chin, denying the sea of emotions wavering within, and stood before Abram and Hagar.

"So, you have returned." She kept her voice even and her gaze on Hagar, unwilling to let Abram sense her turmoil.

Hagar bowed low and prostrated herself at Sarai's feet, startling her. "Mistress," she said, her face to the dust, "I am your servant."

Sarai looked from Hagar to Abram, but her husband's expression told her that Hagar's actions were her own. He had not prompted them. Did he agree with them? Or had his opinion of Hagar changed in the ten days she had been absent from their lives? She waited a moment, trying to read his thoughts, but he only shrugged and crossed his arms over his chest, a clear signal that Hagar was still her maid to do with as she wished. The thought brought a small sense of relief. He still trusted her, was giving her another chance. Perhaps she had not ruined their relationship after all.

"Where have you been, Hagar?" Sarai gentled her tone, not wanting to scare the girl off again.

Hagar did not move or lift her head. "I had determined to go back to Egypt. But at the spring on the road to Shur, the angel of Adonai met me there."

Awe tinged her words, and Sarai's heart skipped a beat, jealousy filling her. Adonai had sent an angel to speak with a slave when He had never once given her any reassurance of His promise?

"The angel told me to return to you, to submit to you, mistress."

The news took Sarai aback. "The angel spoke of me?" Her heart beat with sudden fear. Had Adonai condemned Sarai to this slave? Yet no. He had told Hagar to return and submit to her.

"Yes, mistress. He said I would have a son and was to name him Ishmael."

Abram cleared his throat, causing Sarai to glance up toward him. He motioned toward Hagar still kneeling in the dust, indicating Sarai should bid her rise. Heat warmed her face that she had not thought of it first, that her husband should have to suggest it in front of so many witnesses. She gave a slight nod to him.

"You may rise, Hagar."

The girl slowly leaned back on her heels. Before Abram could do so and shame her further, Sarai offered her a hand to help her up. But when she glanced at him again, she read only approval in his eyes.

"Come, let us get you something to eat. Then you can tell me more about what the angel said to you." She turned and walked ahead of Hagar, fully expecting her to follow, silently relieved when she did. She was not ready to embrace the girl or allow her back into Abram's arms, but she knew if she intended to keep peace in her home and in the camp, she would have to treat Hagar with more respect. She was going to bear Abram a son, and Adonai's visit to the girl told Sarai that perhaps she had done the right thing in giving her to Abram after all.

❊ 32 ❊

The soft breezes of fall accompanied birdsong in the early dawn as Hagar's cries split the sounds in two. Abram strode outside the birthing tent, pacing first one way, then the next. Would the child never be born? The women had crouched around the girl all last afternoon and through the night, yet still he waited for his son to come forth from the womb.

His son. Had a word ever held such joy?

He glanced at Eliezer where he sat on a log bench near the fire, breaking his fast with bread and figs and soft goat cheese. Abram had tried to eat, but as with the wine Eliezer had begged him to drink last night to ease the waiting, Abram refused. What if he was needed to help? And yet what could a mere man do? The women had shooed him far from the tent's door several times. Even Sarai had not come to speak with him, to ease his fears.

A rueful smile tugged his mouth. He had not been fair to Sarai these past few months, and the rift in their relationship was taking its toll. She'd been kind to Hagar after her return. The least he could do was welcome Sarai back into his confidence. He winced at his own hard-heartedness, recalling the wistful looks she often cast his way. How foolish of him to punish her for something Adonai had surely long since forgiven.

More cries came from the tent, some like soft moans, while others wrenched his heart. He turned at a touch on his arm.

"You will not wait long now, my friend." Eliezer smiled, his expression that of a knowing father. "Her cries are coming more often and sharper."

Abram ran a hand over his ragged, dusty beard. He'd hurried in from the fields two days ago at the first sign of Hagar's travail and was in dire need of grooming. "I would ask Adonai why women must suffer so to bring children into the world, but I already know the answer."

"If only Mother Eve had not tasted that fruit." Eliezer chuckled and drew Abram to sit with him on the bench.

"Of course we can blame the women, but they would remind us Adam could have told his wife no." Abram laughed, his tension easing.

"When have men ever been able to say no to their wives?" Eliezer's smile widened at the musical sound of a baby's cry. "And when has a sound ever been so welcome, my father?" He patted Abram on the back.

Abram's heart quickened its pace, and he jumped up from the bench, but Eliezer stayed him with a hand on his arm. "They will bring the babe to you, Abram. It is the duty of men to be patient."

Abram sank back down, but his anxiety did not lessen. Until he held the boy, counted his fingers and toes, looked into his face, he would not be at ease. He shifted, wanting to pace again, but forced himself to relax.

What was taking them so long? The child still cried, making Abram groan within. He should know better than to worry. Didn't all babies cry at birth? He'd heard plenty of them in the camp over the years, Eliezer's own children being no exception.

A servant brought him a cup of goat's milk, and this time he did not refuse. Moments later, he wiped his mouth with the back of his hand and stood.

Sarai emerged from the tent, carrying a wrapped bundle. She approached him and met his gaze. "You have a son, my lord."

She offered the babe to him to bless on his knee. He sat again and accepted the child from her arms, but he did not miss the mixture of awe and longing in her dark blue eyes. He held her gaze, wishing the child was hers, yet glad he had not had to endure such cries of anguish coming from this beloved wife. Could he bear such a thing? Yet as he looked into the face of his son, he knew he would want her to experience the same joy, the same love he felt swell from deep within him.

"Ishmael," he said, placing the babe across his knees and holding him steady.

Sarai lifted the blanket to reveal the babe's fingers. "He is perfectly whole, my lord," she said, covering them again. "We must keep him warm."

Abram nodded, wondering how she knew such things but accepting her appraisal that all was well. He turned his face to gaze down on the child again. "May Adonai bless you mightily, my son. May you live long on the earth and father many sons to follow after you. And may Adonai give you peace."

He looked up at the crowd that had been waiting with him in the circle of the campfire. "My son!" He lifted the boy in his arms and stood. "His name is Ishmael!"

Cheers erupted, causing Ishmael's cries to begin again. He lowered Ishmael and held him against his chest. "Perhaps he needs his mother." He looked at Sarai, reading the pain in her gaze as he handed the boy back to her. "Take him to Hagar."

She accepted the boy and turned to go.

"Sarai." He stepped beside her and touched her shoulder. "It is time you came to my tent again."

She met his gaze, then swiftly looked beyond him. "As you wish, my lord."

He could tell by her reticence that his request was long overdue. He must speak with her, comfort her, and reassure her of his great love for her. Perhaps then she would see the babe as the blessing he was.

He told himself that things would be well now that the babe was safely born. But Sarai's proud posture as she walked with the boy back to the birthing tent told him life with two women in the same household would not be easy. Trouble lay ahead—he could sense it.

Sarai entered Abram's tent as dusk descended over the camp. She had left Ishmael with Hagar and one of the Egyptian servant girls, wanting to do nothing more than fall onto her own pallet and sleep. The birth had exhausted her, and she wondered not for the first time how hard it would be to suffer such anguish. Yet for the joy of a man child, she would go through it. She would die if only to glimpse her own child's face and kiss his downy head. The thought left a lump in her throat. It was not meant to be.

Abram stood at her approach, his arm extended toward her. Sudden shyness crept over her despite her exhaustion. She had not slept in his arms since before Hagar's disappearance over five months before. Why had he called for her now? Had he somehow felt that Hagar would run off again if he showed his favor to Sarai? It made no sense, but she had learned long ago that he was past figuring out.

"Come in, Sarai." He stepped closer, and she placed her hand in his.

The strength of his arms as they came around her brought tears to her eyes. How long had it been since he had held her close? When he rubbed her back and did not release her, she could not hold back the emotions that she'd held in check throughout the birth.

"It's all right, dear one. I'm sorry I have stayed so long away from you." His whispered words held gentleness, and when he held her at arm's length, he brushed away the remnant of her tears with his thumbs. "Please do not fret or worry over Ishmael's birth. Hagar gave him birth, but you will be his true mother. You will always be the only woman for me, Sarai." He bent to place a soft kiss on her lips, and she knew he tasted her tears.

"I only wish it had been I who had given you such a gift, my lord." She sniffed back her emotion and blinked hard, willing it away. "You have reason to be proud today."

Abram nodded and touched her cheek. "There was a time I thought any man could father a son. Now I know what a gift it truly is." His gaze would not release hers, until she glanced away.

"Not every woman can bear such a one. Adonai has chosen a foreigner, while me He has set aside. I am too old for such pleasure now." She took a step back and turned away from him toward his sitting area. She bent to finger one of the cushions. "The fabric is wearing thin on these. You should have told me. I would have stitched them long ago."

Did he think she accused him of neglect? But she did not care anymore. He had his promised son and a woman to raise him. She was nothing more than a wife to him now. A useless wife at that.

"I do not notice such things." He came up behind her and touched her shoulder. "Another reason I was a fool to keep your touch from this place. Forgive me, Sarai?"

His declaration startled and pleased her. She turned slowly and searched his gaze.

"I thank you for giving your maid into my arms, for allowing her to give us a son." He placed both hands on her shoulders. "But you are my wife. My only wife. And I love you."

She allowed a smile and reached to kiss him. "You are all I have."

He took her hands in his and pulled her close, then wrapped

her in his arms and kissed her as he used to in the early days before babies and barrenness constantly occupied her thoughts, back when she was young and in love with this handsome prince, certain she held the power to give him anything.

"Come sup with me, Sarai. Taste the fruit of the vine, and share in my love." His words were like a sweet caress, and she allowed him to lead her to his plush cushions, accepting the wine he poured from his own hand. "This is a night to celebrate and remember," he said, sinking down beside her, cradling a silver chalice between his fingers. He sipped the wine and smiled.

She returned his smile, wishing she could share his joy, wishing she could tell him all the things that still lay like a troubling wound deep within her soul. But he would never understand, and bringing up her jealousies and insecurities now would only dampen his jubilant mood. No. Better to wait until another time when their old friendship had been fully restored, when the babe was not such a fresh reminder of her failures.

She sipped the wine and laughed at something he said, praying to the Unseen One that He might yet look with favor on her, and if not give her a child, then at least grant her peace.

Part

4

When Abram was ninety-nine years old, the LORD appeared to him and said, "I am God Almighty; walk before me and be blameless. I will confirm my covenant between me and you and will greatly increase your numbers."

Genesis 17:1–2

"As for Sarai your wife, you are no longer to call her Sarai; her name will be Sarah. I will bless her and will surely give you a son by her. I will bless her so that she will be the mother of nations; kings of peoples will come from her."

Abraham fell facedown; he laughed and said to himself, "Will a son be born to a man a hundred years old? Will Sarah bear a child at the age of ninety?" And Abraham said to God, "If only Ishmael might live under your blessing!"

Then God said, "Yes, but your wife Sarah will bear you a son, and you will call him Isaac."

Genesis 17:15–19

THIRTEEN YEARS LATER

Sarai fingered the topaz pendant Abram had purchased from visiting merchants, then fastened it to a chain about her neck. Matching topaz earrings dangled from each ear, and her maid had taken care to weave rose-petal pearls into her dark, silver-streaked hair. The ornaments reflected the changes age had brought, and when Sarai examined the effect in her silver mirror, she could not help but smile. Hagar might have her youthful vigor, but even at almost ninety years of age, Sarai's beauty remained.

She placed the mirror on a low table and smoothed the soft fabric of her blue and green robe, forcing her tense muscles to relax. It did no good to think of Hagar in that way. She was not a rival for Abram's affections. Not really. No, it was the boy Sarai competed with. The boy who was supposed to be hers. But the feelings of motherhood had never managed to surface, and Ishmael had bonded too well with his Egyptian mother.

She moved past the sitting room of her spacious tent and nodded to a maid who was busy cleaning and straightening from Abram's visit the night before. That he came to her often just to talk brought some small comfort. They'd grown accustomed to life in these hills. If only Abram could talk of something other than Ishmael.

The voices of the women drifted to her, and she left her tent, head held high. Today she would join Abram as he greeted merchants coming from Mesopotamia, and she hoped to view their wares as well as hear news of Abram's brother and family. It had been so long. Was Milcah still living? Even Melah, though she lived much closer, had not been to visit them in years. Time kept marching on, whether Sarai wanted it to or not.

She spotted Abram standing near the central fire speaking with Eliezer while Ishmael stood nearby. The boy wore the headdress of a grown man now, though at thirteen he still carried the gangly limbs of youth. A handsome boy, he bore a striking resemblance to his mother and carried the same proud tilt to his jaw. The realization prickled, and Sarai felt her muscles tensing again. She rolled her shoulders and drew in a deep breath. If she had her way, Ishmael would not be joining them today.

She marched with determined steps across the compound and stopped within a handbreadth of Abram, waiting for him to finish his conversation. At last he turned to her, but before she could speak, Ishmael came up beside his father.

"Can I go on ahead with Eliezer, Father?" He averted his gaze from Sarai as though her presence was of no consequence. "I can help with the camels." The boy did have a way with the beasts, which had gained him respect even among his elders. But his avoidance of Sarai, his adoptive mother, irritated her all the more.

"Perhaps the boy's skills would be put to better use following one of the herds today. They can always use an extra hand, and the practice would do him good." Sarai hid a smirk at the scowl Ishmael sent her way. It was time he learned some respect, and Abram seemed at a loss for how to teach him. And Hagar did nothing but indulge him. He was wild and unruly, and Sarai had grown weary of Abram's doting on him.

Abram looked from Ishmael to Sarai and back again, his brows knit in disapproval and indecision.

"Please, Father. I run with the herds and flocks nearly every day. How often does a caravan come this way? And all the way from Mesopotamia! I could learn much, Father." The boy placed a hand on Abram's arm, and Sarai knew the battle was lost. To fight against Abram's son would be to put herself in a position where she could be shamed before the boy. Something she was not willing to do.

"It was only a suggestion, my lord. If Ishmael can be of use to you with the camels, then by all means, do as you wish." She flicked a piece of lint from her sleeve and lifted her chin, making sure Ishmael knew by her look that his father still had her ear. She knew what wars were worth winning, and this was not one of them.

Abram met her gaze, his look telling her he knew she meant more than she had said. He turned to Ishmael and put an arm around the boy. "Very well, my son. Run along and catch up with Eliezer. But mind you, stay close and listen to everything he says. Only help where you are needed. It is better to listen in silence and learn."

Joy lit the boy's eyes, and a look of appreciation crossed his dusky complexion. "Thank you, Father!" He gave Abram an impulsive hug and then turned and took off at a run through the camp toward the road where Eliezer had gone.

Sarai did not miss the affection evident in Abram's gaze as he watched his son go, stirring the seeds of jealousy already growing in her heart. She should never have given Hagar to Abram that long-ago day. She should have let them both remain childless and given their inheritance to Eliezer and his children. What difference would it have made who gathered their wealth when they were gone? And yet how could she refuse Abram the joy she saw light his eyes whenever Ishmael entered his presence?

When Ishmael was out of earshot, Abram turned to face her, extending his hand. "Why would you keep him from joining us?" His tone held kindness mingled with a gentle reprimand. "Most of the camp wants to go, and only the most feeble or infant among us will not. You know this, beloved."

She placed her hand in his and followed as he led them toward the road to meet the caravan approaching from the King's Highway. "Sometimes it is hard to compete with the boy." She spoke softly, knowing he heard her, not wanting Hagar or those who had fallen into line behind them to overhear.

Abram squeezed her fingers in a possessive grip. "You have nothing to compete with, dearest wife. You alone are the one I love." He bent his head toward her as he spoke, the warmth of his breath tingling the skin on her neck. "But don't deny me the pleasure the boy brings. We will not have him forever. We have only each other until the grave takes us."

"Don't speak of the grave."

Though Abram still carried a spring in his step, his years were nearing the one-hundred mark, and she could not deny the fear that age brought with it. The fear of losing him. What would happen to her if she lost Abram while Ishmael still lived among them? Would Ishmael inherit Abram's wealth? Would she be at his mercy?

But of course she would.

He tucked her hand into the crook of his arm and placed his hand over hers. "Do not fear the grave, Sarai. Adonai will not abandon us. He will fulfill His promises to us."

"His promises to you, you mean. Isn't Ishmael the fulfillment of that promise? What more is needed of you or me once he reaches manhood? The land Adonai promised will go to him, and you and I will be forgotten." The excited voices of the women and children grew at the sight of the camels approaching just over the rise. Sarai felt her own heart quicken again at the thought of news from home.

At Abram's lengthy silence, Sarai thought he would not answer her question. She glanced at him as some of the older children raced ahead to greet the merchants. It would take time for the camel drivers to unpack their wares, but the thrill of something new interrupted the normal daily routines.

As they came upon the caravan, Sarai looked again at her husband, surprised to find his gaze on her. She came to a halt beside him, waiting.

"I do not know if Ishmael is the fulfillment of Adonai's promise to us, Sarai." His low tones were barely above a whisper, and he glanced around them as though to make sure he was not overheard.

She followed his gaze, relieved to see Hagar move with the throng of maids heading toward the merchants. She looked at him again, startled by the uncertainty in his eyes.

"I always thought the promise would include you." He touched her cheek, and an inexplicable longing filled her. But it was far too late for such misguided hopes.

"I had hoped so as well, my lord, but obviously it was not meant to be."

Abram shrugged, then straightened, as though he realized the conversation held no purpose. Of course Ishmael would fulfill the promises. There was no one else. "I don't know why I entertain such thoughts," he said, taking her hand again and turning them toward the caravan. Camels had already begun to kneel, and she spotted Ishmael trotting along behind the caravan leader, engaged in some conversation she could not hear, as though he were already taking charge of the situation that belonged to Eliezer or his father.

"Come. There is no use discussing it further. In time, Adonai will show us His plan."

Never mind that Adonai had remained silent these past thirteen years.

❋❋❋

The afternoon waned, and the merchants began to pack up their wares for their trip to the next settlement on their way to Egypt. The day had been productive, and Abram's heart had swelled with pride as he watched Ishmael barter with one particularly difficult trader. The boy would do well someday. He had the makings of an able prince, if not for his quick temper. If he learned to keep his fists at his side, men would follow him just for his charm.

He sighed, imagining the time when he would hand over control of his house to his son. The boy still had years of growth ahead. Surely Adonai would not ask it of him too soon.

His feet crunched the stone path from the tents toward the hill where the altar stood bathed in the sun's fading glow. There was still time before the evening meal to offer a sacrifice, and he needed time alone. Time to hear from Adonai. If only He would speak. Years had passed since God had given him the covenant, the promise to give the land of Canaan to his descendants. Since Ishmael's birth, there had been no further word, and with the boy's approaching manhood, he worried. It made no sense to keep Eliezer as his heir when he had a son of his own flesh and blood.

He rounded a bend past a copse of trees, his walking stick holding more of his weight than it had in recent years. Admitting the fact that he was feeling his age was something he did in private with Sarai. No sense letting the boy know how frail his father felt at times.

He passed the sheep pens and took time to select the choicest year-old lamb, then carried it on his shoulders up the low hill to the altar. The sacrifice brought a sense of sadness, an acute awareness of his sins, his many failings, and how far short he came of Adonai's goodness. He knew Adonai could be trusted to keep His word, but it was the details of not knowing, not understanding, that made Abram weak.

He sank to his knees, his face to the dust. *Accept my offering, O God who sees me and knows me. Forgive my frailty. Guide Your servant to do Your will.*

The wind whispered in the trees above him, and suddenly he sensed he was not alone. Lifting his head, he looked up into the face of a man who was clearly not as other men. Abram dropped his face to the dust again, his heart seizing and yet somehow still beating. Fear and love mingled until the overpowering presence cast Abram's fear out of reach. He raised his head again and sensed a silent urging to remove his sandals and stand. He quickly obeyed.

"I am El Shaddai. Walk before Me and be blameless."

Abram did not speak, but he felt his spirit agree, his gaze fixed on the blazing light surrounding the man, his ears ringing with the deep, ageless voice.

"I will confirm My covenant between Me and you and will greatly increase your numbers."

The promise brought with it such an overwhelming sense of relief that God had heard his inner yearnings that he fell to his knees once again, his face to the ground.

"As for Me, this is My covenant with you: You will be the father of many nations. No longer will you be called Abram; your name will be Abraham, for I have made you a father of many nations. I will make you very fruitful; I will make nations of you, and kings will come from you. I will establish My covenant as an everlasting covenant between Me and you and your descendants after you for the generations to come, to be your God and the God of your descendants after you. The whole land of Canaan, where you are now an alien, I will give as an everlasting possession to you and your descendants after you, and I will be their God."

Abram's mind spun with the implications, and he rose up on his knees. *Abraham. Father of many.* What did it mean?

"As for you"—God's voice interrupted his fleeting thoughts—"you must keep My covenant, you and your descendants after you for the generations to come. This is My covenant with you and your descendants after you, the covenant you are to keep: Every male among you shall be circumcised. You are to undergo circumcision, and it will be the sign of the covenant between Me and you. For the generations to come, every male among you who is eight days old must be circumcised, including those born in your household or bought with money from a foreigner—those who are not your offspring. Whether born in your household or bought with your money, they must be circumcised. My covenant in your flesh is to be an everlasting covenant. Any uncircumcised male who has not been circumcised in the flesh will be cut off from his people. He has broken My covenant."

Abraham nodded his understanding, waiting.

"As for Sarai your wife, you are no longer to call her Sarai; her name will be Sarah. I will bless her and will surely give you a son by her. I will bless her so that she will be the mother of nations. Kings of peoples will come from her."

Sarai a mother? Abraham's strength failed him even as laughter bubbled from somewhere deep within him. His knees would not hold him, and he fell facedown to the earth once more. *Will a son be born to a man a hundred years old? Will Sarah*—the new name came easily to his heart—*bear a child at the age of ninety?* The idea seemed ludicrous. Impossible.

"If only Ishmael might live under your blessing!" Surely it made more sense to bless the child he already had. Yet he could not deny the increase of his heartbeat or the excited sense that God could indeed do as He had promised.

"Yes, but your wife Sarah will bear you a son, and you will call him Isaac. I will establish My covenant with him as an everlasting covenant for his descendants after him. And as for Ishmael, I have heard you. I will surely bless him; I will make him fruitful and will greatly increase his numbers. He will be the father of twelve rulers, and I will make him into a great nation. But my covenant I will establish with Isaac, whom Sarah will bear to you by this time next year."

The words rang in his ears, matching the pace of his heart. Sarah would bear a son. How God would quicken a dead womb was more than he could fathom. But he did not question the promise. He waited, his heart and ears attuned to every sound, realizing in that moment that when the voice had spoken, there had been no other noise. No wind, no birds, barely a breath from his lips. And then suddenly the blinding light disappeared, the wind picked up, and birdsong floated softly downward from the trees.

He slowly stood, new life pouring through him, his strength renewed. Leaving the walking stick behind, he made his way back to camp. El Shaddai had told him to circumcise every male in his household. He would not sleep until the task was accomplished.

34

Melah lifted her face from the cool tiles of the temple to Ningal and rose from her knees, feeling every aching joint. When had her body betrayed her so? She was older now, nearly seventy, but the years since the loss of her son felt like they had passed times ten. No children had followed his death, and her daughters were now grown and soon to marry. Her future sons-in-law were good men—as good as any that could be found in Sodom. So why did the future seem so dark?

She glanced at the shimmering idol, her offering of fruit and nutmeats sitting untouched in a golden bowl at its feet. Ningal had abandoned her long ago, but she could not bring herself to walk away.

Heaviness settled over her as she backed from the sanctuary and turned at the door to step into the sunlight. The temple courtyard buzzed with the chanting of priests, and cones of incense tainted the air with sickening sweetness. In the paved street in front of the gated court, donkeys pulling well-laden carts trudged past, and young children raced by, shouting curses and scooping up stones to throw at some unfortunate person who had angered them.

Melah glanced at the Egyptian slave Lot had secured for her

and nodded once. She pulled her cloak over her head, clutching the folds tighter at the neck, and made her way toward the merchants' stalls. Cries of anguish pierced the air, an all-too-familiar sound. The boys' stones must have found their mark. She hurried on, ducking to the side of a cart, keeping close to the buildings. She did not wish to see a child beaten to death. When had the city become so violent? Would her son—had he lived—have been part of the crowd casting stones or the one destroyed by the hatred of bullies?

A shiver worked through her as the sounds of anguish died away. Where were the city guards at such a time as this? Why didn't the magistrate or the king do something to quell the cruelty? If things were this bad in daylight, she couldn't imagine what atrocities took place after nightfall.

She glanced behind her again at the Egyptian, relieved to see he kept up with her hurried pace. His size alone would scare any who might approach her, and he was useful for carrying her wares back home. If her daughters could have been roused from their beds, she would have brought them as well. But they had spent the night with friends who stayed too late and drank too much, and Melah had left her maids behind to clean up the mess they had made.

A few more turns and she at last reached the market district. The bartering over fresh fruits and vegetables never took long, but the haggling over fabric and a new water urn took longer, and sweat dotted Melah's forehead by the time she finished. She ended up filling her arms, along with those of her slave, and hurried home before the midday meal.

Flower stalls caught her attention as they moved toward home. She would need baskets filled with some of the cultivated lilies for Kammani's wedding next spring. Surely Pirhum, her future son-in-law, would have the house finished by then. She clucked her tongue, wishing she could use a goad on both young men to get them to hurry so her daughters could be safely married.

The thought made her pause mid-step. She glanced ahead to where the pinnacle of Ningal's ziggurat could easily be seen, like a beacon guiding her home. And yet she knew Ningal had not been the one pushing Lot to secure men to wed their daughters. If not for Melah, the girls would never leave home, never breed and give her grandchildren to love. Though at times, she wondered if they might not have found better husbands in a town outside of Sodom. If the rumors were true . . .

She shuddered, hurrying on. At least Lot was faithful to her. His faith in Abram's God would not allow him to be like the other men around him. Regret filled her. She wished she could have shared that faith.

Thundering hooves suddenly shook the hot pavement, startling her. The Egyptian shoved her to the side, barely in time to escape the prince's chariot as it rattled past, followed by another reckless sea of horses and chariots filled with shouting and laughing young men.

Screams pierced above the racket, and she turned toward the sound, her stomach roiling at the sight of a young child run over by the flying wheels. The driver did not bother to stop or take notice. Why must they race through the city during the busiest part of the day, with no warning to clear the streets to protect the people?

"Are you all right, mistress?" The Egyptian touched her arm, snapping her thoughts from the horrid sight.

As the dust settled, she looked warily down the street, relieved to see no more sign of the brash young men, only normal early-morning travelers and merchants. "I am well. Thank you."

She glanced at the child lying in the street, his cries gone silent. Someone should go to him, find his mother. She waited a moment, relieved when a young woman raced to the boy, screaming his name. At least someone would care enough to bury him.

Shaken, she turned away and hurried on. Lot had been right. Sodom was not a safe place for a woman alone. Or for children.

Her feet flew past the temple, the priests' chanting somehow louder this time.

Up ahead, her house came into focus, but she did not stop until she entered the courtyard and the Egyptian shut the gate behind them. Stepping into the house, she set her basket of vegetables on a long table, grabbed a sharp knife, and set about chopping, her fear and horror pouring out through the rhythm and strength of the blade on wood. She was through going to market, and her girls would never set foot there without ten guards to watch them. It wasn't safe. No. Safe was inside the house where she could shut out the noise of the city, and with it the brutality she could not bear to witness ever again.

Abraham closed his eyes, listening to the leaves brush against one another in the welcome breeze, cooling the heat on his skin. The awning of his black goat's-hair tent cast him in shadow, though his spot here near the great oaks of Mamre afforded him a wide view of the valley below. Birds chirped merry songs, no doubt enjoying the breeze as much as he did. A dove's mournful call rose above them all.

He moved gingerly, still healing from the rite of circumcision he'd performed on himself and his household the week before. Ishmael and the younger men had recovered days ago, but he still moved with measured steps. The reminder never ceased to bring a sense of humility to his heart. God would keep His promise after all. If only he had waited and not succumbed to a loss of faith.

He glanced beyond his tent toward his family, spotting Ishmael, bow slung over his shoulder, headed with a friend toward the hills where they would hunt small game. A surge of pride rushed through him. His faith had not been perfect, but he would never regret fathering his firstborn. God Himself had said He would bless Ishmael. Abraham took comfort in that fact.

He courted a smile as the two young men disappeared from sight, then turned his gaze toward the entrance to his campsite, where the great oaks stood guard like towering sentinels. The breeze flickered, then suddenly died like flames blown out. Birds grew silent as if anxious, holding their breath. Abraham blinked, shading his eyes from the sun's overpowering glare.

But it was not the sun causing the ethereal glow, as it stood behind him now, to the west. His eyes quickly adjusted to the brightness, and in its midst he saw three men standing near the oaks. He pushed to his feet and grabbed his walking stick, his heart thudding hard and fast in his chest. Anticipation mingled with recognition, and he hurried closer to his guests and bowed low, his face to the ground. A thrill raced through him, and suddenly every part of his body tingled with life. Joy filled him as he lifted his gaze to theirs.

"If I have found favor in your eyes, my lord, do not pass your servant by. Let a little water be brought, and then you may all wash your feet and rest under this tree. Let me get you something to eat, so you can be refreshed and then go on your way, now that you have come to your servant."

The glow dissipated like water into mist, and Abraham felt himself lifted without a touch to stand before them.

"Very well." They seemed to all speak at once yet with one voice. "Do as you say."

Abraham quickly found a servant to bring water to wash the feet of the men, then whirled about, the walking stick left behind, and ran as a youth to Sarah's tent. He burst through the door without announcing himself and found Sarah nestled among the cushions, mending something. She startled, dropping the garment.

"Quick! Get three seahs of fine flour and knead it and bake some bread."

He rushed out of the tent without waiting for a reply. She would do as he asked without question. Would the visitors stay as they had said? His heart beat the rhythm of a joyous dance as he lifted his robe, tucked it into his girdle, and ran unhindered to the hills outside of camp, where his herds of cattle grazed. One of the herdsmen met him and led him to the choice calves kept especially for guests or sacrifices. The meat would be young and tender, a savory offering to present the three men.

"Kill it and prepare the meat over an open fire in the camp. Do not delay."

"Yes, my lord." The man signaled another servant to help him and led the calf toward the place of slaughter.

Abraham hurried toward the women's area of the camp and roused Lila from her midday rest. "Milk one of the goats and prepare some fresh curds for my visitors. Quickly."

She gave him a brief nod. "Yes, my lord." She hurried off.

As Abraham left Lila's tent, he spotted Sarah near the ovens, kneading dough to set to rise. In a few hours, all should be ready, but he chafed like an old woman, half fearing his guests would not wait. Yet even as the worry came, it disappeared, as though his visitors had somehow silently reassured him.

Abraham glanced toward the trees near his tent where they still waited. They sat in a circle conversing among themselves, the two listening intently to the one who stood out as the leader. The one who Abraham knew in a place deep within him was Adonai come in the flesh. How God could become man was beyond his ability to comprehend. But he did not doubt. God could do anything.

The thought lingered with him as he hurried back to the fire pit, where chief cuts of the calf now roasted. He carried a heavy wooden platter to a nearby rock, waiting. Would God speak to him of the promised child? The one He had said would come through Sarah's womb? He laughed as he pictured Sarah with a small babe on her hip. A spirit of adventure filled him, much as he'd felt the day God had told him to pack his things and move away from Ur. Change was upon him again, and he was not afraid. He would embrace whatever God had for him.

He turned at the chatter of women's voices, clearly hearing Sarah's in their midst. A servant turned the meat and checked for any remaining blood, then stuck a two-pronged fork into the thick slabs and pulled them from the fire onto Abraham's wooden plate. Sarah approached with Lila at her side.

"Here is the bread you requested, along with the milk and curds, my lord." She handed him a basket and a skin of milk. "Would you like me to go with you?"

Abraham shook his head. "No. Not yet. Go to your tent and wait until I summon you."

She bowed slightly in acknowledgment, then turned with Lila and walked back toward the camp. Abraham scooped up the basket, skin, and platter and headed toward the trees. He breathed a sigh at the sight of the men, wondering at his foolishness for worrying they would not keep their word. He set the food on the ground before them, then stood nearby.

"Where is your wife Sarah?" they asked him.

"There in the tent." He pointed to the large goat's-hair tent closest to his.

"I will surely return to you about this time next year, and Sarah your wife will have a son." The one Abraham sensed was Adonai spoke, making the hair on Abraham's arms tingle.

Abraham glanced behind him in the direction of the tent, catching a glimpse of Sarah in the entryway. A hand covered her mouth, though no sound came out.

"Why did Sarah laugh and say, 'Will I really have a child, now that I am old?' Is anything too hard for the Lord?" Adonai looked at Abraham, His gaze holding mild reproach. "I will return to you at the appointed time next year, and Sarah will have a son."

Sarah stepped from the shadows, and Abraham glimpsed fear in her eyes. "I did not laugh," she said, though Abraham noticed the way she avoided the man's searching gaze.

"Yes, you did laugh." The voice of the Lord held rebuke, and Sarah's cheeks colored in shame. She had lied, and Adonai knew it. Had she so little faith then?

Sarah lowered her head and stepped backward into her tent again, as though she could not bear to remain in Adonai's company. Could she not hear the kindness in His words? Such a lie might have brought a slap from their father, justly deserved. If her faith was so weak as to lie to Adonai, perhaps she needed time to think over His rebuke and her response to the promise she had so long been denied.

He watched her but a moment, then turned as the men stood, their meal complete. The Lord gave Abraham a steady look, then broke contact as the group directed their gazes toward Sodom. They moved forward, and Abraham fell into step beside Adonai, every part of his being yearning for them to stay, to fellowship, yet knowing they must go.

"Shall I hide from Abraham what I am about to do?" Adonai's quiet voice touched Abraham's soul. He slowed to keep pace with the Lord, while the other two men moved on ahead. "Abraham will surely become a great and powerful nation, and all nations on earth will be blessed through him. For I have chosen him, so that he will direct his children and his household after him to keep the way of the Lord by doing what is right and just, so that the Lord will bring about for Abraham what He has promised him."

Abraham's heart rang with the cadence of song as he sensed the Lord's joy in the words. But as they came to the edge of the hill overlooking the valley to the east, where Sodom and the plains of the Jordan Valley spread out as a lush garden before them, the mood shifted, the air no longer sweet.

Abraham looked at Adonai, whose feet had stopped moving. His expression filled with myriad emotions, none of them pleased, yet all of them saturated with love.

What is it? he longed to ask, yet held his tongue. God could read his thoughts. He would speak in His own good time.

They stood in silence a moment longer, the Lord's gaze shifting from Sodom to Abraham. "The outcry against Sodom and Gomorrah is so great and their sin so grievous that I will go down and see if what they have done is as bad as the outcry that has reached Me. If not, I will know."

At this, the two men who were still some distance ahead picked their way down the slope toward Sodom. Abraham watched them go, fear rushing through him. *Oh, Lord, what of Lot?* But his silent question brought no reply.

Drawing strength from Adonai's presence, that He still stood close by, Abraham quietly approached him.

"Will You sweep away the righteous with the wicked? What if there are fifty righteous people in the city? Will You really sweep it away and not spare the place for the sake of the fifty righteous people in it?" He paused a moment, but at the Lord's silence, he rushed on. "Far be it from You to do such a thing—to kill the righteous with the wicked, treating the righteous and the wicked alike. Far be it from You! Will not the Judge of all the earth do right?" He stepped back a pace, surprised at his boldness, yet thought he saw approval in the Lord's gentle gaze.

"If I find fifty righteous people in the city of Sodom, I will spare the whole place for their sake."

Shame filled him that he should have been so quick to assume otherwise. And yet as images of Sodom's inhabitants whom he'd once rescued from foreign kings flitted through his mind, he wondered. Would they find fifty righteous people there?

He glanced at the Lord out of the corner of his eye, emboldened by an acceptance he could not explain. He cleared his throat. "Now that I have been so bold as to speak to the Lord, though I am nothing but dust and ashes, what if the number of the righteous is five less than fifty? Will You destroy the whole city because of five people?"

"If I find forty-five there," He said, "I will not destroy it."

"What if only forty are found there?"

"For the sake of forty, I will not do it."

Abraham glanced down the mountain. The two men were mere specks on the horizon now, nearly to the gates. How had they gotten down there so fast?

A sigh troubled his chest, and he told himself not to speak, but the words would not stay within him. As he counted Lot's family and servants in his mind's eye, he came up far too short of good men and women. "May the Lord not be angry, but let me speak."

At Adonai's nod, he hurried on. "What if only thirty can be found there?"

"I will not do it if I find thirty there."

"Now that I have been so bold as to speak to the Lord, what if only twenty can be found there?"

"For the sake of twenty, I will not destroy it."

Abraham could no longer see the men as they crossed the Jordan Valley and were surely bordering Sodom's gates. What would they find? Lot, Melah, and their two daughters made four. Surely there were more than that. Friends of Lot's or sons-in-law?

"May the Lord not be angry, but let me speak just once more." He looked into approving, fathomless eyes, as old as the ages yet somehow new. He paused once again, sensing that after this there would be no more words. "What if only ten can be found there?"

"For the sake of ten, I will not destroy it."

In the space of his next breath, Adonai vanished from Abraham's sight. Abraham stood a moment longer, knowing only one prayer remained for his nephew's wicked city. *Oh, Adonai, please spare Lot*. He closed his eyes against the grief at both the loss of Adonai and Sodom's coming destruction. For despite his pleas, he could not count even ten people whose lives could save their city.

Melah shifted on her couch, closing her eyes against the throbbing at her temples. Heavy curtains had been drawn against the daylight, but by now the light creeping in at the edges had faded to a soft orange hue. Lot would be home soon, expecting a feast. Did the man ever tire of eating? He'd grown plumper than he'd been during his days as a shepherd, sitting in the gate with the elders of Sodom, demanding richer foods, moving less with each passing year. And he rarely spoke a word that wasn't laced with sarcasm or said in jest.

She couldn't blame him, really. This town was obsessed with food and drink and making merry, with buying and selling and entertainment of every variety. Sometimes the pace was wearying. Still, she could not help a sense of pride at all the city had accomplished. Even Ur and Harran had not grown so prosperous or allowed for such a life of ease.

She opened her eyes, adjusting to the dusk, the throbbing in her head releasing with her musings. Life was good here despite the violence. She would just send her servants to fetch whatever was needed from the market. There was little need for her to take such risks at her age. She had earned the right to rest.

A door banged at the front of the house, and male voices drifted to her. Hurried feet, probably those of her lazy maidservants, rushed past her room, and giggles from her daughters roused her curiosity. Lot often brought visitors home, though few ever ventured into Sodom these days. No doubt rumors had spread of the vile practices of the men of the city. Especially when darkness fell. A shudder shook her, and she forced herself up from her plush bed.

She checked her appearance in the bronze mirror through the dim light of the oil lamp, pinched color into her wan cheeks, and squinted at the wrinkles she could no longer hide with oils and ointments. She never could match Sarai's beauty. A veined hand smoothed the fabric of her embroidered robe as she took it from the peg on the wall and slipped it over her shoulders. She could match Sarai's wealth, though, and more. The thought held a hint of a lie, but she lifted her chin and squelched the guilt, moving into the hall toward the cooking room. She found Lot directing the servants.

"Bake bread without yeast, and bring out some of our best cheeses and wine." He looked up. "Melah, there you are. We have guests, and I promised them a meal. Can you see to it?" His helpless expression did not impress her or move her to act, and it was on the tip of her tongue to retort and tell him to make it himself.

The girls burst into the cooking area, hands covering their mouths in an attempt to suppress their laughter.

"Aren't they handsome? Too bad we are already promised. Pirhum is not nearly as finely crafted as either of those two men!" Kammani turned to her father. "Abi, won't you introduce us? The sounds of their voices are like music. I should so like to meet them."

Lot looked askance at the girl, a look Melah had not seen from him in years. He shook his head as though the request disgusted him. Ire lifted the hairs on Melah's arms.

"Why would you deny them? After your guests have eaten, will there not be a cause to introduce your family?" She leveled a gaze at him he could not ignore, one he had succumbed to all of their married life.

He shook his head again and took a step back toward the sitting area where the men waited. "Please, just hurry with the food. These are not ordinary men." He disappeared through the archway.

"Not ordinary men? What sort of men aren't ordinary?" Melah shot the words after him, but he did not respond.

"Perhaps they're like the men of the city who lust after other men," Ku-aya said.

"Wouldn't that make them ordinary?" Kammani moved to the cutting boards and lifted a knife to chop vegetables. At least the girl could be useful when needed.

Melah glanced from one to the other. The girls accepted Sodom's vices as though everything was normal. Had they no concept of wrong?

A check in her spirit made her pause. Was anything really sin? Abram had taught such a concept, but the thoughts had blurred once they moved to the city. She wasn't sure what she believed anymore. Why should her daughters be any different?

She picked a cheese from the shelf and cut thick slices, adding it to the wooden tray where the flat bread waited. Kammani added sliced cucumbers and olives and honeyed melon. It would do. Whoever these men were, they had come unannounced. They would not expect a lavish feast.

Hefting the tray in her arms, she shooed the girls out of sight and walked into the sitting room where Lot waited. One glimpse of the tall, muscular men made her knees weak. When they glanced at her, she nearly dropped the tray and had to steady herself in order to place it on the table before them. She bowed low and backed away without speaking.

They spoke in low tones with Lot while Melah slipped back to the cooking area to catch her breath.

"What's wrong, Mama? Are they not handsome?"

Melah could not speak, wondering at the strange weight in her chest. Though the glimpse had been swift, it was enough to sear her to the core, as though in a moment her conscience had been laid bare, all her pride exposed. She placed a hand to her heart. Who were these men?

A rumble of voices came through the open window, growing louder and coming closer. She moved on trembling legs to the window overlooking the courtyard and was jolted at the sight of men, young and old, descending upon their house. She quickly shuttered the window and hurried to the other rooms to make sure each fastener was securely in place.

Kammani and Ku-aya rushed after her, doing the same without being asked. They met in the hall, their fear matching her own. "What is it, Mama? Why are they here?"

"I don't know." Melah reached to place one arm around each girl, suddenly grateful beyond words for their presence. "Let's go."

She walked them toward the sitting room where they stayed against the walls, listening.

"Lot! Open the door. Where are the men who came to you tonight? Bring them out to us so we can have sex with them."

Horror slid down Melah's spine. She dared a look at the two men, but they appeared unruffled by the noise or the request. Lot bounced up from his seat as though stung with hot coals. He hurried to the door, slipped out, and shut it behind him.

Melah rushed to the window nearest the door, checked the latch, and pressed her ear against it, straining to hear. She felt Kammani and Ku-aya pressing against her back.

"No, my friends. Don't do this wicked thing," Lot said. "Look, I have two daughters who have never slept with a man. Let me bring them out to you, and you can do what you like with them. But don't do anything to these men, for they have come under the protection of my roof."

At the gasps of her daughters behind her, Melah turned and wrapped them in her arms. Soft weeping came from them both, and she shook with their trembling. He was joking as he always was. Surely he was joking.

"He can't do this."

"Why would he do this? We're promised to others."

"We're nothing to him. We were not sons."

Melah's heart stung with every whispered word. "He never means what he says. You know this." He could not be serious, could he? Did he even stop to think what he was saying? The girls would be dead by morning if he gave them to such men. And these men would not think he was kidding. Did he care nothing for his family? Bitterness scalded her throat. Lot was a fool.

"Get out of our way!"

The women jumped at the shouts coming from the men outside. Melah pulled her daughters further from the door and glanced for the briefest moment at Lot's two visitors, willing them to put an end to this madness.

"This fellow came here as an alien, and now he wants to play the judge!" The voice from outside came through the shuttered windows.

"We'll treat you worse than them." Another closer voice was soon joined by others. The door creaked against the pressure of the howling men, and Melah had a fleeting image of Lot pushed against it, begging for breath. Would serve him right for making such an awful suggestion!

"They're going to break down the door!" Ku-aya's cries sparked fear in the room.

"Someone do something!" Kammani's screams brought Melah's arms tighter around both girls.

In the next breath, the two visitors opened the door and dragged Lot into the room, shutting the door behind him. Cries of a different tone seeped through the window now. Melah released her grip on the girls and tread quietly to look. Men stood with hands stretched out before them, groping at air but making no progress forward. Could they not see where they were going?

"Do you have anyone else here—sons-in-law, sons or daughters, or anyone else in the city who belongs to you?" One of the visitors looked straight at Lot, who cowered in a corner and slowly nodded.

"Get them out of here, because we are going to destroy this place," the visitor said. "The outcry to Adonai against its people is so great that He has sent us to destroy it."

Melah looked at Lot's ashen face. Lot returned his gaze to the men. "I have two sons-in-law, pledged to marry my daughters."

"Go now and get them. There is little time left."

Lot rushed to the door, then whirled around and hurried to the back, slipping out of the house. Melah stood still, unable to move.

"We are leaving?" Kammani's voice jolted Melah from her stupor. "How can we leave?"

"They are going to destroy Sodom?"

The emotion in the girls' voices made Melah's eyes fill with tears. She looked around at the walls with her embroidered tapestries, the ornate furnishings, the gold and silver plating over each urn. Costly alabaster jars held fragrant oils. They would need many carts to lug it all with them. The image of goat's-hair tents surfaced in her mind's eye. She couldn't bear to live like that again.

"Take only what you can carry."

She jerked her head to look at the one who had spoken. Had he read her mind? But that was impossible.

"We cannot possibly—"

He shook his head. "There isn't time for more."

The comment both angered her and caused a fresh rush of fear to whip through her. She looked to her daughters. "Come." She hurried to her room, snatched clothing and pots of makeup and ointment and herbs, and placed them in large baskets. Surely a servant could carry some of this.

"He said only what we could carry, Mama." Ku-aya appeared at her side, a small satchel in her hand, her sister behind her.

Defeat mingled with Melah's exhaustion. The back door slammed, and she was acutely aware of the deepening darkness. She dropped her things and hurried to the sitting room, the girls on her heels. Lot appeared out of breath and distraught. A servant brought him a goblet of wine. He took it from the man and gulped it down.

"They didn't believe me." His chest heaved. Had he run the whole way? "They thought I was joking." He cast the two men an imploring look. "I couldn't convince them."

"No!" Kammani rushed at him, beating her fists against his chest. "You must go back, Abi. You must convince them. We cannot leave them here."

"From the moment you met them, you did not speak a serious word to them. Why should they believe you? Why should anyone believe you?" Melah could not keep the scorn from her tone.

"Go back and try again, Abi. You must!" Ku-aya had hold of his arm, her look pleading.

Lot pushed the girls from him. "I tried. It is no use." He glanced at the two men. "Perhaps they will change their minds before we leave." He walked toward the hall to his bedchamber.

"We will not wait long," one of the men said.

A deep shudder worked through Melah, her sense of foreboding rising with each step as she hurried back to her room to continue packing.

Predawn stillness settled over Sodom, the town's night revelries spent, the quiet unnerving. Melah had given the last few hours to packing and unpacking what she would need to start life over again somewhere else. In the end, she had settled on two linen sacks, one weighted down with some of her finest robes and tunics and belts and jeweled sandals. In the other, she'd had to fit all of the creams and ointments, not only to keep her youthful appearance, but to use for healing balms. Lot would have to carry the food sacks. There just wasn't room enough for it all. As it was, their pack animals were too far away to get to in time. The few donkeys he kept for travel were boarded at the stables on the outskirts of the city. They would have to carry their supplies until they could reach the stables.

"Can you stuff these pots into your sack?" She looked at Lot where he stood in the cooking area, one sack stuffed with clothing sitting at his feet, then at the two men who suddenly filled the arch of the door between the cooking and sitting areas. The gray light of the coming dawn peeked around the shuttered windows.

Lot turned from her to the men, ignoring her question. Where would they fit the griddle? She could not possibly make flat bread without a three-pronged griddle. The old way of cooking over stones—she could not even think of doing that again.

"Hurry," one of the men said, interrupting her rambling thoughts. "Take your wife and your two daughters who are here, or you will be swept away when the city is punished."

Swept away? A sense of confusion settled over her. She couldn't leave her home. She'd raised her children here. Her son was buried here. No, wait. Her son was buried in another land, in a foreign cave. No, that wasn't so either. Lot had brought his body back with them and buried him here. She visited his grave every week to offer him food and drink.

A little cry escaped her, and she pressed her hands to her temples. There was still so much to do, so much to gather. "We cannot go without the donkeys. There is too much to pack, and we are too few to carry it all."

She glanced at Lot, who suddenly looked lost and confused himself. Kammani and Ku-aya huddled closer, the four of them standing in the middle of the room, unsure what to do, where to go.

One of the men stepped forward and grasped Lot's and Kammani's hands, while the other grasped Melah's and Ku-aya's. "Come."

They moved forward without another word, the provisions left in the sacks on the floor of their home.

Melah's head throbbed, her mind muddied and struggling to focus. Where were they going? Why were these men leading them out of the city?

They crossed the threshold of the city gate and kept walking past the ring of trees that led toward the Jordan Valley. Dawn had almost fully crested the eastern ridge now, and the men urged them faster with each step, as though everything would change once the day came to light. They stopped at the edge of the plain facing the mountains to the south.

"Flee for your lives! Don't look back, and don't stop anywhere in the plain. Flee to the mountains or you will be swept away!"

Melah hurried to Lot's side and grasped his sleeve as the girls' startled whines came from behind them.

"We can't live in the mountains."

"We brought nothing with us."

"What are they thinking? Abi, please!" They spoke as one.

"Listen to them," Melah whispered, turning pleading, sultry eyes on Lot, knowing he could not resist her.

Lot took a step closer to the men and fell on one knee, hands clasped in front of him. "No, my lords, please! Your servant has found favor in your eyes, and you have shown great kindness to me in sparing my life. But I can't flee to the mountains. This disaster will overtake me, and I'll die. Look, Zoar is a town near enough to run to, and it is small. Let me flee to it. It is very small, isn't it? Then my life will be spared."

Did he think small meant good and honorable? But surely a small town was better than the wild mountains.

"Very well," one of the men said, "I will grant this request too. I will not overthrow the town you speak of. But flee there quickly, because I cannot do anything until you reach it."

Lot bowed and quickly rose, thanked the men, and ran. "Go!"

His shout rang out, jarring Melah from her fear-induced stupor. She whirled about and shoved both girls ahead of her.

"Don't look back!"

Lot's reminder rang within her, the words of the two men searing her heart. She snatched her robes between her clenched fingers and ran after her daughters, the town of Zoar not appearing to grow any closer. She heard Lot's heavy breaths behind her and was comforted by his presence.

The town looked small because it was so far from the plains. What was Lot thinking? And yet running across the plains was easier than climbing mountains would have been.

She slowed her gait, her legs growing weary.

"Don't stop," Lot said. His body was in no better condition than her own. Running was for the young and vibrant. She was too old for this. But she picked up the pace again just the same.

She glanced ahead at her girls, their long hair flowing behind them. They were many paces ahead, and Melah wondered why one of them hadn't thought to grab a sack to carry with them. Had Lot at least tucked gold coins into his belt?

She nearly turned around to ask him, but the men's warning stung her ears. *Don't look back*, they'd said.

She ran faster and didn't.

36

Sarah rose from a fitful night's sleep and slipped from her tent as dawn kissed the last vestige of night's gray. The visit from the three men had left her shaken, and she still felt the sting of Adonai's gentle rebuke. She *had* lied to Him, and He knew it. Whatever had possessed her to do such a thing?

She felt the soft touch of dew against her feet as she moved through the campground and turned toward the place where Abraham had built an altar to Adonai Elohim. Birdsong twittered above her in the oaks' heavy branches as she picked her way up the hill to the place overlooking the valley below. What a failure her life had been. Would she have lied to God if she'd had more faith, been more righteous? How could she possibly have a son at her age? And yet, if she had believed all along . . .

Things had seemed so simple in her youth, when she promised her father she would give Abraham a son. If her mother had lived, perhaps she would have shown her how very little a woman could control such things. But no, her mother would have insisted Sarah never make such a promise, would have told her to accept that the man might want or need another wife. She shook the thought aside, the cobwebs of her mind filling with images of her past, her pride, her faithless sacrifice to the fertility goddess, her miserable failure in giving Hagar to Abraham, and worse, after the visit of the three men, her complete lack of trust in Adonai to keep His own promise.

Don't look back. You cannot undo what is past. She looked from the altar to the valley, wishing she could rid herself of each and every failure. But she couldn't seem to let them go.

Sodom was surely far behind them by now, Melah suspected as Zoar grew closer, sitting at the crest of a low hill up ahead. Kammani and Ku-aya had already reached the ridge encircling the city and suddenly slipped from view. Panic filled her, but she told herself to calm down. Lot was somewhere still behind her. But as she strained to listen, she could no longer hear his heavy breaths. Fear rushed over and through her as a loud roar from the heavens drowned out all other sounds. Sweat beaded her brow and trickled down her back, and her heart beat wildly from the exertion.

Was Lot still behind her? What if he somehow got caught up in whatever was making that awful noise?

Don't look back.

"Lot?" She called his name, keeping her face forward, but the sound of her voice was extinguished in the thunderous roar coming behind her.

Sarah turned toward a sound in the distance and walked closer to the edge of the hill, standing at the tree line overshadowed by a towering oak. Thunder boomed, an angry storm, yet the leaves barely rustled overhead. Fear fluttered near her heart. Abraham had told her what God had said about Sodom's coming destruction, but she had held out hope that He would find ten righteous people there to save the city.

Clouds congealed over the plain, the darkness blocking the dawn, hovering as though waiting to act. Had God found no way to save them? What of Lot and Melah and their daughters? Why had they ever chosen to live in such a vile place?

In an instant the pointing finger turned on her, and she realized with stark clarity that she and Melah were not so very different. If not for Abraham's faith in Adonai, if not for his strength of character and unwillingness to always give in to what others wanted—even her—they could be in Lot's situation. If Abraham had been as weak as Lot, she could be standing in Melah's sandals.

The clouds darkened further to billowing smoke, and in an instant, fire fell from heaven like a thousand lightning strikes all pointed to one spot. Horror filled her at the sight of Sodom's shining city snuffed out and turned to smoldering ash before her. She closed her eyes, but she could not shut the image from her thoughts. All of those people destroyed! Fear swelled in her middle, and she opened her eyes again, shading them with a hand from the bright flashes, knowing deep within her that she was no better than they. In truth, she had been controlling, fearing, despairing, never truly trusting.

Oh, Adonai, why have I not believed?

She turned to face the altar again, unable to watch the fire and yellow smoke raining down on Sodom and Gomorrah and the lush beauty of the Jordan plains.

Don't look back, beloved. Trust and believe.

The words came softly in her ear, like the touch of a father's gentle hand. Emotion clogged Sarah's throat, and she fell to her knees, her heart yearning, seeking, surrendering.

I will stop looking back, Adonai. I want to believe. Please help me to believe.

✳✢✳

Don't look back!

Melah heard the command in her head and forced one foot ahead of the other. Still no sign of the girls, but if she called to them, they would be forced to look back, exactly what they'd been told not to do.

"Lot!" Yet she could still barely hear her own voice above the roar. His heavy breathing was no longer close. He'd grown lazy and carried too much bulk these past few years. What if his heart had died within him as he ran? He could be lying on the road behind her.

The deafening roar blotted out all thought, making her head throb harder with every step. She couldn't do this. Yet the ridge was just ahead. *Lot!* She must know, must see what was happening to her home, to her husband.

Don't look back!

Perhaps it was just a suggestion. One little glimpse should not matter. Most rules were not meant to be kept explicitly, were they? She stopped, waiting, listening. If Lot touched her, she would know all was well with him.

She waited, counting her heartbeats. But his touch did not come, and the smell of sulfur overpowered each breath, choking her.

Just one look.

She glanced quickly behind her, glimpsing Lot's face before it disappeared and blackness enveloped her.

✳✢✳

Lot looked in horror at Melah's back, seeing her as if time had slowed, noting every movement from her head to her shoulder to . . . The rest of her body had not had time to finish the turn when their gazes connected, and she transformed from the Melah he loved into an unmoving pillar.

"No!" He raced forward, throwing his arms around the pillar, feeling only the gritty sense of salt beneath his touch. "Melah, no, no, no!"

He fell to his knees at the base of what had once been her body and rocked with the force of the clamor in the distance behind him. Tears streamed down his face, not just for his wife, but for the choices that had led him here. If only . . . There were so many things he could have done differently, done better.

Oh, God, what will I do without her?

Don't look back.

The angel's words rang in his ears, for he knew without a doubt they could not have been mere men. Why hadn't he been stronger, taught his wife and daughters and sons-in-law the truth? Why had he kept silent when the city grew so corrupt? Why had he stayed?

He stumbled forward, weeping the rest of the way up the ridge, knowing that while Melah did not listen and looked back, he could not afford to do so.

Tears streamed unhindered down Sarah's cheeks, but she made no attempt to wipe them away. She spotted Abraham near the place where the land sloped toward the valley and walked toward him, her heart full. She slipped her hand in his as they both surveyed the destruction of Sodom.

"Do you think Lot and Melah are safe, my lord?" She leaned into his strength, grateful all over again for the faith of this man. The faith that had saved them from Sodom's fall and so much more.

"Adonai promised to save the righteous. He would not force them against their will." He looked at her then. "I hope so, beloved. But I do not know."

She nodded, the heaviness settling over them. She recalled the frustration she'd felt toward Melah's misguided faith, but in that moment all she could feel for her niece was deep concern. She loved Melah. She did. Despite everything. "I hope so too, my lord."

Abraham released her hand and pulled her to him. She rested her head against his chest, feeling his breath. "The smoke is like smoke from a great furnace."

She nodded, overcome with sadness. "So much beauty gone. The plains were so well watered, so green with life."

He sighed, and she knew his own grief went too deep for words. There was nothing to be said. Adonai had revealed Sodom's sin to Abraham, sins of pride and arrogance, of gluttony and selfish ease, of neglecting the poor and needy, leading its people to commit detestable acts of immorality and violence.

"Let's go home," he said, turning her away from the sight. They would long remember Sodom's destruction, but they did not need to glory in it. Better to remember their own sins and keep faith with Adonai.

The thought brought a smile to her lips as Abraham's hand slipped into hers and they walked side by side past the altar, back toward the camp. Adonai had promised her a son by this time next year. Joy filled her. This time, at last, she would believe Him.

❊ 37 ❊

ONE YEAR LATER

Abraham stood in the center of his tent, the side flaps opened to allow the members of the camp to gather near and watch this momentous occasion. His son, Sarah's son, rested in Eliezer's arms, balanced on his knees, while Sarah and Lila stood close by to watch. The miracle still amazed him, that Sarah should bear him a son in his old age. Who would have thought? Yet God had promised.

He picked up a flint knife from a low table to his right, his gaze sweeping the crowd before coming to rest again on his wife and son. The child squirmed in Eliezer's lap, and Abraham could not stifle a soft chuckle that the boy had already brought them so much joy. And now their joy would be complete as he made his son of promise a son of the covenant as well.

A slight commotion near the edge of the tent made him look up. Hagar caught hold of Ishmael's hand and pulled him against her as the boy tugged her nearer to watch. Abraham met his son's gaze with a smile and a nod. The servants nearby made room for them both, and Abraham didn't miss the guarded look of relief in Hagar's dark eyes. She had no reason to fear. Abraham could love both sons with ease.

Stepping closer to Eliezer, he nodded to his trusted steward to unwrap the boy's body, exposing his soft flesh. Abraham marveled again at the perfection in one so small, then quickly, so as to cause little pain, he removed the foreskin from his son's future manhood.

The boy's lip quivered, followed by a lusty cry. Abraham smiled at Eliezer even as tears filled his eyes, knowing the covenant had been given to humble men and remind them where their dependence must lie. He held up a hand to Sarah as she moved forward, intending to bandage and comfort her son.

"Wait for the blessing, beloved."

She paused mid-step, clearly distressed with each pitiful cry, but she did not move again. He looked from her to their son again, blinking at the image the boy made. How like a sacrifice—so helpless, so dependent on those who cared for him. Was this what circumcision was to show him? He'd been a grown man during his own circumcision, as had all of the men in his household, all old enough to feel the pain and understand the reasons. But this child, only eight days old, did not know the reason such pain had been inflicted on him, did not understand the covenant, the obedience and surrender this sacrifice required.

Oh, Adonai, my heart yearns that Isaac should know You. Set Your blessing on him. Make Your face shine upon him.

He glanced up, catching Sarah's impatient look and hearing Isaac's cries, and looked beyond them both to the edge of the trees where the Lord had come last year to renew the promise. And there He stood again. As He had promised to return, so He waited beneath the shade of the oak's spreading limbs. Abraham felt the pull of Adonai's gaze as warmth and love poured through him, invigorating him with sudden, overpowering joy.

"Blessed are You, Adonai our God, ruler of all things great and small, who has sanctified us with Your goodness, who has given us Your righteousness." He held his hands aloft toward the angel of the Lord. "And you, my son, shall be named Isaac, for God has kept His promise and blessed your parents with laughter."

Sarah stepped forward and touched his upraised arm. "God has brought me laughter, and everyone who hears it will laugh with me." She hurried forward then, laid strips of linen over Isaac's exposed, bleeding skin, then quickly bound him and lifted him from Eliezer's knees.

"Behold our son, Isaac!" Abraham said, smiling.

"Amen!" The crowd spoke as one and then burst into laughter, some cheering, others dancing.

And Abraham and Sarah laughed.

Note from the Author

In Sarai's story, Sarai and Melah lived in similar circumstances and faced similar problems, but when it came to how to live in faith, they made opposite choices. One followed after the gods made with human hands. The other followed the God she could not see. The Bible commends Sarah for her faith, and I have no doubt she believed. But as with each one of us, sometimes doubt creeps in and our faith wavers. In those moments, we might make choices we live to regret. I think Sarah understood regret most deeply, especially when she gave Hagar into her husband's arms.

But as Sarah discovered at the end of the story, God remains faithful whether we believe Him or not. This faithfulness was clearly shown in the covenant God made with Abraham—when the firepot moved between the carcasses of the animals Abraham had sacrificed. In a covenant, normally both parties would pledge to keep their side of the agreement. But God's covenant with Abraham was one-sided. God alone would keep His promises. Abraham could add nothing to them. He was given the choice to believe

God or not. He chose to believe, and God "credited it to him as righteousness" (Gen. 15:6).

In the end, it comes down to choice. Abram and Sarai made some hard choices to leave their father's household and follow God into the unknown, looking for a city whose architect and builder is God. He blessed them for their obedience. Abraham became the father of many nations, and he is the father of all who believe. Kings and princes came from Sarah's line.

He who promised is faithful.

May our choices lead us to the same obedient faith in Him.

In His Grace,
Jill Eileen Smith

Please note: As with all of my biblical fiction, I strive to follow the Scripture as best I can. Where there is room for interpretation or scholars have disagreed, I have made an educated choice based on research. Portions of the story not in Scripture are purely from my imagination. Any errors are my own.

Acknowledgments

"Thank you" never seems like enough, and each year my gratitude rises for the wonderful people God has put in my life. I wish I could include each one, but because of space I am limited. Please know that you all are greatly appreciated.

Special thanks to the talented team at Revell for another great experience in bringing *Sarai* to print. You all make my job a joy!

To my agent, Wendy Lawton—I sure do appreciate you!

To my editors, Lonnie Hull DuPont and Jessica English—the stories are always better after you edit them!

To my critique partners, Jill Stengl and Kathleen Fuller—brainstorming sessions are more fun with a friend. Thank you for all of your wise suggestions.

To my son Jeff—for brainstorming the initial plot and for the great suggestions regarding Sarai's and Melah's character arcs.

Special thanks to Pastor Cliff Johnson for the use of his Jewish library. The books you pointed my way were most helpful and appreciated.

To my readers and influencers—thank you for loving these stories and writing to tell me so.

To my family, friends, and prayer team—you are a precious, priceless gift.

Randy—you are my inspiration. There is no better man than you.

Jeff, Chris, and Ryan—you are gifted writers in your own right, and I can't wait to see what God does with your work!

El Roi, the God who sees me—thank You that You watch me still.

Jill Eileen Smith is the bestselling author of the Wives of King David series. When she isn't writing, she enjoys spending time with her family—in person, over the webcam, or by hopping a plane to fly across the country. She can often be found reading, testing new recipes, grabbing lunch with friends, or snuggling one or both of her adorable cats. She lives with her family in southeast Michigan.

To learn more about Jill or for more information about her books, visit her website at www.jilleileensmith.com. You can also contact Jill at jill@jilleileensmith.com. She loves hearing from her readers.

Meet Jill Eileen Smith at
WWW.JILLEILEENSMITH.COM
to learn interesting facts and read her blog!

Connect with her on

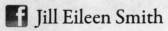 Jill Eileen Smith

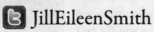 JillEileenSmith